Double Black

Double Black

A SKI DIVA MYSTERY

Wendy Clinch

MINOTAUR BOOKS

A THOMAS DUNNE BOOK
New York

A THOMAS DUNNE BOOK FOR MINOTAUR BOOKS.
An imprint of St. Martin's Publishing Group.

TheSkiDiva.com™ is a trademark of TheSkiDiva.com LLC and is used by permission.

DOUBLE BLACK. Copyright © 2009 by Wendy Clinch. All rights reserved. Printed in the United States of America. For information, address St. Martin's Press, 175 Fifth Avenue, New York, N.Y., 10010.

www.thomasdunnebooks.com
www.minotaurbooks.com

Library of Congress Cataloging-in-Publication Data

Clinch, Wendy.
    Double black / Wendy Clinch.—1st ed.
        p. cm.
    "A Thomas Dunne book."
    ISBN 978-0-312-59326-1
    1. Women skiers—Vermont—Fiction.   2. Ski resorts—Vermont—
Fiction.   3. Murder—Investigation—Vermont—Fiction.   4. Vermont—
Fiction.   I. Title.
PS3603.L545D68 2010
813'.6—dc22   2009034743

First Edition: January 2010

10 9 8 7 6 5 4 3 2 1

For Jon Clinch,
my favorite skiing buddy,
my best friend,
and the love of my life

ACKNOWLEDGMENTS

Writing this book allowed me to indulge my passion for two things: skiing and a good story. All the same, I couldn't have done it without a tremendous amount of help and support. Much love and gratitude to the following:

My dad, Sid Harris, for getting me involved in skiing many, many years ago; my mom, Rita Harris, for patiently allowing it; all the women at TheSkiDiva.com, for their spirit and inspiration; the great team at Thomas Dunne, in particular, Marcia Markland and Sarah Melnyk; my agent, Jeff Kleinman; and last but not least, my husband, Jon Clinch, and my daughter, Emily Bryk, for more reasons than I can say.

Double Black

ONE

When Stacey Curtis found the dead man on the bed, she knew it was time to get her own apartment.

The writing had been on the wall for a while and she'd ignored it for as long as she could. These empty condos on the mountain were convenient—they had clean sheets and plenty of hot water and maybe even a packet of somebody's left-behind instant oatmeal to toss in the microwave come morning—and it seemed like a shame to let them sit unused. Especially when she was new in town, just sprung from an engagement gone bad, and living out of a tip jar.

A tip jar and an '87 Subaru, to tell the whole truth.

But everything changed when she flicked on the light and found this total stranger in this strange bed, blood everywhere, and the jagged oily chain from a chain saw yanked tight around his neck. She knew right away that it was time to move on.

At first she thought the thing around his neck was barbed wire. Why not? She didn't exactly make a study of it, not that she'd have recognized the chain for what it was if she'd found it in the hardware store. Stacey Curtis, born and raised in the Back Bay and only recently arrived here in the Green Mountain State minus any kind of support system, had no experience with that sort of thing. Chain saws, that is. Or murder.

No wonder she spent a few minutes in the Italian-marble master bathroom before she called 911.

At least they had 911 up here in the woods. She didn't have a lot of confidence that it was going to work (Wouldn't that have been great? You call 911 and you get that voice saying your call cannot be completed as dialed? What do you do next?), but she pressed the buttons and listened and the call went through just like that. God knows where the dispatch center was. Boston, for all she knew. India, for that matter, although the operator sounded like a Yankee. Stacey held the phone in a hand that was still gloved and gave the Yankee Indian lady a name that was not hers and told her that the problem was a dead man. A dead man in the bed. A dead man in the bed who looked for all the world as if he'd been strangled or something at least. Yes, strangled. With some kind of a spiky chain.

She stood in the bedroom door with the portable phone to her ear and she tried not to look at the dead man but she looked anyhow. The chain was all kind of dug into his neck and one bent-up end of it was lying across the pillow.

Yes, she said, there was blood. No, he wasn't breathing. Yes, she'd just come in the door and found him that way.

She turned her back on the dead man and doing that gave her the creeps even worse so she turned back, because at least this way she could keep an eye on him.

What address? She didn't know, exactly. Snowfield Condos. Building D. That much she was sure of. As for the unit number, she mumbled something about how the shock must have blanked out her memory and took the cordless and went to see what it said on the door. Going back inside the condo took everything she had, what with the dead man on the bed and all, but she did it rather than stand out there in the hallway where somebody might see her. She closed the door and told the lady that yes, she'd wait for the sheriff. And then she hung up the phone, grabbed her pack, pulled her cap down over her ears, and got the hell out.

So she'd have to sleep in the Subaru. She'd done it before. And come morning she'd hit the slopes and come afternoon she'd go to work and one way or another it would all blow over.

By the time Stacey started her three o'clock shift at the Broken Binding, Tina Montero had it all figured out. A local from the ground up, Tina knew everybody in town and didn't mind talking about them. She'd been the Binding's best customer for years. She'd lied about her age and downed her first beer at the Binding in the sixties, back when the place was brand-spanking new and the distressed barnboard paneling was only for show. Back when it was called the Broken Binding for the first time. She'd held on through a brief period in the seventies when a group of German investors rechristened it the Edelweiss and gave it a new dining room with a hokey Bavarian theme. She'd endured a number of dark years that followed, when the 'Weiss (those in the know said "Vice") passed from hand to hand until a drunk with a snowplow took the sign out for good and the place reached its low point as a biker bar with no name that anybody knew for sure. And now that Pete Hardwick had arrived as its savior—Pete Hardwick with his investment banking fortune, Pete Hardwick who gave the Broken Binding back its original name and décor in a move that could only be described as retro sentimentality—Tina Montero felt right at home.

"I used to babysit for that one," she said as she took her usual place at the bar. "And if you want me to tell you about him in a single word, it's *pain-in-the-ass.*"

Stacey always felt this way when Tina started a conversation. As if she'd arrived right in the middle of something, something that she wasn't entirely sure she had any interest in. "'That one'?" she asked.

"The dead one."

"Oh, *that* 'that one.'"

"David. David Paxton. I babysat him. His brother was older. I babysat David."

"So you said." Stacey had been hearing about the dead man all day long—on lift rides and in the ladies' room and over the boot dryer outside the cafeteria—and although she would rather have put it out of her mind, she kept alert to any rumor that might involve a young woman and a 911 call and some shadowy prowler in a beat-up Subaru. Four or five fresh inches of snow had fallen overnight, though, and between the skiers and the plows she was pretty certain she'd left no trace.

Tina was still going on, clarifying. "He was the younger one, David. By maybe five or six years. I don't know exactly. Ricky was older, anyhow."

"I thought he went by Richie."

"Old habits die slow, honey. I always called them David and Ricky. Like the Nelsons."

Stacey shook her head, trying to dislodge the reference and failing.

"That old TV show," Tina went on. "*Ozzie and Harriet.*"

"Still nothing," Stacey said.

"Never mind. Anyhow, that younger one was a royal pain in the ass."

"So you said."

"Not like his brother. Ricky was always sweet as pie. At least to me."

"His brother. Richie."

"David was sharp, though. You got to grant him that. Sharp as a tack."

"I'll bet."

"A lot of good it did him." She raised her chardonnay in a sorry toast. "He crossed somebody and brought it on himself."

"You think?"

"If I know him. And I know him."

"You *knew* him."

"If you know the child, you know the man."

"I suppose."

"Besides, what man isn't just a little boy anyhow?"

"You've got that right." She was thinking of her failed engagement.

Tina tilted her half-empty glass and ran the bottom in circles on the coaster. There was something else on her mind and she would not be long in letting it out. At last she righted the glass and looked square at Stacey. "You know something? They say there was a woman involved."

"They say that?" she said, wiping at a glass. "Who?"

"People."

"How come?"

"The 911 call. Word is, there was some gal made it. Nobody knows who."

"Really."

"Folks say he'd already been dead a while, though."

"Who'd know that kind of thing?"

"Dead a while when she called, I mean. A day anyhow. Maybe more."

"Who'd say—"

"I can't tell." Zipping her lip. "Folks who ought to know, is all."

"Hmm."

"Speaking for myself, though—if there was a woman, I don't think she had anything to do with it. *If* there was a woman. David crossed somebody and got himself killed and maybe some gal knew about it but she sure as heck didn't do it. I think maybe she knew about it and she got cold feet. Who wouldn't? Imagine that body laying there all by its lonesome. Just all by its lonesome in that bed. Imagine that."

Stacey winced. "Don't make me."

"If any woman could know about a thing like that and didn't call the sheriff, I'd be surprised."

Stacey dragged her attention back to the job she was being paid to do, back to the bar at the Broken Binding, where nobody was dead and life went on. "You want another chardonnay?"

"In a minute." Tina was building up to something and she wasn't going to let a second drink get in the way of it. "Anyhow," she said, "if you want my take on it, that's as much as there's any woman involved. To begin with, David wasn't like that."

" 'Like that.' " Stacey was lost all over again, trying her best to catch up.

"*Like that* with women."

"Like that with women—"

"I'm sorry, honey. I forget you haven't been around as long as I have." Tina pushed her glass to one side and leaned forward over the bar, her décolletage straining for what would not be the last time this evening. "David was *queer*," she said. "Folks knew that when he was still in the Cub Scouts."

Before the après-ski rush kicked in, Stacey went back into the cooler for some alone time. She kicked herself for having not spent at least part of the day looking for an apartment, but between the four or five inches of new snow and the dead man who wouldn't stay out of her head there was just no way she could stop skiing early. And now here she was back at the Binding, having cleaned herself up as usual in the lavishly equipped employee locker room that those big-spending Germans hadn't been able to live without and the bikers hadn't been able to ruin no matter how many lines of coke they must have snorted off all those stainless-steel countertops. God bless 'em, those Germans built things to last. Maybe when the Subaru finally gave out—*if* it ever gave out—she'd find herself a nice used VW.

So here she was, taking a moment for herself in the cooler. The cooler full of cases and kegs of beer and God knows what-all premade and raw stuff for the kitchen, the cooler that stayed a steady thirty-eight degrees night and day. Thirty-eight degrees was a lot warmer than it was going to be overnight in the Subaru, and the steadiness of it was a comfort. It was high time she had something steady in her life, even if she had to put on her jacket and go into the cooler and sit on a keg of Magic Hat to enjoy it. She stayed there as long as she dared, loaded up her apron with a pile of lemons and limes, and went back out to brave the crush.

TWO

Back in late November, six months before the wedding, Stacey had found Brian in bed with a mutual friend—a stealth slut whose name she still couldn't bring herself to say out loud. She didn't even give them the satisfaction of making a scene. She just eased the door shut and loaded up the ski racks and made for the Mass Pike. Two hours later she was hanging a right toward Vermont.

She knew it was strange for a woman of twenty-six, but as she gripped the wheel and watched the mountains loom up out of the darkness she realized that never in all her life had she felt this entirely free. And it wasn't just because she was flying up Route 91 all alone. She'd made that drive many times before, and even though Brian had never been in the passenger seat—he'd never made time to go to the mountains with her; he'd always had something more important to do—nonetheless he'd always been very much in her heart. He would be home working or whatever, and she'd be feeling guilty about having left him behind. Guilty about going off to have a little innocent fun all by herself.

Guilty. Now there was a laugh.

For all she knew, he'd been sniffing around what's-her-name even then.

A person can get some real thinking done between Boston and Vermont, with the roads freshly cleared and a radio that was getting only static and an old Sheryl Crow cassette stuck in the tape player. (Literally stuck. Sheryl Crow was now the soundtrack of her life, for better or worse.) The real issue wasn't whether or not Brian was even then thinking about running around on her—*running around on her while they were still engaged, damn it! was there even a word for cheating in that big a hurry? was there even a word for betraying a marriage that hadn't happened yet?*—the real issue was that he'd never lowered himself to enjoying the things that meant the most to her. And that, she decided, was a kind of faithlessness that was bigger and more hurtful than anything. That was the kind of faithlessness that she wished she'd been smart enough to recognize before it bit her on the butt.

The truth is, like so many women, she'd thought she could change him. She'd thought time and circumstances could change him. So she'd ignored the red flags.

And look where it got her.

Free at last.

As furious as she was at Brian, the thought kept coming back. She'd done it the hard way, but she was free at last. And she promised herself that she'd never make the same mistake again.

She turned on the tape deck and jacked up the volume. All she wanted to do—at long, long last—was have some fun.

Make no mistake: Arriving in this little town as a refugee had been different from arriving as a weekender. She spent the first two nights in a motel, even though she knew she'd have to abandon that luxury soon enough. And *luxury*, quite frankly, was hardly the word for it. The place was called the Trail's End, and it looked the part.

Ski bumming, on the other hand, had a long and colorful history that she'd always found attractive beyond words. Free spirits living in their cars, trekking from mountain to mountain with no destination more specific than the latest and deepest snowfall. It was the stuff of legends. But did ski bums work? And if they did, where? On the mountains and in the bars. Simple as that. They put people on chairlifts all day or they poured drinks for them all night. Maybe both.

Lucky for Stacey, it was late November and everybody in town was still hiring like mad.

Also lucky for her, she got the word on her first lift ride—there'd been a fresh snowfall overnight, and she couldn't bring herself to go looking for a job—that the mountain was in some kind of financial trouble. Three old men occupied the chair with her, three red-faced members of the seventy-plus club, and for every opinion that one of them had the others had two more. The basic word was that the mountain had been on hard times for years. A big operation from out west—SkiAmerica—had apparently offered a buyout this past summer, but the Forest Service had their underwear in a knot over some technicality and was holding things up. Who knew what was next? A hostile takeover? Bankruptcy? The seventy-plus club felt sorry for anybody who depended on Spruce Peak for work, that was for certain.

Stacey decided that the life of a lift attendant might not be for her, and when the day was done she went for strictly business reasons to the nicest bars in town. Both of them. The rest was Broken Binding history.

The life of a ski bum wasn't exactly everything she'd pictured, but what was?

It still beat the heck out of being engaged to Brian.

She skied every day until one-thirty or two, she started work at three, and when her shift was done she slept in the car behind Bud's Suds, in the lee of the pizza joint. The two buildings came together there in a corner that the wind couldn't reach, making a little haven that stayed pretty well free of the worst snow. Whatever came straight down came down, but that was it. She parked there every night until a two-pound ring of master keys showed up in the dust behind the jukebox at the Binding. They were labeled like so many Christmas presents. Moyer's Hardware, Cinco de Taco, Vinnie's Steak-Out, and a smorgasbord of condominiums, from The T-Bar on the low end to Snowfield on the high. Not to mention most of the other businesses in town, plus a lot of the most exclusive private residences. Five- and ten-million dollar places, every one of them.

She'd been cleaning up at the end of her shift when she bumped the ring with the vacuum. Nobody'd swept that far behind the jukebox in years, you could bet on it. But she'd been raised fastidious, and even living out of the back of the car hadn't changed that. She knocked the dust off the keys and asked around—she even left them in a dish on the bar for a few days—but nobody knew where they'd come from. Tina Montero had a theory that they belonged to this good-looking long-haired guy from Troy who'd dabbled in property management two or three years back, but he'd vanished one summer just like that and she couldn't remember his name and what difference did it make anyhow. Gone was gone.

After another few days of sleeping in the car Stacey had worked up the courage to claim the ring of keys for her own. The first one she tried said BLACK BEAR in tiny and very neat letters written in ink on what looked like a patch of adhesive tape. It was just like all the others in that detail; whoever that cute long-haired guy from Troy was, he had nice handwriting and had obviously started out with the best of intentions. After she and Pete Hardwick closed up the Binding for the night, she scraped the new snow off her car and drove up to the Black Bear Condos and parked around back. Sure enough the key worked. She swung the service door open against the snow and stepped inside and her nerve failed and she stepped outside and closed the door again and let it lock behind her. She went back to the car to give things a little more thought. There were two other cars in the lot already, and a light on in one window. That meant that one other unit could be occupied, one out of maybe twenty or so altogether besides the one with the light. What were the odds that she'd pick that one? She figured she could improve her chances by keeping an eye out for damp places on the carpets. She would certainly knock on any door before putting the key in the lock, which would save some potential embarrassment. And she had to be ready with a story. Something about how she was there from the maintenance company. To see about a leak in the toilet, maybe. That would be good. Unless the person who came to the door recognized her from the Binding, by which point the charade would be over, so what difference would it make? Or unless the person worked for the management company himself. What then?

This was all Brian's fault, damn him.

Damn him damn him damn him.

She beat her fist on the steering wheel and the ring of keys jangled on the seat beside her.

On the other hand, though, she *was* skiing every day of the week.

And if one was Brian's fault, wasn't the other?

No. Definitely not. She would not give him that. Brian had made their bed and then he'd slept in it with another woman, and whatever good had come of it was Stacey's own doing.

The realization actually made her feel pretty good again. Master of her own fate. Daring, almost. Certainly independent, and in the middle of an adventure she'd never imagined she'd have the courage for. So she picked up the keys and weighed them in her hand and got back out of the car. She opened the service door and went inside, and for a moment she stood there in the dark just listening—

surrounded by cleaning supplies and heating pipes and a gas fur-
nace that whooshed on right then and scared her half to death—and
then she went through the next door into a brightly lit hallway.
She avoided the side of the building where she'd seen the light in
the window, and she went instead down a hallway that branched
off in another direction.

There were no signs of life anywhere—no wet boots, no damp
doormats, nothing—so she rolled the dice and they came up lucky:
the first warm bed she'd had since leaving Boston.

From then on Stacey Curtis would never again sleep in her car,
not until the night when she stumbled on the dead man with the
chain around his neck. She'd have blamed him on Brian, too, but
there were limits on everything.

THREE

How many murders did Vermont see in a year? Closer to none than a person might think, but not close enough for Guy Ramsey, who kept a running tally in his head. Twelve was the average for the twenty-three years he'd been on the job. Twelve murders was pretty close to none but it wasn't there yet. And speaking of close, not a single one of those twelve times twenty-three had happened anywhere near this close to home. Guy Ramsey had never actually had to mess with a murder, and he hated the idea that something new might be starting up. Not after twenty-three years in the sheriff's office.

He'd called in the troopers from Rutland and they'd done their job as if it was something they did every day of the week. They made sure to call it a homicide and everything, like it was old hat, even though he guessed they might have gotten that part from watching TV. They did it all by the book, you had to assume that much, but then again you couldn't be sure around people who'd had so little practice. There were twelve state police barracks in the state and twelve murders a year to go around, which meant one apiece. Even the best trained people could lose their edge at that rate. What kept these guys busy for the most part—and this included Ramsey, he didn't deny it—was passing out speeding tickets to drivers of the big shiny black Hummers that burned up the roads out of Connecticut. That and running D.A.R.E. programs.

But they'd put up yellow tape and they'd fingerprinted everything in sight and they'd had jars of Vicks VapoRub on hand just in case the body had had time to go bad. They'd taken pictures and they'd taken the bedsheets and they'd taken the chain from around David Paxton's neck. He'd watched them do this last like he was hypnotized by it, like the chain was a snake coming slow out of a basket. It was black with old oil and dried blood and it hadn't come away easily. Ramsey watched it jerk loose a link at a time and he wondered what kind of person would have put it there to begin with. Dug it in so deep. The busted chain from a chain saw here in this nice tidy condo right up against the slopes, the farthest place from a woodlot you could think of. He wondered what it meant, if it meant anything at all or if it were even intended to. And he wondered if this thing he was watching unfold might be just the beginning of a development he wasn't going to enjoy very much. Twenty-three years on the job meant he still had a bunch of years to go.

This stuff had been on his mind all night and all day. He hadn't rested and he didn't know how he would. He turned the cruiser up the little dirt road that led to his house and let it drift to a stop in front. It was a private road. Vermont was etched all over with private roads, a condition that sounded more hifalutin than it was. Private roads like this one were gravel and plain dirt, muddy in the spring and dusty in the summer and expensive to keep clear once the snow began to fly. Mostly they were named after the person who'd built the house at the end of them, which in this case was accurate. RAMSEY ROAD, the sign said. RAMSEY ROAD, PVT. There was a time when he'd liked the sound of it, back when he and his brother and their old man built the house with their own hands. But today, with this new problem up at the Snowfield Condos, it kind of felt to him like a target hung around his neck. He thought about taking down the other sign tacked up to a tree at the spot where Ramsey Road turned off 100, the little sign hand-lettered on a paper plate that his wife had put up, reading ROOM FOR RENT. In past years they'd had no trouble renting out that back bedroom to some kid from Australia or New Zealand who'd come all this way for the pleasure of standing in the cold and putting people's butts on chairlifts, but this year they'd had no takers. He thought it might be time to pull it down, but it was starting to snow again and he was already stamping off his feet on the porch and he didn't feel like going back out.

Megan was busy in the kitchen and the kids were up in their rooms doing their homework and nobody was around to say hello to Guy while he stood in the little front entryway shaking out his hat and coat. He hung them up and put his gun in the cabinet he'd built over the coat rack for that purpose. He wondered how long it would be before anybody noticed he was home. While his mind was going in that direction he wondered how long it would be before somebody who happened to be attracted by that RAMSEY ROAD sign out front—the kind of person who might strangle somebody with the chain from a chain saw, let's say, just for the sake of argument—could stand in that little entryway before somebody took notice and did something about it. Then he turned the rusty lock behind him—it was jammed and wouldn't throw—and walked into the kitchen.

"Hey there, handsome." She'd always greeted him the same way. Childhood sweethearts, they'd grown up three houses away from one another in the village and begun dating in junior high school. The quarterback and the head cheerleader. The king and queen of the prom. They went to different colleges thinking it might do them some good, and they were brokenhearted every day of the four years it took. By the end of the next summer they were married and that was that.

Over supper he told them pretty much everything. The kids were certainly old enough to hear. Anne was seventeen and Jim was two years behind. Anne and Jim. When he looked in the paper and saw the names of kids being born these days—Alexis and Brittany, Jared and Brandon—he felt like the last of a dying breed, as if he and Megan were the very last adults on earth who remembered what normal names sounded like. He wondered what kind of oddball monikers his grandkids would get saddled with, and he wondered whether they'd seem normal to them. Probably.

He ate his supper and he told them about the scene in the Snowfield Condos. How there had been no forced entry, either by the person who had killed David Paxton or by the person who called 911, assuming they were different individuals who'd entered at different times. Which a fair-minded person could assume, given the condition of the body.

"We're eating lasagna, Dad." This from Anne.

He told them how the troopers had been utterly cool and collected, as if this kind of crime scene was all in a day's work. All in a day's work for *anybody*, much less a couple of carloads of troopers from the Rutland barracks, which shared a driveway with the Department of Motor Vehicles and for good reason. He told them about the yellow crime scene tape and the fingerprinting equipment. He didn't mention the Vicks VapoRub and he didn't mention how deeply the chain had cut into Paxton's neck or how slowly it had come away. They were eating lasagna, after all. He'd been reminded of that once already.

Jim took the last slice of garlic bread and tore it in half. "You think they'll ever get 'em?"

"I hope so." He didn't know what to think about his son's choice of words. About the suggestion that somebody else would track down the murderer—as if the local sheriff had no dog in that fight. Frankly, he held the same bias that the boy did. He hoped somebody else would get 'em, too.

Tina talked her into it and Stacey looked up the number in the book they kept in the drawer beneath the cash register. Imagine that—a town where they put the sheriff's home phone number in the book.

"The house is a little out of the way," said Tina.

"That's fine."

"Like I said."

"I don't mind."

"I'd drive a little farther than that for work, but not much." Tina was in the massage therapy line these days, and among her customers were a few retirees and shut-ins who couldn't make it to the office that she and the chiropractor shared. "If I were still selling real estate, I'd describe it as *secluded*."

Stacey held her place in the phone book with one finger.

"'Course, you'll be safe enough. With the sheriff around and all."

She wondered if Tina knew her better than she knew herself. "I'm not worried," she said. "I'm a big girl."

"They've got bears out there."

"I've seen the signs."

"Not in the wintertime. They're hibernating. But come spring you'll have to watch out."

"I don't think living in the sheriff's house would protect a person against bears."

"Come the middle of April you might think different."

"I'm not—"

"I'm just saying," said Tina, sipping her chardonnay.

"Okay. I'll keep an eye out. I'll put it on my calendar. April. Bears."

She told a waitress she was going on break, and she took her cell phone out into the parking lot. Mobile service was spotty around here, but people said that you could get a signal outside the Broken Binding if you stood on a certain little rise about ten feet beyond the last handicapped space. She went there and climbed up on a snowbank and looked at her phone. Two bars. Nope, one. Wait— make that two. She keyed in the number as quickly as she could and pressed Send, and then at the last second she clicked the phone shut before the first ring. What if Tina was right, and she wanted this particular room just for the safety of it? It was a long way from sleeping in your car to sleeping under the sheriff's roof, and she hated to think that the dead guy with the chain around his neck had scared her into anything but self-reliance. Especially if it meant relying on another man.

Then again, she could keep an ear to the ground over there. She could find out if there was any more word about the woman who'd made the 911 call. That might be a good thing to know. So she clicked open the phone and pressed Send again, and this time she didn't hang up.

FOUR

She left work and stepped out into starlight. There was so much more of it up here than there was in Boston. It was gorgeous and overwhelming at the same time, and it made you feel weirdly insignificant. Small and vulnerable and above all exposed, like you were just some little animal hiding in the fields, holding your breath while predators sniffed around for your scent. Space aliens, maybe. Or bears.

She started the car and thought about the big ring of keys in the glove box. No way she'd use them tonight. No way she'd unlock another random condo. Tomorrow she'd drive out and check out that room in the sheriff's house and take it pretty much regardless, but tonight she'd bunk behind Bud's and the pizza joint one last time. Anything but risk turning another key in another lock. And hey, sleeping in your car was the way of the ski bum, wasn't it? Space aliens and bears notwithstanding.

She pulled into Bud's lot and went around back and crunched over a hard crust of snow that would be there until spring, following her own tracks from last night out of the main lot and into her safe corner. Out of sight and out of the wind, she cut the lights and switched off the engine and sat for a while listening to the world's worst classic rock on the radio. It was either that or NPR, and she'd had enough bad news to last a while. The windows started to fog and the starlight disappeared. The inside of the car began to cool down in a hurry. So she switched off the Marshall Tucker Band, climbed between the seats into the back, and crawled into her sleeping bag. Thank God for microfleece. Thank God for layers and layers of microfleece. She could ski in it, work in it, sleep in it, and then drag herself out of her trusty down bag come morning and repeat the process. It never wrinkled and it never wore out, no matter how often she put it through the giant industrial-strength washing machines at Bud's Suds. Plus it came in basic black, which went with everything.

She drifted off wondering if she'd have laundry privileges at the sheriff's place.

Some time while she was asleep a cold front moved in, and she roused up to the pinging of sleet on the roof of the car. The sound was high and ringing, not entirely constant, like water torture done with shards of ice. She lay in her sleeping bag listening to it and picturing the car getting slowly glassed over. She imagined what lay ahead on the mountain. They were certainly finished running the groomers by this hour of the night—however late it was—so this slippery crud would just build up on top of the snow and stay nasty. She hadn't realized how quickly she could get spoiled by the luxury of skiing every day, even if the rest of her living conditions weren't all that fantastic. Before, when she'd lived in Boston and made the trip only once or twice a month, any conditions on the mountain had been good. Not so anymore. She tucked her head down farther in the sleeping bag and smiled, thinking that she'd rather be spoiled this way than any other. Thinking that she had it coming. And letting that happy idea block out the sound of the sleet and the image of the dead man and the distance of the stars.

She drifted off figuring that she was the only person awake in town, but there must have been at least one other. One other to take some sharp implement and begin scraping a thin line clear around the glass of the car. Beginning with the driver's side window. Just a single surgical line in the ice, narrow as a vein, revealing nothing behind it for the utter darkness of the empty lot. It might have been a tire iron or a knife blade or maybe even just a key, cutting through the new coating of ice and rousing her with the hard high cry of metal against glass. All she could do was huddle in the sleeping bag, watching it come toward the back of the car where she lay.

It moved slowly and steadily. She watched the thin line move along the window and realized all at once that she had forgotten to lock the doors, and she wondered if she dared move to hit the power button for fear that whoever was out there with that tire iron or hatchet or God forbid chain saw would hear the thunk of the locks going down. It was a decision that didn't take long to make. And when she lashed out one hand and hit the switch and drew herself back into the bag all in one continuous motion, the line carving itself in the glass did not falter. It continued all the way to the rear hatch where it hesitated as if deciding something, and then it started up again across the liftgate, perfectly even and level and parallel to the defroster wires. She held her breath. It paused again at the other edge and then it started up the passenger side. She exhaled and watched the windows fog some more. Good. That was good. Still, if whatever it was that was carving this line had been a welding torch, it would have sliced the car in half by now. And Stacey inside it, like a sardine in a can.

It stopped at the leading edge of the passenger window, and it did not continue across the windshield.

And that was it. No other sound, no other interference with the car, nothing. Not so much as the crunch of footsteps on the snow and ice in the parking lot, heading away.

Stacey shut her eyes and tried to believe that she was dreaming, but it did no good. She resolved to start the car and drive to the gas station—there was a convenience store there that she was pretty certain was open twenty-four hours, and if it weren't still open at least there were lights—but at the last moment she realized that there was no way she could move the car with the windows iced over.

She sure wasn't getting out to clean them off.

She shut her eyes again and pulled the sleeping bag over her head, but she didn't go back to sleep for the longest time. She thought that maybe she would never manage to sleep again.

Morning dawned late. There was no sun, and the clouds were still spitting something ugly and hard. From inside her bag Stacey rubbed at the condensation on the glass only to find it frozen. She groaned and reached out and turned the key in the ignition, drew back her arm and lay still until she quit shivering, and then reached out again to jack up the fan and push the heater control as far into the red as it would go.

When the car had warmed up but not too much she wriggled out of the bag and breathed on the window and rubbed at it again. She picked a spot right about in the middle, just where the line had been cut in the ice during the night. She rubbed there and she rubbed in a few other places, and the condensation came away, but if there was any sign left in the ice on the outside of the glass she couldn't spot it. Not the slightest thread or break, not the smallest lingering variation in the way that the gray light passed through from outside. So she threw on her frozen jacket and put up her hood and got out of the car to see what she could see, and out there it was even more hopeless. Whatever had happened hadn't left a trace, either on the windows or in the lot around the car. Not as far as she could see.

She got back into the car and waited to stop shivering, but it took a while.

If anything could take her mind off this stuff, it was a morning on the mountain. At least her job came with a season pass, compliments of Pete Hardwick and his investment banking money. Spruce Peak wasn't anybody's idea of the best in the East, but it was something. And as long as you got started early and knew where to look—which by now Stacey did, both of them, in spades—you could still manage to find more fun there than was strictly good for you. She'd never have let it slip to Pete, but she'd have pretty much worked for the pass alone.

She left the car running in front of Judge Roy Beans and went in for her usual double espresso. The pause that refreshes—isn't that what the old Pepsi bottles said? Well, this wasn't much of a pause, and the refreshment was more on the order of antifreeze applied directly to her circulatory system, but it did the trick every morning. The counterman (she didn't know his name; not yet, anyhow) handed it to her in a squat little paper cup and she dosed it with Sweet'N Low and knocked it back in a single gulp. It went down fast and smooth and she stood there at the counter for a moment letting it work, like some needy drunk at a whiskey bar. She drew the back of her hand across her mouth. Then she crumpled the cup and trashed it and went out again.

The hard weather had kept the out-of-state contingent home this morning. You could always tell the road conditions in Connecticut by the size of the crowds at the base lodge, and this morning the driving must have been lousy. The only people booting up were old-timers, the seventy-plus club that was here regardless of the weather. Coming into the base lodge during the early part of the season felt like going to an out-of-the-way McDonald's at seven at the morning: Nothing but escapees from the nursing home,

swapping stories they'd told each other a million times. Alzheimer's
was a blessing and a social lubricant to these old codgers. And codgers they were, for the most part. There was hardly a woman among
them, motherhood and failed interest and osteoporosis having
taken all but the hardest core. Stacey threw her bag on an empty
table, dropped her boots, and headed down to the ladies' room
where she could wash her face and brush her teeth and plug in her
cell phone for a few minutes' charge. She wondered when Brian
would realize that he was still paying *that* bill, and every time she
made a call she half expected it not to work at all, never mind the
lousy service up here in the woods. So far, though, so good. It kind
of made her want to pile up some minutes.

The first lift ride was miserable, and her parka had acquired
a good thick crust of ice by the time she slid off the chair at mid-
mountain. She shivered and scraped off her goggles, and just the
idea of scraping ice made her shiver again; not from the cold, but
from the idea of whatever claw had been scrabbling at her make-
shift bedroom window in the night. Things got better on the peak
lift, though. The higher she went the higher she got above the crud
and the better the mountain looked. There was actually some sun
breaking through and a few flakes of snow blowing in from somewhere at the top, and it occurred to her as she slid off and arranged
her poles that there was a lesson in that somewhere. A lesson in
sticking to it. A lesson in having faith. The chairful of golden old-
ies who'd unloaded ahead of her were indistinguishable from
younger men in their parkas and helmets and goggles, and as one of
them gave a whoop and they started making turns downhill she
realized that they handled themselves on the mountain as well as
anybody. They certainly took the same joy from it that she did, and
that was another lesson in perseverance, wasn't it? She thought of
her mother and her grandmother, osteoporosis victims the both of
them, and she vowed that she'd start drinking more milk. Maybe

get some calcium tablets at the drugstore if she remembered. Even a full-time free-at-last ski diva had to look out for the future.

Then she started downhill and forgot about everything.

Everything.

She forgot about the weather, she forgot about getting old, she forgot about her faithless fiancé. She even forgot about the dead man with the bloody chain around his neck and whatever Evil Claw had carved a thin cruel line into the ice on her car.

It all disappeared, every brain-clogging bit of it, and her world was clarified and lifted up until it consisted of nothing but snow and speed and long linked turns.

It was a beautiful thing, and she was determined to make it last just as long as she could.

FIVE

She was due to look at that room for rent at one, and she was only a little late. The Ramsey place was farther out of town than she'd imagined, farther out than she'd been before. Driving out there, she thought how four-wheel drive would probably come in handy. Then again, the sheriff probably got special treatment from whoever took care of the roads. Either that or he'd have some kind of extremely capable vehicle that she could count on to blaze a trail. Wrong on both counts, as it turned out. The road as it wound farther and farther out among the tall pines wasn't in the best of shape even now, and parked where he'd slewed it into the drive was a standard-issue police cruiser, big as a whale and probably just as hard to keep going in a straight line. Around the side of the house was another car, probably his own, probably driven by his wife—a beat-up Dodge minivan missing most of its paint. The house was missing some paint, too, and one part of it was wrapped in raw Tyvek that fluttered in the light wind. That kind of thing was common enough in the Green Mountain State. A lot of construction projects seemed to take forever. And a lot of homeowners did them on their own, in their spare time. Still, she looked at the minivan and the Tyvek and she didn't wonder why they might be eager to rent out a room. Even the little bit she could afford to pay would probably help.

As she approached the house somebody raised a slat in the Venetian blinds with two fingers, and no sooner had she caught sight of it than it dropped again. A man's hand, no doubt belonging to the sheriff himself. Either he was no sophisticate in matters of surveillance or he didn't care that she saw him. Or maybe he did care, and he wanted her to know that he had his eye on her already. There was probably nothing wrong with that.

The woman opened the door and put out a hand and introduced herself, and right away Stacey felt pretty much at home. It wasn't that this was much like any home she'd ever known. She'd grown up an only child in an enormous but sterile apartment, with a mother who worked long hours at her law firm and a father who traveled constantly for Gillette. He used to tell her that he sold razor blades door to door, but by the time she was in middle school she realized that a person couldn't sell enough razor blades in one lifetime to support their expensive habits for six months. By that time, though, she didn't much care what he did. And besides, he wasn't around enough to explain it. As for the home she'd been putting together with Brian when the ax fell in the person of that tramp—that tramp she'd actually gone to the movies with the night before; *to the movies,* if you can believe it, to see a chick flick that Brian was just too manly to bother with—well, the less said about that setup the better.

The Ramsey place was overly warm and crowded with furniture and it smelled like the fire that was burning in the pellet stove. She knew she'd take the room if they'd have her, and not just because it beat sleeping behind Bud's Suds in plain sight of The Claw or The Chain Saw Killer or whoever it was. Probably just kids. Yeah, that was it. Unless it was somebody who'd seen her leaving the Snow-field two nights back. She hadn't thought of that until now.

Stacey went a little vague with the thought and Megan had her fixed up with a mug of tea before she knew what hit her. The sheriff's wife was already in the middle of extracting her life history when Guy emerged from the next room. The one with the Venetian blinds. That would turn out to be their bedroom; Stacey's would be farther back, in the part of the house done up in Tyvek, although she wouldn't really give much thought to the geography of it. The kids' rooms were upstairs.

"Guy, this is Stacey Curtis. She's here about the room."

He moved into the kitchen with them—he took up most of what was left of it, which wasn't much—and leaned against the refrigerator, noncommittal. "Pleased to meet you."

"So you're the sheriff." She raised her mug.

"That's what it says on the car."

She lowered the mug but held on to it, pointing with one finger. "The badge, too. And the uniform."

"I can't seem to keep any secrets around here."

"Stacey's from Boston."

"You just up for the winter?"

"I really don't know. I'm a little unsettled right now." That was the understatement of the year. She pressed her lips together and gave a pained look, as if she was afraid of being difficult. "Is the room, I mean, do you—"

"We like to keep it to the season if we can. Guy's mother uses it in the summertime. She's in Florida now."

Guy cocked an eyebrow. "Mostly people only come for the winter."

"But it's definitely empty until May," Megan said. Which wasn't exactly an offer, but might have passed for one.

"So," said Guy, "you working at the mountain?"

"Actually, at the Broken Binding."

"Pete's done a good job down there."

"It's a nice place."

"Eight or ten years ago it was rough as they come. I was down there breaking up fights more than I was home."

"Really?"

"Really."

"You'd never know it."

Stacey drank her tea and Megan drank hers and Guy leaned against the refrigerator in the pose of a person who has just realized he ought to be somewhere else. But there was still one question in the air, even if he hadn't asked it. Megan did, finally, and coming from her it was anything but confrontational. "You said you're a little *unsettled?*"

"A little."

Not a word from Megan, just a look that asked the question all over again.

"Temporarily."

The same look and the same silence.

"Let's just say I'm not getting married this summer after all."

Megan's eyes widened.

"I'm out of here," said Guy.

He stopped as he left the driveway to take down the hand-lettered paper plate, folded it into neat quarters, and put it in his jacket pocket. Then he pressed the tack back into the wood and rolled up his window against the weather, which had started to spit again, and headed down the road. He felt a little foolish for having wanted to come around to see the girl, but you never could tell. Not these days.

Megan showed Stacey the room, and although there was something of the third hand and even more of the mother-in-law about everything in it, it looked fine. Kind of cozy, in a way that Stacey hadn't experienced very much in her life of some privilege. Brian would have scoffed at it, and if it had been a bed-and-breakfast they'd found themselves checking into he would have insisted that they leave and look for some other place. The one window had only a thin curtain over it and no blinds or shade, an absence that made her a little uncomfortable. A person outside could see right in. On the other hand she could hang up a bath towel if she wanted. Besides, she'd changed in the Subaru more times than she could say anyhow.

Anyhow, there was nothing out there but woods.

Woods and space aliens and bears and now maybe The Claw.

They went back to the kitchen and poured more tea.

"So what do you think?"

Stacey put both hands around her mug as if she needed the warmth all over her body, and squeezed her shoulders together. "Oh," she said, "I'll definitely take it."

"Great. When do you want to move in?"

"Right away, if that's OK with you."

Megan sipped. "As soon as you want."

Having come from the land of the annual lease and the thirty-day notice, she thought Megan might think her answer a little strange: "How about right now?"

But she had nothing to worry about. Megan was already an old hand at this. "Let me get my shoes on," she said, "and I'll give you a hand."

"Are you sure?"

"Absolutely."

"You don't mind?"

"Mind what?"

The modest jumble of stuff in the back of the Subaru would turn out to be the conversational break that Megan hadn't entirely known she'd been waiting for. Stacey popped the liftgate and looked a little sadly inside at the sleeping bag and the microfleece and the stash of energy bars. At the hats and the gloves and the pair of boots cocked sideways to dry over the heater vents.

In Megan's mind, no excuse was necessary. She looked from the mess to Stacey and back again, and she summed it all up. "Looks to me like somebody left in a hurry."

The vague sadness on Stacey's features melted a little and she smiled through it. "You think?"

"We've had a lot of young people rent that room, but never a runaway bride."

"You are so onto me."

"A runaway bride in basic black. That's different, too."

"You don't know the half of it."

Unloading the car took two trips, and they weren't straining themselves.

"So how long were the two of you together?"

"Forever. Two years in college and three more in grad school."

"I'll bet your parents put a little pressure on."

"Not really. Well, I don't know. Maybe a little." Stacey bent to gather some odds and ends and put them in a plastic bag from the grocery store. "It's hard to say."

"After five years, they probably figured—"

"Right. I kind of started figuring that, too."

"So you made it happen?"

"Yeah. And then I made it not happen."

"At least you know your own mind."

"I do now."

They went in the house and went to Stacey's room and put everything on the bed. Then they went back out. Megan unlatched the ski racks and raised them up. "Five years, you said?"

"Yeah."

"Five years is a good long while."

"I know."

"But it's not forever." Taking the skis and leaning them up against the car.

"I guess not."

"And don't start thinking it is." She opened a little home-carpentered closet on the wall of the house and put the skis inside.

"I don't know." Stacey shook her head and stood by the car with her arms full, and in her stance anybody could have seen the loss of all that time. "It sure seems like it."

Megan set her straight. "I've been crazy about Guy since we were five years old. Now *that's* forever."

Stacey had to allow that she was probably right about that.

SIX

People in these little Vermont towns still looked out for one another, still pulled their own weight and some of their neighbor's if they needed to, still came together when one of their own passed on. That's how it went with David Paxton. His funeral the next day didn't start until two but St. Paul's Lutheran was packed tight by a quarter to one, and the whole village was more or less shut down for the better part of the afternoon. Skiers up from the south couldn't get a cup of coffee at Judge Roy Beans and a sandwich at Mahoney's and they couldn't pick up their freshly tuned skis at MountainWerks. They couldn't even give a handout to Danny Bowman, the gray-skinned and white-haired vet who'd been a fixture in town ever since the Army had shipped him back from Da Nang in 1969, because Danny was at the funeral too. They stood in the cold and they sat in their cars and they scratched underneath their wool caps, wondering what in the world was going on. The mountain itself didn't close, but there was black bunting draped around the base lodge in David's memory. The out-of-town snowboarding crowd dug it in a goth sort of way, and it got traction in the blogosphere for a week or two until everything blew over and Spruce Peak reclaimed its reputation as a family place.

Stacey hadn't been able to make up her mind about attending the service. She kind of wanted to say good-bye to David Paxton, thinking that by seeing him off she might free herself of the sticky image of him in that bloody bed with the chain around his neck. But she was still a proper Bostonian and she didn't have anything to wear. (She had plenty of black fleece, and black was the color of the day, but still.) On top of that she wasn't sure that a stranger in town had any business barging in on a funeral. Even if, in her particular case, she actually had reasons galore.

In the end, Pete Hardwick made up her mind for her. He posted word that all hands had to be on deck at the Binding by one o'clock, the late shift included, because Andy Paxton had booked the dining room for a reception. It would start the minute the funeral was over. No graveside service and no burial, not today, not with the ground this hard. Stacey didn't want to think about where they'd keep the body or for how long. So she took a few runs and went back to the Ramsey place for a shower and turned around and headed back into town.

She threaded through the heaviest traffic she'd seen since Boston, cars parked everywhere and the lights on Guy Ramsey's cruiser strobing away just because. Guy himself stood in the street in front of the church, directing people and cars with one of those long orange flashlights that always made her think of *Star Wars*. He took note of her car and caught her eye and waved her on past with the press of one finger on the flat brim of his campaign hat, knowing where she was bound. The brotherhood of those called upon to do their jobs, even at a moment like this.

Inside the church, wrapped in her best coat despite the steam heat and the press of the growing congregation, Megan Ramsey sat with

Anne on one side and Jim on the other. She had taken off her gloves and was holding hands with each of them as if no power on earth could cause her to let go. Nothing like somebody else losing a son to make a person gather her own children close.

The casket was the best that loads of money could buy—a world-class beauty of solid oak and brushed nickel, it must have weighed three times what David weighed—and it was sealed up tight as a drum. That fact got plenty of tongues wagging right off, even in the hushed confines of St. Paul's. So it was true what people said. About the chain saw. And about how David's body had deteriorated while it lay in that awful bed for God knows how long. There was obviously no fixing him up, and it probably would have taken a turtleneck sweater to cover those wounds.

The truth was simpler and sadder. His father simply couldn't look.

The elder Paxton sat in front, the halo of his white hair dipping now and then as he dabbed at his eyes with a handkerchief. His shoulders were narrow in his black suit. Paxton was all height, not much width, and when he had arrived the undertaker and the pastor had both wondered under their breath at the frailness of him. It wasn't a side of Andy Paxton that you saw much. He was a man of the world and a man of the woods, educated at Choate and Amherst for the purpose of self-betterment and educated at his father's knee for the purpose of running Spruce Peak. He was as skilled at felling trees as at negotiating labor contracts. He was comfortable anywhere. And even at seventy he could still skin up Spruce's highest peak without resting and shoot back down through the deepest woods before lift-riders a third his age had found their first stashes of powder. But today he was broken; and he was leaning on his wife, Marie, for support; and Marie was broken, too.

They'd met in college. She was a city girl, a native New Yorker, and fifty years in Vermont hadn't changed that as far as the natives were concerned. Start life as a flatlander, and you stay a flatlander forever. Fifty winters and fifty mud seasons hadn't been able to buy Marie a membership in their homegrown club and another fifty wouldn't get her any closer, particularly since she'd had the big-city nerve to marry the wealthiest bachelor in town.

Then again, maybe she'd been admitted today—courtesy of David. It was the furthest thing from her mind.

The receiving line took forever and the line of cars between the church and the Broken Binding was steady and unbroken enough that a person could have walked to the reception on it. Bumper to bumper and slow as molasses. The undertaker used up his supply of little magnetic funeral flags early, but it didn't make any difference because there was barely a car in town that wasn't already in the line.

For Stacey, the first hour of the reception was an absolute cakewalk. A couple of martinis, one scotch, and a string of Manhattans (she had to check in the book for the recipe). That was it, unless you counted the one bottle each of merlot and chardonnay that she'd opened up just in case. The heavy action was in the dining room, and the drink of choice for that first hour was hot black coffee.

An open bar was an open bar, though, and sooner or later things took their usual course.

Guy Ramsey posted himself on a stool at the entryway, between the bar and the dining room. He wasn't in his uniform—perhaps he'd gone back to the office and changed—but his posture and the look in his eye said "on duty" clear enough.

As Stacey watched, one middle-aged couple paid the last of their respects and threw on their coats and fled toward the door. They were both perfectly steady on their feet but the man buttoned up his face as he passed the sheriff, looking even from Stacey's spot behind the bar as if he were holding his breath. As if he were reluctant to exhale until he was out the door and gone.

She called over, "You think everybody'll get home all right, Sheriff?"

"Guy."

"You think they'll get home OK?"

"I hope."

"I do, too."

Guy pulled back the lace curtain that covered the little window in the door, and he tilted his head to watch the couple make their way to their car. "I don't run a taxi service, but sometimes I wish I did."

"Either that or a tow truck."

He let the curtain go and turned back and smiled at her. "You've got that right."

SEVEN

The Manhattans, as it turned out, were for Andy Paxton. The old man stood along the wall by a display of photographs of his son—photographs of the whole family, really; they were always together, by the look of it, skiing and boating and picnicking by waterfalls—he stood along the wall and solemnly put away one drink after another. The alcohol seemed to have no affect on him whatsoever. He was as dry and as sober after two hours as he had been when he'd arrived. It was as if something had been removed from him, some vital part that would have processed the fluids that he was methodically pouring in, and all he could do was try to fill himself up to no avail.

Guy watched him and thought about starting up that taxi service.

Unlike her husband, Marie was altogether too occupied to eat or drink. Someone had possession of her hands from one minute to the next, squeezing them and stroking them and pressing them together like dried flowers. She and Andy started the reception together but soon drifted off in different directions, he to his post by the photographs and she toward whatever eddy the movement of the crowd took her. At the moment she was sobbing on the tailored breast of her daughter-in-law, Jeanette, Richie's wife.

Meanwhile, Richie himself, the only son that she and Andy had left, loaded up his plate at the buffet for a second or third time and headed toward the bar. "Haven't eaten since we got the news," he said to someone. Richie was every bit as tall as his father and just as slim, built like a whippet and raised that way, too. He'd always been high-strung and furiously athletic. Given his low weight and his brother's recent death, no one could have held an extra plate or two of lobster ravioli and roast beef and scalloped potatoes against him. Or another Corona Light, for that matter. Which is what he had in mind as he made his way toward the bar.

Chip Walsh stopped him. The young man stopped him with a hand thrust out in sympathy and friendship, but Richie chose not to accept it. Richie chose quite theatrically not to accept it, in fact. He went so far as to swap his plate of food from his left hand to his right so as to avoid shaking hands, leaving Chip standing in the entryway with one arm out and a look of consternation on his face.

Chip Walsh was the only person in the room not dressed in black. He wore a wrinkled pair of dirt-brown Carhartts and a shirt of plaid flannel faded to nothing, under an army-green Arc'teryx jacket that would have cost more than everything else he owned if he hadn't found it on closeout three or four years back. Chip wasn't from around here, although he looked it. He was from somewhere down in Maryland, somewhere not far from D.C., where his father was an oil-company lobbyist and his mother spent her time lingering over society lunches. Chip had escaped from all that to come live by himself in the mountains. He was a ski patroller in the winter and he led canoe and mountain bike trips in the summer. He knew he couldn't keep it up forever, but right now he was content to live in the kind of self-imposed poverty that only youth can endure. Unlike some people, he hadn't been reduced to sleeping in his car. Not yet, anyhow.

Stacey had never seen Chip before, at least not without his helmet and his goggles and his official red jacket in which he looked pretty much like every other patroller on the mountain. He didn't visit the bar at the Broken Binding much and he sure didn't look like the kind of guy who could afford to eat in the dining room. He looked like the kind of guy who got a couple of slices or maybe half a rotisserie chicken and ate in front of the TV. Definitely not premium cable, though, and that was fine with Stacey. She'd had her fill of guys who sprung for premium cable. Brian, for example. Premium cable was perfect for him. Seventy-five channels, and nothing to watch.

Stamping off his boots out there in the entryway, sunburned and yellow-haired and dressed in the colors of the woods, Chip stood out like a beacon in that relentless sea of black. Stacey looked up at him from her work and looked back down again and looked back up against her will. He and Guy were talking. And then here came Richie Paxton with a plateful of food and Chip turned to him and was ostentatiously shunned and something about the transaction made Stacey even more curious about him than before. Not necessarily in a positive way, but hey: She'd made worse mistakes.

Richie came right on past, into the bar. Chip looked at Guy and shrugged and watched Richie go. He looked as if he was thinking about taking off his jacket or at least going into the dining room to pay his respects to Andy and Marie but then something passed across his face and he went into the bar instead. He followed Richie, who must have heard his footsteps, because he turned, spun on his heel, and said, "You come for the open bar, Woodchip?"

"I came to pay my respects."

"You and everybody in town. Free food and drink always brings a crowd."

"Richie."

"I should remember that. Maybe we'll do a free wiener roast sometime next season. Guarantee a big opening day."

"Richie, I'm sorry about your brother."

"You're sorry? What did you have to do with it?"

"*I'm sorry.* It's a manner of speaking."

Richie turned away and called the rest over his shoulder. "The sheriff's right there. Confess to him if you're confessing, Woodchipper. I'm occupied." He'd reached the bar and he put his plate down on it and demanded a Corona.

Stacey fetched a glass and a coaster, and then she opened the bottle and pushed a wedge of lime into its mouth.

Richie looked as if she'd bitten him. "I asked you for a Light."

"No. You said—"

"I know what I said. Repeat after me: *Corona. Light.*" He pushed the bottle with its little wedge of lime back toward her. "Anyway, sweetness, it's time to be on your best behavior. In case you didn't know, I'm the *bereaved.*"

"I did know. And I'm very—"

"In other words, this whole clambake is courtesy of yours truly."

"Yes, sir. I understand."

"That's better. Now, some time ago I ordered a Corona Light, if it's not too much trouble."

When she looked up again, Chip Walsh had cleared out. Not a moment too soon, as far as she was concerned. If Richie Paxton was going to humiliate her, he could do it without Chip in the audience.

When Andy and Marie began shrugging into their coats and moving toward the door, Guy slid down from his stool and vanished into the dining room. He turned up a moment later with his hand on Chip Walsh's shoulder, and the two of them caught up with the

Paxtons. Guy whispered something to Andy and then squeezed Chip's shoulder and smiled. He reached in his pocket and took out his wallet, but Chip held up a hand and shook his head. He might have caught Stacey's eye with one last look into the bar, but it was hard to say.

Richie turned on his stool and witnessed the end of the transaction, Chip softly taking Marie by the hand and elbow and then accepting a set of car keys from her husband, the three of them stepping outside into the early dark. Richie pointed to the door with his thumb and leaned toward Stacey. "He's a smooth one, for all the rough edges."

"Is he?"

"Look at him. Acting like the son they never lost."

"I think it was the sheriff's idea."

"Now that he's got their keys, I just hope he doesn't rob the place."

"Is that any way—"

"At least we've got witnesses."

"Is that—"

"Is that any way to talk about a nicely put together young man who's driving my parents home because I'm too drunk to do the job? Too drunk and incidentally *too bereaved*? Is that any way?" Drinking off the last and motioning for another. "It is. Yes, it is. And if you doubt it it's because you don't know the Woodchip like I do."

"Woodchip."

"Chip. Chip Walsh. He's from the big city, and he came up here to save the trees."

EIGHT

A shiver crawled up Stacey's spine as her headlights raked across the dark and empty lot in front of Bud's Suds. She turned on the radio and the dome light in self-defense, and in that little moving bubble of dim light and Sheryl Crow music she began to feel better. She wouldn't be doing her laundry at Bud's anymore and she wouldn't be camping out behind the place, either. Let The Claw find somebody else to pick on.

There was a streetlight where she turned off the main highway, but the narrower and less-traveled road into the country was completely dark. Here and there a light burned in some cabin or cottage, screened from the road by trees, but that was it. Her headlights only went so far, and turn after turn presented blind spots that promised moose or deer or worse. Reflectors at the ends of driveways and private roads loomed like the eyes of predators. She drove as fast as she dared, wondering how this long and twisting stretch could have seemed so very different by daylight. She hadn't even noticed it.

Secluded, Tina had said. "Secluded" must be Realtor-speak for way the hell out in the boonies where no one can hear you scream.

Megan had left the light on in the entryway as she'd said she would, which was a comfort—not only the light itself but its guarantee that there was somebody else in the house, somebody else waiting for her mindfully enough to light up the place a little. Stacey parked the car and went inside and tried to lock the door behind her but the works were jammed. She latched the bathroom door shut with its little metal hook and brushed her teeth and washed her face and unlatched the door again and went out. There was another hook just like it inside her bedroom door, and she latched that one before she shut out the light and climbed into bed.

Come morning there was a new angle all over the Rutland newspaper. Guy was at the table muttering over it with a cup of coffee in his hand when Stacey came down the hall.

Richie Paxton—he was Richard in public—had given an interview the day before. The truth is he hadn't actually given it as much as he'd jammed it down the reporter's throat, and although the reporter had been less than enthusiastic about making the drive down Route 100 and setting up shop with his notebook and his recorder at a booth at Judge Roy Beans, he'd done his duty. Spruce Peak was an important and reliable advertiser, and you couldn't afford to alienate management.

The reporter had been expecting a reminiscence about the dear departed, but he didn't get much of that. What he got instead was a rant—complex and all but incomprehensible—about a conspiracy to deprive the Paxtons of their livelihood. It was a story worth the drive from Rutland, that was for sure, but the reporter hadn't come close to being able to print all of it. The central theme, at least as it showed up in the paper, was the environment. Nothing new there. Spruce owned half of its acreage outright, and leased the other half from the Forest Service. It had been that way for generations. But aside from some maintenance buildings, the Peak Lodge at the top of the main lift, and the lift hardware itself, every single manmade structure on the premises was built on Paxton land because it was just too difficult to get permits for anything else. Even a first-aid hut could become a federal case. So the base lodge and the ski school shed and the mountain offices—not to mention the barns for the groomers and the pumping stations for snowmaking and the half-dozen condo buildings owned by the family—were confined to resort property. There were other bits of private land here and there, accessible from roads through dense woods that opened now and again on magnificent custom houses, but even those were entirely built out.

And there, according to Richie, was the rub.

The tree huggers, he said, were set on keeping Spruce Peak from expanding. They were dedicated enough to take the life of his own little brother, David, in order to derail things. Poor David, who lived all by himself in his little parking-lot-view condo at Snowfield. No wife, no kids, no house in town. No high-end custom home with a view of the slopes. It was the way he liked it—he'd always been a solitary man of simple needs—but in the end it made him into the weakest member of the herd. The one that the tree huggers could pick off the most easily, according to Richie. David's death was a warning, he said. The first volley in a battle that was only going to get worse.

The reporter had asked if he was referring to the offer from Ski-America, the Denver operation that had been sniffing around the mountain. They'd bought up resorts everywhere, but so far they hadn't made any progress with Spruce. Thanks to the Forest Service and that technicality. Something about runoff.

Richie said the tree huggers didn't mind SkiAmerica *per se*. What they didn't like was SkiAmerica's money, which they thought might outlast the patience of the Forest Service, letting the trails of Spruce Peak expand back into wilderness acreage now off-limits and beyond the lease. When he'd said *wilderness* he'd clearly put a pair of ironic quotation marks around it, and the reporter had quoted his gesture. By *wilderness*, he clarified, he meant land that had been made use of for as long as these mountains had known white men—and not just by legitimate users like hunters and loggers, but by every kind of troublemaker from Prohibition-era bootleggers to growers of high-quality marijuana.

He went on to hint at a connection between the marijuana grown in those remote and sunny mountain vales and the true motives of the granola-eating tree huggers—small-time dope fiends and major-league smugglers all, whose lives would get difficult when the engineers and loggers arrived to start cutting new ski trails. He suggested that these perverts and criminals were aided, perhaps unwittingly, by dupes in the Forest Service regional office.

He added that the use of a chain saw chain to murder his brother was suggestive in the extreme. Things like this were all about imagery, he said, all about sending a message. "Like putting a dead fish in bed with some mob guy," was how he put it.

And he concluded by insisting that he himself, without a doubt, was next on their hit list.

At the breakfast table, Guy finished his coffee and dropped the paper with a scornful look. "The man's gone hysterical," he said. "If anybody in that family ever hugged a tree, it was David." He looked up at Stacey, who stood pouring herself coffee at the counter, and he slid the paper in her direction. "You may as well get the details on the local sideshow. Read all about it."

She saw the name in the headline. "I met Richie yesterday."

"I saw," he said. "Lucky you."

Stacey couldn't believe how long the car took to warm up. And she'd been sleeping in it? Incredible, the things a person could get used to. And incredible how easily you could slide back into the old habits and comforts of civilization.

The heater was barely wheezing by the time she turned onto the main road and made for the mountain. Past the fire station and the VFW and MountainWerks, where the lights were on and the walkways were freshly salted for the arrival of the early morning crowd. Past Bud's Suds and the pizza joint. Then a quick stop for her double espresso. She appreciated that Megan and Guy let her help herself to their coffee, but it was watery and half scorched. Watery and half scorched Maxwell House drip grind, to be frank. It wasn't even even Dunkin' Donuts, that familiar and nearly drinkable New England staple.

Pushing open the Judge's door for the first time in a condition other than frozen-solid and bleary-eyed, she caught a flash of familiar blond hair in a back booth. It was that patroller from the Broken Binding, she realized, the one who'd taken the dead man's parents home. Chip. Chip Something. All she could think of, thanks to the poison that was Richie Paxton, was *Woodchip*. Great. She felt like a bird-watcher, alert to the slightest flicker of plumage and armed with a set of ridiculous names. Warbler. Nuthatch. Woodchip.

She went to the counter and stood behind some bottle blonde up from Connecticut in a Bogner one-piece jumpsuit. The one-piece was glittery and geometric and had *Saturday Night Fever* written all over it, although it was probably fresh from the toniest shop in Manhattan. Stacey with her basic black fleece and the same old yellow Columbia jacket she'd been wearing night and day for weeks felt a little surge of superiority, as if she were a hard-core old-timer already. She stood at an angle to the counter and like an idiot she looked at the patroller in the back booth thinking the rest of his name would come to her. And then she looked away from him toward the blonde in the one-piece, who was in the middle of ordering a half-caf low-fat caffe macchiato. Stacey thought it sounded like a designer handbag and the counterman just looked stumped. Then she glanced again toward the patroller in the far booth, her mind far less on him than on solving the puzzle in her head. But with all the looking it wasn't long before she got herself noticed. Chip was giving her a little wave of his hand when the counterman presented her with her usual squatty paper cup.

She took it with her left hand and acknowledged Chip with her right. Just the slightest upward tilting of her hand to match his. Then she went for the Sweet'N Low. Whoever had been sitting opposite Chip in the booth got up and left as Stacey tore open the pink packet, and she caught the movement of a large shape from the corner of her eye. A reflexive glance brought the line of her vision into contact with Chip's again and kind of made it apparent that she'd better go over and say hello before he got the wrong idea. Or any idea at all.

"Hey." Looking up, twirling his spoon in his mug.

"If it isn't the Good Samaritan."

He squinted in thought. "Oh. Yeah. I try."

"Those were the parents." It wasn't really a question, just an assertion that they were on the same page. "David Paxton's parents."

"Yep. They're good people."

"It's a shame."

"Terrible."

She gave him her name and he gave her his, as if he needed to. Then he pointed toward her little cup and said, "I don't guess it'll take you long to drink that, but if you want to sit down . . ."

She perched on the end of the bench, noncommittal. Just to take a load off.

"I see they let you out of the Binding every now and then."

"Only so I can take a few runs."

"Somebody's got their priorities straight."

She indicated his patrol jacket. "Somebody else does, too."

"It's a job."

"It's not a job," she said. "It's an adventure."

Chip smiled. "Only on a bad day."

She asked him why he wasn't up opening the mountain and he explained he'd had to drive Andy Paxton's Land Cruiser back to his own place last night and then arrange a swap this morning. How he'd driven up to the Paxton homestead to get Andy, and how they'd gone together to the Binding where he'd left his Wrangler. "You should have seen my roommates when I fired up that Land Cruiser," he said. "Me. Mister Eco-Friendly. Mister Green Jeans."

"He drives that white one I see around town?"

"That's it. The white whale."

"Moby Dick."

"It's an incredible piece of machinery," he said. "I swear. You could live in it."

"I'll bet you could."

"And the *leather*. It's like a dozen cows gave their *lives* for those seats. And if they'd known how gorgeous it was going to be and how great it was going to smell and how warm it would be once you turned on the heaters, they wouldn't even have minded."

"The cows."

"The cows. It's this gorgeous creamy color. Soft as butter."

"All in memory of the cows."

He laughed, half at her and half at himself. "In memory of the cows." Toasting them with his empty mug.

"You're an inspiration, Mister Green Jeans."

"Hey, I can appreciate it without approving of it."

"How does that fit with the guy being a good person, like you said?"

He didn't take it as a challenge, which was nice. Instead he just looked across the room as if the answer were over there somewhere, and after a minute he said, "I don't know. I guess you can have more money than you know what to do with, and still be all right."

"I guess."

"Not that I know from experience. My dad's loaded, and he's kind of a rat about it."

"Really."

"Yeah. So I think maybe it's hard, but it's still possible."

"It's not that you just feel sorry for him? Andy Paxton?"

"No."

"Not just because of his son. Not just because of David."

"No." He shook his head, and then reached to put his gloves on. "You ever meet him?"

"David?"

"David."

"No."

"Too bad." With a gloved hand he pointed to her cup. "You gonna drink that?"

Between the paper cup and the small amount in it, her espresso had gone cold. She drank it in a hurry, two big swallows tops.

"David was working that same deal," he said. "Trying to be a good person in spite of all the money."

She crumpled her cup and stood. The caffeine hit her bloodstream like a roman candle and there was something else there, too. Something else she wasn't entirely thrilled about feeling. She leaned forward and tossed the cup into the trash. "See you out there."

She parked a million miles away and booted up in the crowded lodge, and he parked in the employee lot and booted up in the empty patrol shack, but they hit the lift at the same instant. She decided it was either kismet or some angle on his part or the random result of her having delayed everything over that double espresso. Regardless, they took the same chair up. There was the usual lift talk about gear and the weather and how gorgeous the conditions looked. Then—because they had to get down, didn't they?—they took a run together, and one turned into a few, and a few turned into a few more, and before they knew it the morning had slipped past in one long lovely blur of white.

At noon, they stopped for lunch at the Peak Lodge. Stacey's usual was a couple of energy bars, washed down with tea made with free hot water and a tea bag from the grocery store. When the resort was charging three bucks for a large coffee and six for a cold veggie burger, you learned to improvise. Chip was chivalrous with his employee discount and offered to get her whatever she might want at half price, but she figured that four-fifty plus tax for coffee and a veggie burger was still out of line. So no, thanks.

As she sat with the tea steeping in its big doubled paper cup and her bare hands clasped around it for warmth, she was pretty sure she caught him looking at her left hand. It would have been perfectly normal. She'd been checked out that way many times before, although this was the first time she registered it since the ring was gone. (No doubt it had happened in the Broken Binding a hundred times, between curious locals and out-of-towners up for a good time, but she'd been both on the clock and one hundred percent not interested. So she'd paid it as much attention as she paid the football games showing with the volume down on the big screen above the register: exactly none.)

This, though, was different.

She sat with the cup in front of her and she caught his quick downward glance and she didn't move a muscle in response to it. She felt the absence of the ring on her finger as if it were something she'd put there intentionally. And as she did, she reflected on how the ring had never failed to snag on her glove liner and how in turn that protruding spot on the liner had never failed to snag on her ski glove. Whether she was putting them on or taking them off, it was a constant irritant and reminder. The diamonds on it were enormous—*diamonds* plural, plural and then some—and they hadn't just signaled her status to the world but signified it to Stacey herself by catching on every last thing she owned, from slips and dresses to long johns and glove liners.

Not anymore.

Chip sprinkled his chili with parmesan cheese from a shaker meant for the lousy pizza, crumpled a packet of saltines on top, doused the whole mess with hot sauce, and dug in.

She winced at the look of his lunch and warmed her hands and thought of the last time she'd worn that ring. She should have dropped it in the apartment when she left Boston, but she hadn't had the presence of mind. So somewhere on the Mass Pike between there and Worcester, when it sparkled in the oncoming headlights, she tore the traitorous thing from her finger and dropped it into one of the cup holders. The one where she kept change for tolls. Even there it was an annoyance, since she had to keep separating it from the quarters and dimes that actually had some value in her life, but that's where it stayed until a couple of weeks later when she finally moved it with a handful of other odds and ends to a zippered pocket of her backpack. It seemed a little safer there, although she couldn't say from what. Still, she hated carrying it around, hated knowing it was there—hated knowing it was *anywhere*, really— and now that she wasn't living in the car anymore she should prob-ably put it somewhere in her room.

"Where'd you go?"

She blinked.

Chip was smiling at her, a little smear of chili on his chin. "Just now? Where'd you go?"

"Thinking."

"I could tell."

She tugged at the wrapper of an energy bar, but it wouldn't open. He asked if he could help and instead she used her teeth.

"Ow. I guess you were thinking about getting some dental work."

"Just thinking." She left it at that.

He dabbed at his chin with a napkin and asked where she was from, as if he'd read her mind. On the other hand, in a place as full of short-timers and misfits and new arrivals as this, it was as good a conversation starter as any. The Green Mountain State, she'd been quick to realize, was like some remote island in the south seas in that it had two classes of people: natives whose families had lived here forever, and a mixed bag of refugees who washed up on its banks after their luck had run out somewhere else.

"Boston." Her voice had none of that flat braying sound of the old Irish beat cop in the movies. It was softer and rounder and more suggestive of privilege, and so he was not surprised much by the explanation that followed. "I finished grad school and thought I'd live a little. You?"

"D.C." Pushing his empty bowl to one side. "I came for the waters."

The words rang a bell, but she had to think for a minute before she could place them. "*Casablanca*," she said at last.

"Hey. We'll always have Paris." He broke his brownie in two pieces and offered her half of it on a paper napkin. "Want some?"

She did.

"You know," he said, looking up at the ceiling with its exposed latticework of dusty beams, "if the sale of this place goes through, this lodge'll be only the halfway point."

"Really."

"If that. The plans are huge. This place'll stretch all the way out to Saddleback Mountain."

"*If* the sale goes through." She chewed on the brownie.

"Oh, it'll go through, all right. As long as the Forest Service gives it their blessing. Which they will."

"And you're sure about that because—"

"Because my father's a lobbyist for the oil companies. At the end of the day, the agencies always cave. He'd be out of work if they didn't." He picked up his empty cracker packet and shook the last crumbs into the palm of his hand and tossed them back, followed by a swallow of Gatorade. "It's the will of the people. The people with the money, anyhow."

"Speaking of Andy Paxton."

"He's different. I think he's been dragged into this whole Ski-America thing kicking and screaming, if you want to know the truth."

"He stands to profit big time."

"How much more does he need?"

"It doesn't matter," she said. "At a certain point, money's just a way of keeping score." Brian had liked to say that, and it was one of the few things in life about which he'd been correct.

"True enough." Chip collected their trash onto his tray and slid it toward the end of the table. "But it's also a powerful force. It can move mountains, and it can wear them down."

Stacey stood and zipped her jacket and pulled on her helmet. "Maybe we'd better go, while there's still a mountain out there to ski on."

NINE

Skiing with a patroller was like surfing with a lifeguard, and Stacey made the most of it. She was anything but a cautious skier to begin with, but after lunch she tackled runs she'd never quite dared before. Chutes and steeps and tight little stretches of trees where one late turn meant disaster. All of them at top speed, which was her normal pace. She didn't feel as if she had anything to prove to Chip, and she wasn't setting out to impress him either; it was more like she didn't want to make him drag his feet on her behalf. That and what the heck: If she wiped out big-time, there'd be no waiting for somebody to notice and call for help.

Today was her day off from the Binding, so instead of quitting at one she hung on until the end. Chip and another patroller actually got the very last chair—the one with the flag on it, indicating that nobody else had loaded up and the lift could shut down safely—and he waved to her from it as he rode up for the final sweep. She shouldered her skis and trudged off to the lot, good and tired for once and even a little wobbly in the knees.

• • •

Tonight was laundry night. Better yet, it was laundry night somewhere other than Bud's Suds. Which meant not only that Stacey's clothes might get clean for a change, but that she didn't have to sit on the bench in that ice-cold plate-glass fishbowl while she waited for the machines to finish. In that ice-cold plate-glass fishbowl, now that she thought about it, outside of which The Claw was probably lurking with his one wild and bloodshot eye fastened on her.

In short, laundry night felt like a red-letter occasion for a change.

She was down in the basement folding the first load, the door cracked open behind her at the top of the stairs, when Guy got home from work and sat down in the kitchen with Megan. She heard her say, "Hey there, handsome." She heard him open the fridge and pop open a beer and she heard the legs of his chair scratch across the linoleum. She heard him sigh and she heard his boots hit the floor like weights.

Small talk came next. She tried not to listen, and did pretty well. Mutterings and murmurs, the names of the kids, something about a homework assignment. Partial sentences spoken in the way of married couples everywhere. Questions asked and questions answered, to judge by the way their voices rose and fell. Humming to herself and moving wet wash from washer to dryer and letting the doors slam as they might, she wasn't in the least stealthy about her presence at the bottom of the stairs. And in the kitchen Megan and Guy didn't acknowledge her and talked on as if they were all alone in the house, the way they must have always done no matter who was renting the back room. Two people in their own house with nothing to hide.

After a while Guy began to talk about a conversation he'd had with the troopers about David's murder, and downstairs Stacey cleared her throat in case they cared. They seemed not to. He went on. She cocked an ear and took a step or two closer to the stairs.

There was no forced entry, not by the killer and not by the woman who'd called 911. And they were probably not the same individual, since the body had had a head start on the caller by between eighteen and twenty-four hours. The condo was practically wallpapered with fingerprints, although most of them had good reason to be there. They belonged to David, of course. To his brother and his parents. To the cleaning lady and the Snowfield caretaker. The chain didn't have any prints on it at all, or at least none that the forensic guys could extract from the dried blood and smeared grease, but it did have plenty of residue from what looked like a pair of ordinary work gloves. Residue that could have come from anywhere, of course, and could even have been there all along. Probably had been. There was some coarse gravel on the floor that didn't match the pea gravel outside the Snowfield. Once again it could have come from anywhere, although given David's fastidious nature it had probably been tracked in by the killer or, more likely still, the woman who'd called 911. The only thing truly out of line in the whole place was a woman's ring on the bedroom floor. Alongside the bed, just under the dust ruffle, as if it had fallen a few feet away and bounced. It didn't belong to the mother and it didn't belong to the cleaning lady. It bore some latent prints that so far didn't seem to match any others in the condo. But it was probably nothing.

Megan disagreed. A woman's ring on the floor of David Paxton's condo was definitely *something*. She reminded Guy that they were talking about David, not Richie.

Yes, he knew that. He hadn't forgotten. But still.

When Stacey couldn't rationalize staying in the basement any longer, she picked up her laundry and headed up the stairs. She slipped through the kitchen with smiles for Megan and Guy, and padded in her stocking feet down the hall to her room. She closed the door and put everything away in about ten seconds. And then, idly, thinking about her lunch with Chip and about Guy's mention of the ring that the troopers had found in the condo, she unzipped her backpack and stuck in her hand to dig out her own ring—the one that she should have left in Boston weeks before.

It wasn't there.

It wasn't there, and right away she broke out in a sweat.

She ransacked her backpack. She opened every pocket and pouch, turned everything inside out that would go inside out, and shook the whole thing until her bedspread was littered with pennies and candy wrappers and the crumbs of a dozen energy bars. She found a couple of ChapSticks that she'd lost track of and a pair of sunglasses with one lens missing and the other broken, but those were the only surprises. The ring was nowhere.

And in a heartbeat, she was pretty sure she knew why the sheriff hadn't minded her listening in from the basement.

TEN

A ndy Paxton pulled the headlamp over his helmet and switched on the bright white LEDs. "This always makes me feel like a coal miner or something," he said. "How about you? You all set?"

Chip switched on his own lamp and said that yes, he was good to go.

Since the arc lights were on overhead and the fluorescents were still lit inside the empty base lodge, their headlamps weren't necessary just yet. That would change soon enough. And when it did, they'd be wearing their heavy gloves and wouldn't want to take them off just to flick on the LEDs. Like the Boy Scouts said, *Be Prepared.* They hoisted their skis and stepped away from the lodge and dropped their skis onto the snow and clicked in. Their shadows stretched up the beginner slope, a pair of black silhouettes cut from the harsh white glare of the arc lights, and step by step they started gliding forward, skinning up the hill in the gathering dark.

Andy cut his head to the left, toward his young friend, raking the snow with the beam of his lamp. "Thanks for this."

"Thanks for what." It was not a question. It was Chip's way of explaining to this man old enough to be his grandfather that being out here in the middle of the night with him was exactly the thing he would most like to be doing right now. More than anything else in the world. And that the death of the man's son just a few days back had nothing to do with it.

"Right," said Andy.

"We haven't gotten out enough, I don't think."

"Not like last year."

The year before, Chip's first full winter on the mountain, they'd done this two or three nights a week. But last winter had been mild. This year the weather pattern had been different—snow most nights, and heavy clouds or at least a high overcast when it didn't snow—and what they were about to do required as bright a moon and as many stars as the New England sky could muster up.

High up on the mountain a battery of groomers moved down an open face in a carefully choreographed sweep, preparing one more run for tomorrow's skiers. Their halogen headlamps lit the snow ahead of them and turned it blue against the night sky.

"That'll be the end of it," said Andy, pointing with his pole.

"I didn't know they were still up there."

"This is the last pass. I've had my eye on them."

That suited Chip fine. The whole purpose of their skinning up the mountain in the dark was to have it all to themselves, and the full-throated roar of a half-dozen diesel-guzzling Cats kind of spoiled the vibe.

Andy was already beginning to pant a little. It was easy to forget how old he actually was, although he'd never quit on you. "You ever been in the cab of one of those things?"

"Me? No."

"They're regular Cadillacs. Leather seats, satellite radio, CD changers. The whole nine yards."

"I had no idea."

"I didn't either. Not until I started seeing the invoices. Man, oh, man. Let me tell you."

Chip had grown up among people of privilege, but he'd never seen one quite like Andy. Within his experience, Andy Paxton had a unique ability to drop the odd fact relating to his wealth as if the dropping of it were purely accidental and the fact itself were entirely amazing, even to himself. As if he hadn't grown up on his father's and grandfather's mountain with precisely these expectations. To tell the truth, Chip had fled home and made for the woods because if he hadn't yanked himself from his own parents' grip he'd have never achieved the kind of freedom that came so naturally to Andy. He'd have been one of those guys walking around cocktail parties drinking scotch older than he was, letting slip the names of the boards of directors he'd been invited to join during the past week.

Chip had come to the mountains not to save the trees, but to save himself.

Taking these nighttime runs with Andy was part of his therapy. They were also their little secret, although he supposed that Marie knew what Andy was up to, and Andy had never exactly said that they should keep it to themselves. Still, there was about these nighttime adventures a kind of primitive and unspoken secrecy that he didn't dare violate. Even afterward, when they swung by the Broken Binding for a hot toddy—a hot toddy! Andy warmed up with hot toddies! They went down easy enough, that was for sure—they'd arrive in their own cars and make like they'd just run into each other.

It was a long way up to the peak, and when they cut off the bunny slope toward the main mountain the going got steep. They were out of the glare of the arc lights around the base lodge now. They had risen up from the bowl of light that filled the bottom of the valley and set off into the darker reaches of the woods. Although they stuck for the most part to marked and groomed trails, the most direct way to the summit required taking some narrow passages through the deep woods, some of them used by maintenance guys on snowmobiles and some not even known to the most experienced tree skiers and powder hounds on the mountain. These places, the deep black upward angles where snow-laden trees blocked the moonlight, were where their headlamps came in handy.

Chip let Andy lead the way and set the pace. Now and then they paused to rest. For all his own skill on skis, and for all his youth, Chip was always ready to catch his breath whenever Andy called it.

"The boys used to make this run with me," the older man said as they stood together on an outcropping and looked down at the mountain and the town below. The burning pool of arc light around the base lodge had been reduced by distance to a half-hearted little puddle. Down along the access road, the last of the groomers slipped into their barn in strange and utter silence. Lights gleamed along the streets of town at restaurants and shops and gas stations, and the taillights of cars blinked red at the town's one and only traffic light. "Their mother had no fondness for having us up here in the dark. Either the boys or her loving husband, for that matter."

"I'll bet."

"Richie quit on me first. Then David. At about the same age, now that I think of it."

"Growing up."

"And a long time before that, I used to do it with my own dad. God rest his soul."

"The view from here must have been different then." Chip turned the conversation because he didn't think these guest appearances by the dead were likely to do Andy any good.

"Oh, you bet it was different. The base lodge wasn't much to look at. None of the condos were there, or even those two lower parking lots. That was all just woods. Used to be an old fellow had a house back in there, just a lean-to, really, didn't even have a road to it. He'd just whack his way in and out through the underbrush. Us kids thought he was peculiar, maybe crazy."

"Man."

"We were terrified of him, to tell you the truth."

"I don't doubt it."

Andy stood in complete silence for a minute, just looking, possibly at something that wasn't even there anymore. After a while he said, "This was in the forties, the time I'm talking about."

"A lot has changed."

"You have no idea." He stamped the tip of one pole into the snow and turned and continued on up the hill, following the bright white beam of his headlamp into the moonlit darkness. Chip followed close.

Stacey checked every garment she owned. She emptied the chest of drawers she'd just filled up and she spread everything on the bed and one by one turned it all inside out and back again. She checked every pocket and found them all empty. She discovered two socks glued by static inside the legs of some long underwear and peeled them free and rolled them up but that was it. So she folded everything and put it all away again and sat on the bed in a kind of woeful fury, thinking. She went to the basement, slipping through the kitchen again with an embarrassed smile, and checked the washer and dryer even though she knew it was hopeless. Then she returned to her room and started again—emptying the drawers and checking the far corners of them as if she'd lived here for years, yanking all of her clothes inside out and checking them again. She made frustrated little sighs and mewling noises in spite of herself and she hoped that the sounds of Megan putting supper on would drown them out. The engagement ring had to be somewhere. It wasn't in an evidence bag in Rutland, that was for sure. It just couldn't be.

Which left a couple of alternatives. The car, and the Broken Binding. With the kind of brilliant and imaginative illogic that lights up the nuttiest scenarios for anyone in search of something lost, she could practically *see* it there. In the glove box, in the cup holder, under a seat. In the locker room, in the liquor well, by the cash register. She threw on her coat and grabbed her keys. She'd start with the car, and if it wasn't there, she'd drive to the Binding and put this thing to rest.

The daughter, Anne, was setting the kitchen table when she left her room. Megan was at the stove, and Guy was nowhere in sight. Megan spoke. "Shall we set a place for you?"

"Oh, no thanks. Really."

"It's just spaghetti and meatballs. Plenty to go around."

"You're too good to me."

"It's your night off."

Anne stood absolutely motionless, waiting for her mother and Stacey to come to some kind of terms that would let her finish setting the table. Stacey could see a little fire of impatience building up behind her perfectly amicable smile, and she wondered if Megan saw it, too.

"Oh, I know. Believe me, I know. Tonight's the night I get to live on something other than hot wings and Chex Mix."

"Yecch." She nodded to her daughter, who squared up the fourth place setting and left it at that. "Make the most of it, OK?"

"I will." She let herself out onto the frigid glassed-in back porch, and with a blast of even colder air she stepped out into the dark.

Since the sheriff would be sitting down to his supper just inside the kitchen window any minute now, she couldn't exactly ransack her car while it was parked alongside the house. So she fired it up and headed for town. There'd be more light there, anyway—either at the gas station or in the lot at the grocery store or just in front of the tall steamed-over windows at Bud's—more light that would make finding the ring easier.

She gunned the Subaru and navigated the ruts and icy patches in the road, eager to get started. So eager, in fact, that once the car had warmed up a little she took off her right glove and began to explore the nooks and crannies of the console. Nothing. Damn it.

The gas station was crammed full of SUVs with New York and Connecticut tags, all of them idling on pricey gas and crusted from front to back with the mixture of snow and sand and salt that had covered every car in town since November. The parking lot at the grocery store was the same. *Flatlanders*, Stacey thought. She could imagine them clomping up and down the beat-up linoleum aisles, some of them actually still wearing their ski boots as if idiocy had been declared a badge of honor.

So she gave up on the gas station and the grocery store and doubled back to Bud's Suds. The lot there was pretty much empty, just a couple of rusty old pickups with Vermont plates, although a few out-of-state cars were parked in a jumble in front of the pizza joint next door. College kids from Massachusetts, lying about the day's runs over a slice and a beer. She pulled right up to Bud's, cut the engine, and switched off the headlights. The windows of the laundromat were fogged up on the inside as usual and frosted over some on the outside too, but still they gave off enough light that she could have searched the car without using the dome light. Not that she did. She switched it on and took off both gloves and slid open the ash tray, picturing the ring hiding there underneath the usual tangle of elastics.

Nothing.

She looked up at the bright windows. Behind them a vague

shape or two moved, just gray masses against the hazy yellow light of the old fluorescent bulbs that hung from the ceiling in rank after buzzing rank. Many times she'd been inside Bud's Suds, sitting on the damp plastic benches waiting for a load to finish, when the air was so wet and foggy that clouds of it rose up and made the old fluorescent fixtures snap and sizzle. It was as if the place had its own weather, and none of it good.

She dug again in the console now that she could see, and she emptied everything from it onto the passenger seat just in case. Scrap by scrap by scrap. Lift tickets and receipts from Boston parking garages and crumpled shopping lists. Empty Tic Tac boxes and stray pennies and coupons long expired. But no ring.

Movement in Bud's window caught her eye and she looked up once more. Vague dark shapes again, one of them maybe growing a little bit sharper and smaller as whoever it was seemed to come nearer to the glass. For a few seconds she watched it approach and coalesce, like a film of some kind of gas explosion run backward in slow motion.

Then she opened the glove box. Not to search it—not yet—but to fish under that fistful of abandoned keys for the little flashlight so as to give the console one last going-over. She thumbed it on and found it not quite dead but almost. It was a good thing she didn't need to change a tire. That's what the flashlight was for, according to her father, who'd put it there in the first place. Changing a flat tire. As if she'd have had the first idea. As if her mother had ever changed a tire in her life. She shook the flashlight and it died a little and then it kind of came back to life a little on its own and then it faded again almost completely. So she switched it off and dropped it on the passenger seat with the rest of the junk.

When she looked up this time, there was a face in Bud's window. It appeared through a wiped-clear spot in the hazy glass, lined and drawn and pale as smoke. It possessed a pair of close-set eyes beneath an overhanging brow, leathery crocodile skin yanked tight over underlying bone by hair that its owner kept gathered into a steel-gray ponytail, and a mouthful of tobacco-stained teeth scattered around its jaw like tombstones.

Stacey saw it and felt immediately exposed and in peril, as if by sitting there under the dome light she had identified herself as some kind of prey. Her instinct was to switch off the light and conceal herself, but that would have been worse. And as she stared back at the wizened hungry face, a bent and arthritic hand rose up beside it in the smeared-clear spot, and the fingers of that hand waggled just the slightest.

Hello.

ELEVEN

Andy Paxton and Chip Walsh, on top of the world.

Even in the late evening and under a black sky as clear as glass, there was a steady wind up there. There always was. It bit their cheeks raw as they stood stripping the skins from their skis and folding them into their backpacks. The two of them worked in silence and by moonlight, in a bright open patch of snow near the top of the main lift. Once the skis were ready they took off their headlamps and put on goggles with clear lenses and put on the headlamps again. Thirty yards downhill the Peak Lodge stood empty and dark, just an angular blot against the whiteness of the moonlit snow.

Andy sighed. "I guess the day's going to come when I won't be doing this anymore."

Thirsty from the long climb, Chip took a bottle of water from his pack and drank off half of it. "It'll be a while, I think." He supposed that Andy was lamenting his advancing age. "And if I can keep at it even half as long as you have, I'll think I've done all right."

"I'm talking about trespassing on my own mountain, sonny. One day I'll be trespassing on somebody else's."

"Oh, that." He put the bottle away and hoisted the pack and squared it on his shoulders.

"Yes. That."

"That would kind of be your call, though, wouldn't it?"

"Maybe not so much as you'd think."

Chip looked sideways at Andy so as not to hit him with the full force of his headlamp. In his clear goggles he could see the town below reflected, a thousand little lights tailing off to nothing in the distance. And then without another word of explanation the older man took off down the hill, and Chip had no choice but to follow.

The figure eyeing Stacey from behind the window had a name: Danny Bowman.

Danny had helped the U.S. Army cut the A Shau Expressway through the mountains of South Vietnam, and it was the last steady job he'd ever had. Uncle Sam could not have found duty less suited to a Green Mountain boy than clearing vast tracts of hot and stinking jungle behind the wheel of an eighteen-ton Rome plow, unless it was killing Vietcong soldiers with an assault rifle. So just in case, Uncle Sam had made sure that Danny Bowman had the chance to do some of that, too. He hadn't been right since.

Stacey knew him only as the gray-haired ghost that haunted various warm and welcoming spots around town. He always seemed to have a cardboard cup of coffee in one hand, maybe the same cup, by the looks of it, since it was generally a mottled gray and brown, dripped all over with several days' worth of spillage. It was at least as dirty as the hand that clutched it. He may have been re-using it to save trees, as far as she knew. More likely he had sources for hot coffee in places where they only counted the cups.

He lifted that nasty cup to his lips now and sipped from it, his eyes still on Stacey. She gingerly raised one hand and hazarded a tepid wave back, which seemed to satisfy him. His breath over the hot coffee fogged the clear spot in the window a little more, and behind that fog his eyes went blurry. To Stacey it was a blessing. Those eyes of his looked to her like holes burned into a ratty blanket.

She put her back to him and flipped the passenger seat forward and crawled into the rear. Better to stay safe inside the car than let herself out and back in again, out in this lonesome parking lot with those burnt blanket eyes fixed on her. On the way over into the backseat she locked the doors just in case.

There was nothing back there except the junk she'd expected. A couple of near-empty cans of windshield deicer, a glass scraper, a snow brush. A uselessly out-of-date road atlas. She remembered as she looked that she'd been meaning to get one of those collapsible shovels to keep back here, too, and she scolded herself for wanting to add to the crap on the floor when she ought to be finding something and taking it out for God's sake. She scolded herself for hurrying through the search just because the creepy vet was eyeing her—she shot a veiled glance up that way and sure enough, he was still there, still looking her way—and she told herself to take her time. Go slow. Don't get rattled. She reached over to pick up the weak flashlight again and knelt on the floor mat and focused her attention on the space beneath the seats.

Nothing.

She switched off the fading light and explored with her hands, like a blind man.

Nothing.

Once again, in the same places and in the same way, just a little bit more desperately this time.

Still nothing.

She was breaking a sweat in the cooling car. She took off her fleece cap and tossed it forward between the seats and looked out and saw Danny's face, in profile this time, partially reblurred by fog collecting again on the window. Just the act of looking his way seemed to draw his attention, and he turned his face toward her. She winced, as if she'd touched him.

She was getting to the end of the line, and she knew it. If the ring wasn't in the wayback, and she was quickly losing faith that it might be, then it must be at the Broken Binding somewhere. *Somewhere.* She could think of a million places, all of them unlikely. Rather than go down that road she unlocked the back door and stepped out into the parking lot and popped the liftgate. Her heart sank. Hadn't she and Megan just emptied this same cargo area a couple of days ago? There was nothing left there. Nothing. She knew it. She knew it even as she flicked on the flashlight and pushed her fingers into every nook and cranny where they'd fit. She kept her eyes on her work rather than risk drawing Danny Bowman's attention again. And when she was completely satisfied—or dissatisfied—that the ring was nowhere to be found, she turned and sat down on the cargo mat and laid the flashlight down beside her. Between the Subaru's old springs and her weight and the slant of the parking lot, it rolled rearward, hung up for a second on a plastic lip, and then tumbled out into the snow.

Which gave Stacey an idea. What if the ring had done the same? What if it had fallen out of her pack into the back of the car, and then rolled out somewhere? It was a stupid idea, she knew. Stupid and futile. Stupid and futile and desperately attractive, given that the alternative was to imagine it sitting in an evidence bag in Rutland, all decked out with her fingerprints.

Problem was, it could have rolled out anywhere. The muddy lot at Spruce. The gravel lot at the Binding. The paved lots at the grocery store or here at Bud's or behind one of the dozen or so condos she'd hijacked back when sleeping in a borrowed bed had seemed like a good idea. The odds were best at the Binding, since that was where she parked the most—although she didn't usually open up the liftgate there. Then again, she could picture the ring rolling out from any open door of the car, in that desperate way that a person who's lost something important can imagine the most ridiculous scenarios for finding it.

Then again . . .

She sat and wracked her brain until it hurt.

Then again, if you put together frequency of parking in a given spot with frequency of opening the liftgate, one place did present itself. Just one place. The little windless spot around back, between Bud's and the pizza joint.

The ring had to be there. It had to be there on the frozen ground where a layer of ice built itself up from nothing, where little tatters of snow flew past and snagged on one another, and where no car other than hers had ever had a reason to go. She stood, bent for the flashlight, and closed the liftgate. Then she started the car and drove around back.

In contrast to the way they had bushwhacked straight up the hill, Andy and Chip stayed to open slopes on their trip to the bottom and wound their way in the most indirect route possible. That's the way it was when you skied without benefit of a chairlift: You minimized the work and you maximized the joy. They crossed under the main lift a time or two, and Chip took some pleasure in imagining how his buddies on the ski patrol would puzzle over their paired tracks on the first lift ride tomorrow morning. They'd dissect the evidence like one of those guys on *CSI*, guessing the size and configuration of the skis that the trespassers used, observing that the tracks were made some time after the groomers had finished, analyzing the relative techniques of the two individuals who'd been out here on these empty and treacherous slopes. Andy's tracks would betray the ingrained habits of an old-school schussmeister. Chip could see that even in the dark. It was all he could do to keep pace.

Halfway down they stopped. Not to rest, but to make it last. They stood on a narrow catwalk near the top of one of the lower lifts, gulping in the night air and blowing out breath in great white clouds.

The older man pointed toward the town in the valley below, his glove a shadow against the stars. "Down there?" He shook his head and his headlamp sent its beam wobbling out into the darkness to die. "Once upon a time I could have told you who was sitting behind every single one of those windows."

"I'll bet you could have."

"I delivered their newspapers. On my bike. Summer and winter both." He thought for a minute, marveling at something. "I bet I could have told you what half of those people were watching on the television."

"No fair. This was before cable."

"You're kidding. This was before *color*."

"So they were watching, what, *Bonanza?*"

"This was before *Bonanza*. They were watching Milton Berle, something like that."

Chip wiped his goggles clean of the spray that Andy's skis had kicked up.

"Now that I think about it," Andy went on, "most of them were probably still listening to the radio. But anyhow, those times are gone."

Chip looked his way but couldn't see anything past the bounce of his own headlamp off the older man's goggles.

"Sometimes I think I shouldn't care about letting the mountain go. Sometimes it feels like it's already gone."

"Like I said before, it's your choice."

"Not exactly. I mean, I'd love to pass the place on to my children, that's for sure." There it was, *my children*, the phrase lying there like a dead man, and neither Chip nor Andy was going to acknowledge it. "But if you take the long view, in the end it's not really my call."

"You can't please everybody," said Chip.

"You know what my Richie calls it? My son, Richie? You know what he calls selling our mountain to those bookkeepers from Denver?"

"I can't imagine."

"He calls it *monetizing.*"

"Wow."

"Wow, indeed," said Andy. And then he said the magic word again. "*Monetizing.* Now there's a word to suck all the romance out of a person's life, don't you think?"

"I do," said Chip. "I do." He tried it out himself. "Monetizing." It sounded like a curse.

"My own son," said Andy. "And the only one I've got left."

With that he dug in his poles and lit out for the bottom. Chip followed, and the night rushed by in a blur of black and white, and it was as beautiful as a dream.

Stacey stopped short of the little patch where she'd always parked, with the headlights pointed in. She put her hat and gloves back on and got out of the car. In the glare of the headlights she was a black shadow against the white concrete walls of Bud's and the pizza joint, her shadow indistinguishable from herself as she bent and shuffled along the frozen ground, looking down, looking for the faintest glimmer of white gold and diamond amid so many counterfeits. She crossed and recrossed the same area again and again, and after her third or fourth futile pass she straightened up and put a fist to the tight muscles of her lower back.

"I seen you." The voice came from somewhere beyond the white glare of the headlights. It had the advantage of her for sure.

"You what?" Talking to the black night itself.

"*I seen you.*" Footsteps on the ragged ice. A shape materializing alongside the car. "I see lots of things, on account of I keep my eyes open."

"I'm just trying to find—" She wondered what it was that she was explaining and who it was she was explaining it to.

"Not here. I ain't talking about here." A few more scuffling footsteps and Danny Bowman rounded the front of the car and leaned against the warm grille. "I'm talking about that other night. Up to the condos." He set his coffee cup on the hood. "*I seen you then.*"

TWELVE

Stacey stood in the cold glare of the headlights and wondered how she would get back into the car. How she would get around him in order to do it. He leaned against the hood like some lazy black shadow, entirely at his ease. She didn't think he was wearing a coat, but she couldn't be sure. If he wasn't, he might want to get back inside Bud's, where it was warm, in a hurry. He *might*. Then again he might not. He reached for his coffee cup and drank some and she watched the movement of his arm but still couldn't tell for certain. Not with the blazing headlights in her eyes.

"You're Danny," she said.

"That's right." Another sip. The coffee steamed. "I guess everybody knows old Danny, huh?"

"Yeah. Everybody knows Danny."

"Not everybody knows *you*, but I do."

"I'm Stacey." It was kind of a preemptive strike.

"I know that."

"You do."

"I do," he said. "You might not think it, but I know a few things."

Stacey looked down at the icy pavement between her feet and gave it a kick.

Danny narrowed his sunken eyes. "What're you looking for?"

"Nothing."

"You're looking for something."

"Nothing. Nothing important." She watched him and he didn't move. "A receipt, is all. I thought it might have blown back here."

"Nah."

"It could happen. But it's not here, and now I've got to get going." She took a tentative step forward and in return he put the coffee cup back down on the hood of the car. As if he meant to keep it there for a while.

"I didn't mean 'nah, it couldn't happen.' I meant 'nah, you ain't looking for no receipt.'" Both of his hands were on the hood now, comfortable as could be. "It don't smell right. First you're someplace you got no business, and then you're back here looking for something you won't say what it is."

"Really. I've got to go."

Danny put a finger to his nose and blew out like a farmer with a headful of chaff. Mucous sprayed the ground at his feet, and one wet clot of it landed on a headlight.

Stacey thought of a tomcat, marking its territory. It was better than thinking of Danny's snot freezing on her car.

Danny stood and gathered up his coffee cup, almost gentlemanly for a change. He stepped toward the passenger side, leaving Stacey an open passage to the driver's door. "I ain't surprised you got to go," he said. "Seeing's you don't come around here the way you used to."

It was an observation that froze Stacey to the ground.

He went on. "Where you staying these days, anyhow?"

She nearly told him it was none of his business, but thought better of it. "I'm renting a room from Guy Ramsey. You know. Guy

Ramsey? The sheriff?" As if this individual who was apparently hot on her trail with her engagement ring in an evidence bag were suddenly her knight in shining armor. As if she had any time for knights in shining armor.

"I know him. I know his house, too."

"I'll bet you do."

"Nice place."

"It's fine."

"Convenient."

"Not really." She wondered as she said it if she were betraying how far they stood at this very instant from Guy Ramsey. And from whatever protection he might offer.

"Convenient for the sheriff, I mean. When it comes time to put cuffs on somebody who didn't have no business at that condo."

"You can't be serious."

"I'm serious, all right."

She took out her key and headed toward the car.

"I'd say I'm a hundred bucks serious."

Stacey couldn't believe her ears. It was as if by mentioning money he had deflated himself, like a sorry little balloon. How ludicrous, to think his testimony would have meant anything to Guy Ramsey. She charged toward the car, got in, and yanked the door shut behind her. She jammed the key into the ignition, and that small movement gave her an idea.

By the time they were cruising down the beginner slope to the lodge, the sweat that Andy and Chip had raised on the climb had frozen them half to death. Layers of wicking microfleece and breathable Gore-Tex notwithstanding, there was only so much warmth a body could retain while moving at top speed down a moonlit slope. That penetrating and unrelieved chill was the main difference, aside from the low visibility and the incredible privacy and the amazing quiet,

between their nighttime adventure and an ordinary sunny day on
the mountain.

The arc lights were still on at the base lodge and the fluorescents
were still on inside—they never went off, burning constantly like
the eternal flame at the Tomb of the Unknown Skier—and the
brightness of them hurt their eyes as they drew near. Still, rather
than spoil the quiet by speaking, they clicked out of their skis without a word and trudged off to the parking lot with their equipment
over their shoulders. Heading for the Broken Binding, in separate
cars as always.

The key. It was the key—and the jamming of it into the ignition,
hard—that made her realize.

Danny was The Claw. No two ways about it. It was Danny who'd
visited her iced-over Subaru in the middle of the night and freaked
her out by scraping that line around the glass. How stupid of her not
to have thought of him before. He was everywhere in this town,
that's for sure. Everywhere he could find a warm place to sit and a
free cup of coffee to nurse all day. And maybe some tourist who'd
hand over a buck out of either pity or fear.

She threw the car into reverse and spun the wheel and watched
the headlights rake his bent figure in the dark lot. When she cleared
Bud's she yanked the shifter and hit the gas as if the devil himself
were on her tail, not just some creepy gray-haired vet with bad teeth.
Because what the heck, you could never tell.

The Broken Binding was a mile away on the south edge of town,
perched where it could catch the Connecticut crowd both coming
and going. With no ring in her possession and Bud's lot in her rearview mirror, it seemed like a long way off.

And with Danny even aware that she'd been at the Snowfield
the night she found David Paxton's body, it seemed even farther.
She jacked up the heat in the car and checked the rearview and felt

a shiver run down her spine. *When else had he been watching her? And to what end?*

A front-end loader backed out of the gas station with its beeper going, as if everybody on earth had to watch out for it regardless of who had right of way. She saw it coming and swerved around it and kept thinking about Danny.

Where had he been, the night he saw her leave the Snowfield?

She couldn't imagine.

Oh, yes, she could.

The lights of the Broken Binding were visible ahead and she gunned the engine a little, hurrying the Subaru on. Making like a runner sprinting in at the end of a long race.

Because if Danny was The Claw, was he The Chain Saw Killer, too?

THIRTEEN

"Can't stay away, can you?" It was the throaty growl of Tina Montero, lifted up to pierce the din the instant Stacey stepped through the door of the Broken Binding. So what if there were laws against smoking in public places anymore? Tina had wrecked her lungs and her larynx a long time ago. All the same, even she had to admit that cutting down was good for her wind when it came to the massage therapy business. Now *that* was work. And even though she was a substantial woman with plenty of weight behind her, some of those hard-driving ski types showed up with knots in their legs and backs that took more oomph than came easily.

Stacey walked between crowded tables toward the jammed bar, unzipping her jacket as she came and feeling like the fat guy from *Cheers*. Who'd have thought it? A proper Bostonian, armed with a BA from Smith and an MA from Williams and brought up to ex- pect only the most elevated things in life, right at home in this crowd. Well, pretty much right at home. Certainly more at home here than over in the lot behind Bud's, being accosted by that Danny Bowman. And as of this moment more at home here than back at the Ramsey place, where they probably thought she was in cahoots with The Chain Saw Killer.

"I can't stay," she said to Jack the bartender and Tina the regular and anyone else who cared to listen, as she lifted the hinged shelf and let herself behind the bar. Although the alternatives as to where she might go didn't seem all that attractive.

"Didn't ask you to." Jack was an old-timer who'd been here since the Edelweiss days. He was compact and trim and strictly business, and he'd stuck so faithfully to his station behind the bar that you'd think the only things in the world that had changed in all those years were his failing eyesight and his graying hair. He was cutting up limes. He lifted his eyebrows and indicated the room she'd woven her way through, pretty well shoulder to shoulder tonight. "Although now that you're here, I guess we could use the help."

"We'll see," she said, making a beeline for the register.

"What's up?"

"Forgot something." From the corner of her eye she caught sight of Tina at the end of the bar, heavily made up as usual and meticulously overcoiffed, speaking in low tones to some out-of-towner wearing a garish ski sweater of a style that went out with Jean-Claude Killy. The sweater probably stank of mothballs—when these guys pulled them from their packs in the base lodge, the whole place smelled—but Tina probably didn't notice it over her own perfume.

The area around the cash register was a whole lot less jumbled and messy than Stacey had been picturing it on the way over here. Not that anyone had tidied it up; on the contrary, it was only in her mind—fueled by the wishful idea that she might find the ring underneath a pile of receipts or a stack of menus there—that it was a mess in the first place. And now, it looked to her as pristine as a surgical suite. She stood at the register and moved some pens around and checked behind the *Old Mr. Boston's Bartender's Guide*. Nothing but a rubber band and a paper clip. She gave the register a little frustrated push and then she pulled it back into place and looked behind it. Nothing at all.

"What'd you lose?" Jack, done with the limes and pulling a bottle of cheap gin from the well.

"Nothing. A ring."

"Haven't seen it."

"Yeah. Well, I probably didn't lose it here to begin with." She let her gaze fall down to the perforated rubber mat that covered the floor behind the bar, every inch of it awash in melted ice and spilled beer and soapy dishwater, and she didn't see any sign of the ring there, either.

"Maybe check the lockers," Jack said. "And if you want to put in a couple of hours after you're done, I don't think Pete'd mind—"

"I might," she said, turning to go.

Chip came in first. His face was ruddy from the cold, and the impression made by his goggles had just faded out across his cheeks. He also had a killer case of helmet hair, jammed under a wool cap. He scanned the room as if he were looking for somebody and failed to find them. He stuck his head in the dining room and looked there, too, and then he stepped into the bar. There was one table unoccupied, the tipsy one in the corner by the jukebox with a bunch of cocktail napkins jammed under one arm of its pedestal. Two empty beer bottles and a glass filmed with what looked like the remains of a margarita sat in damp pools on the top, along with a five-dollar bill and a near-empty bowl of Chex Mix. The fancy kind with the wasabi peas that taste like they've been in a sack behind the bar for something like a thousand years. Chip hung his coat on the back of one of the chairs and bussed the table himself, because it never hurt to make friends with the waitstaff.

A waitress saw him putting everything in the tub by the kitchen door, which was still swinging a little from Stacey's exit. "Thanks, Chippy."

Here or in the first-aid hut or in the patrol shack, he never knew what it was going to be. Chippy or Chipster or the Chipmeister or something else. Chips Ahoy. Chipparooni. Sometimes he wondered how long he'd have to live around here before the locals could settle on the best way to nickname his nickname. "Hey," he said, wiping his hands on a towel. "No prob."

She indicated the table by the jukebox. "You gonna be over there?"

"Yeah." Like where else would he be, the place was so packed.

"What're you drinking?"

He scanned the taps and pointed vaguely and said he'd do the Long Trail.

"Right. You got it."

A fresh bowl of that awful Chex Mix arrived first and he worked on it. Between the salt and the climb up Spruce he was thirstier than he'd expected and he drank the beer fast when it came.

The swinging door to the kitchen opened and Stacey came through.

Jack the bartender took exactly half a look at the expression on her face. "No luck, eh?"

She shrugged.

At the end of the bar, Tina dragged her attention away from the guy in the awful sweater. "Sweetie, it wasn't your—"

"My engagement ring?"

Tina put a hand on the sweater guy's paw, the one that was holding his beer. "Did you hear that? An engagement ring. At her tender age."

The sweater guy laughed, a little nervously. "Hey. We all make mistakes."

Tina shook her head and clucked a little but did not take her hand away. The sweater guy gave his beer a thirsty look.

Stacey let herself brighten. "Mistakes," she said. "I've made a couple."

"But she broke it off," said Tina.

The guy nodded knowingly. "Smart girl."

Stacey wished that she could agree more completely. She looked around the bar and saw a dozen glasses that needed servicing. Given the alternatives—stay here where there was life and conversation and plenty of give and take, or go home where there was the sheriff and no engagement ring to be found anywhere—she told Jack she'd stick around till closing after all.

Somebody came along and wanted the chair opposite where Chip was sitting but he wouldn't part with it. A sunburned stranger, raccoon-eyed where his goggles had been, in town for the weekend or the week. He wouldn't think anything when an old white-haired dude showed up in a few minutes and this chair happened to be the only empty one left in the place. But Stacey saw the transaction between Chip and the flatlander, since it always paid to watch the traffic in the bar ebb and flow, and she took note of it. She took note of how the chair stood empty while Chip finished his beer, too, and she took note of how Andy Paxton arrived a few minutes later and took the vacant seat as if it had his name carved into it. He hadn't been in the Binding since David's funeral.

The waitress made straight for their table, with all the solicitousness of a kid collecting for UNICEF on Halloween. She greeted Andy with her head tilted to one side and her lips pursed and the same look on her face that moms in Band-Aid commercials use. He was probably getting a lot of that these days.

He ordered a hot toddy. There was a time when Stacey would have had to consult *Old Mr. Boston's* for the recipe, but she'd made enough of them by now to remember. Always for old-timers like Andy, and maybe once for Andy himself. It was hard to remember for sure—this had been back in November, when she was just finding her way and learning faces—but she was pretty certain that that time he'd been sitting with Chip, too.

The old man looked vigorous but a little tired, and unlike Chip's his face still bore goggle imprints. She could see them from behind the bar. As she stood there working on the drink she wondered if he'd been out on a snowmobile this late, maybe ridden over here on one, but he didn't seem the type. The snowmobile guys with their bulky camo coveralls and their giant stiff gloves that looked like something out of a cheap science fiction movie didn't mix much with the ski crowd. Stacey had been quick to detect a socioeconomic dividing line that ran straight through the middle of the middle class. Below it, you motored through the mountains on a Ski-Doo; above it, you used snowshoes or skis. Come summer it would break the same way, with noisy little ten-horse fishing boats on one side and kayaks on the other. Andy Paxton had kayak written all over him. The long, streamlined kind built for touring, stable and steady and expensive as hell.

Stacey finished the drink and thought about taking it over herself but changed her mind. She caught the waitress's eye and leaned against the back bar to make the most of a lull between orders. Crossing her arms and letting her mind drift. The noise and the crowd and the crush of orders had taken her mind off her problems for a while, but everything came rushing back the instant she stopped moving. The ring. The sheriff. The Claw. The Chain Saw Killer. She tried to figure a way she could tell Ramsey about the confrontation she'd had with Danny, until she realized that it was basically just an impulse to rat him out for playing a stupid prank on her while her car was parked. Probably parked illegally, now that she thought of it. And what satisfaction would she get out of turning him in? Guy certainly wasn't going to put the cuffs on Danny for scraping her windows with a key or a quarter or a coffee spoon, for God's sake. And even if he did, the whole business would just start the sheriff wondering about what kind of trouble a homeless stranger like her might have gotten into besides sleeping in her car in a private lot where she had no business.

Damn.

And what if Danny were to tell him that he'd seen her leave the Snowfield Condos that night? She could just see the sheriff's mind at work on *that* one. Didn't they say that the bad guy always returned to the scene of the crime? He'd figure she'd done the killing or at least had some part in it, and gone back later either because she'd lost the ring or else just to gloat or some sick thing like that. He'd figure that she had either (A) had second thoughts about strangling David, or (B) just wanted to show off by taunting the cops, and had made that 911 call, then vamoosed.

He'd figure above all else that he was harboring a killer in his own house. And maybe—wouldn't it be kind of ironic if Danny was right after all?—maybe he'd decide that having her right there in the back bedroom would be convenient when he finally put together enough evidence to make an arrest.

All of this went through her head in less time than it took for the waitress to carry that hot toddy over to Andy Paxton's table and set it down. It's amazing how fast a person's mind works. Even a person who thinks she's turned out to be just about the stupidest girl in the whole world. Not to mention the unluckiest.

"Hey, Stacey." Down at the end of the bar, Tina was snapping her manicured fingers. "Stacey, child. Wake up."

"Wow. I must have zoned out for a second."

"If it's not too much trouble, I could use another chardonnay." She pushed away her empty glass and added, "Sleeping Beauty."

"Hey." She pasted on a smile that was part professional, part relieved to be back in the immediate world. "I wasn't asleep. I was thinking." She leaned away from the back bar and grabbed a fresh glass and pulled the wine bottle from the ice. While she poured she looked toward Tina and saw that the stool alongside hers was empty. No ugly sweater guy, no coat, nothing. "What happened to your new friend?"

"He had the same problem you had. He was thinking."

"Thinking." She brought the beer over and stood holding it.

"Yeah. He was thinking maybe his wife wouldn't like the stunt he was about to pull, as I understand it."

"Tina. A married man."

"The story of my life," she said, a little ruefully. "But they're never married to me, thank God."

From the corner of her eye Stacey saw Andy and Chip nodding toward each other over their drinks. What did the two of them find to talk about? Employer and employee stuff? It didn't look it. Ski enthusiast stuff? That was more likely. Something else? Who knew. She wondered how many people here in the Broken Binding—or in the whole town, for that matter—had any idea that Chip the Ski Patroller and Andy the Mountain Patriarch had as much in common as they did. The thought gave her a tiny but definite sense of belonging, a small but comfortably warm feeling that she had made a connection in this little mountain town where she was otherwise a stranger.

"Are you going to set that glass down anytime soon?" Tina pointed a bloodred nail at it.

"Oh. Sure." Reaching for a coaster as if that was the thing she'd paused over. "Sorry."

Tina turned on her stool a bit and glanced over her shoulder, following boldly where it seemed Stacey had been careful to be not quite looking. "Aha!" she said, and spun back. *"Now I get it."*

"Get what?"

"What you're all incompetent about, honey."

"I'm not incompetent. I'm filling in. I'm a little tired."

"I'm sure you are. And with Mr. Chips over there and all, I bet you're not exactly heartbroken over losing that engagement ring, either. Just don't do anything stupid on the rebound."

"*Tina.*"

"Or maybe you already did?"

"*Tina.*" She blushed, and it was visible even in the dimness of the bar.

"Hey. I'm just saying."

"Me, too," said Stacey. "I'm just saying I'm not the one putting moves on married guys from out of town."

Jack the bartender turned away from the cash register, looked from the empty stool to Tina, and chimed in from over his shoulder: "At least you could wait till closing time before you chase 'em off. The guy was turning out to be a healthy tipper."

Now it was the older woman's turn to blush, and that suited Stacey just fine.

"You heard me before," said Tina. "My life is full of married men. I seem to have some kind of magnetism. It's not my fault."

"Sure," said Jack.

"They're drawn to me like flies to honey."

"It's a curse," said Stacey, her gaze drifting out toward that certain table once again.

"Careful," said Tina.

Stacey's eyes narrowed, but not at Tina's remark. There had been a shift in the mood at Chip's table, and he and Andy were bent toward each other in a slow-burning kind of fury. Chip's mouth was pulled tight into a thin line and Andy was pointing a long arthritic finger at his chest and speaking to him very rapidly. The older man pushed his empty glass aside and leaned forward a little more, and

Chip shrunk back by the very same amount, as if the two of them were linked together by an invisible prop. Chip spoke a word or two and gave his head a slight apologetic tilt. He raised his shoulders and his eyebrows together. Andy's fury didn't alter one bit. His face was dark. He glared at Chip as if he wanted to spit nails at him. Or, worse, as if he had once wanted to embrace him and had just realized that he never, ever would.

FOURTEEN

Morning for Guy Ramsey was a ritual that never changed in the slightest. He started by boiling water for oatmeal, the real old-fashioned kind that needs to cook for half an hour. While the oatmeal bubbled and burped away on the stove he brushed his teeth and took his shower. Stacey could have set her clock by the noises of the tap in the kitchen and the shower upstairs, and when the pipes started groaning Megan was always downstairs herself, putting the coffee on. She'd be gone again about the time the shower stopped running. That gave Stacey a window of about five minutes to throw something around herself and duck into the kitchen for a mug of coffee before Guy appeared again, wrapped in a blinding-white terrycloth bathrobe, to check on the oatmeal and cut up a banana into a bowl. He'd douse the banana with orange juice and sit eating it at the kitchen table, slowly and methodically, while the oatmeal finished cooking.

This morning Stacey didn't duck out for her coffee on schedule. Instead she got dressed and waited for Guy to come down and finish his banana, and then while he was doctoring his oatmeal with raisins and butter and maple syrup she came out and filled a mug.

"Hey," he said.

"Hey."

"You up early or late?" He said it with a puzzled look, knowing only that she wasn't normally visible at exactly this time.

"Actually I think I'm on schedule, pretty much. Just thought I'd kind of mix things up. Get dressed before I got my coffee."

"Suit yourself," he said. "Go crazy."

"Yeah. Go crazy. That's me all over." She stirred in some sugar and sat down at the table.

He pulled out a chair and sat, too, squaring the steaming bowl in front of him. He stirred with one hand and with the other pointed toward the cupboard. "There's more—"

"Thanks. No. Long as I have my coffee."

"Right. I get enough of that as the day goes on."

She laughed. "You don't eat a bunch of donuts or anything, though, do you? I mean . . ."

Guy smiled a little. "I'm watching my cholesterol."

"Maybe it's big-city cops that eat donuts."

"Maybe. But in the movies, those guys eat apples they've stolen from street vendors."

"Right." She picked up her spoon and spun it in the mug again. "Must be the state police then."

"Must be."

She felt like an idiot with this donut business, but it was as close as she could come to bringing up Guy's work. What she really wanted to do was get near the question of what he knew about David Paxton's murder—not to mention the 911 caller and the ring—without acting like she was up to anything. And here was her opportunity. "You'd think they wouldn't have time for donuts," she said, "what with murders like David Paxton's to solve."

"Solving's one thing and investigating's another," Guy said from a mouthful of oatmeal. "Besides, it's not entirely up to them."

"Sure. Like you're working on it, too, and all."

"Not exactly, no. I'm not."

"No?"

"Oh, I hear stuff. I help out if they ask. They float things by me sometimes on account of I know pretty well what's what around here."

"I'm sure you do." She tried to conceal just how positive she was of that.

"But between the uniforms and the BCI, they've got it pretty well covered."

"BCI."

"Bureau of Criminal Investigation."

"Criminal Investigation. Isn't that pretty much what—"

"You'd think, from watching the television. But there's less of that to law enforcement than you might think from TV. At least most of the time. Most of the time it's speeding tickets and direct-ing traffic." He started on his breakfast.

Stacey sipped her coffee and wondered if he was being cagey. Making like he had essentially zero interest in either the murder or her. Not to mention her potential part in it. She thought maybe he was, playing dumb that is, and the thought made her worry that she might begin acting suspicious or anxious or something. The thought made her worry, in fact, that she was *already* acting suspi-cious, with the whole stupid donut gambit and all. She wanted to ask him about the things she'd overheard—particularly about the ring—but that idea was seeming less and less credible the longer she sat there at the table.

Guy tugged at his bathrobe and studied his oatmeal. It seemed that he was making sure he had at least one raisin in every spoonful, but Stacey couldn't be sure. What kind of person would do that? Then again, maybe it was just uncomfortable to be sitting across the table from her instead of eating his breakfast in privacy. He seemed edgy, anyhow, whatever the reason. Edgy and on his guard.

Or maybe it was just Stacey's imagination.

The hot coffee was making her sweat.

Sitting there in her fleece, she remembered that one of the reasons she favored a double espresso over a regular cup of coffee—whether at Judge Roy Beans or someplace else—was that a double espresso provided twice the caffeine with a small fraction of the heat. The kitchen was warm, and she was afraid she was about to start steaming up the windows. Not only that, but she realized that enough dead time had passed in their conversation that bringing up police work again would *definitely* sound suspicious.

Guy got her off the hook. "So what's new at the Broken Binding?"

"The usual." What a sparkling conversationalist.

"It's generally pretty quiet over there, from my point of view."

"Yeah. Quiet." Against her better judgment, she drank more coffee. "Especially during the week."

"Yeah." Scraping his bowl. "That's good, though."

At which point inspiration hit. "The big talk, of course, is the David Paxton thing."

Guy quit scraping. "I'll bet," he said. "Murder has a way of getting people excited."

Was he looking at her funny? He sure was hard to read. So she offered up an answer that didn't amount to much. "You've got that right."

"Especially in a small town like this one," he went on.

Was he insinuating that she had come up here like some homicidal maniac on the run from the big city? Like the Boston Strangler on a road trip? "I'll bet that's true," she said, and then she thought better of it. "I mean, it would be scary enough anywhere. . . ."

"Sure." He sat nodding his head, maybe with the kind of irony she'd seen TV cops use. Or maybe not. And then he said it again: "Sure," pushing back his chair and rising and heading for the sink.

Stacey opened her mouth. She thought she might be losing her mind, that she might be getting ready to throw away every scrap of protective coloration she had, but it was a case of now or never. Wasn't it? She put her hands flat on the table and said, plainly and offhandedly, the lie that had come into her head: "The talk at the Binding is that the police found some evidence."

Guy didn't even look up from rinsing his bowl. "Really?" he asked. "What kind?"

"Oh, they probably don't know what they're talking about."

"What kind? Did they say?"

"Different things."

"What kind of things?" Still not looking up.

In for a dollar, in for a dime. One lie begets another. But this one was pretty good: "It depends on who you listen to. Fingerprints. A glove. Distinctive footprints. A watch. A ring."

"Really?"

She ran back over the list in her mind, hoping that she hadn't overdone it with the jewelry. Hoping that she hadn't overdone it with—what was she thinking, anyhow?—the subconscious O.J. references. At least she hadn't called it a bloody glove. "Yeah," she said. "Like I said. Different things."

"Wow," he said. "Fingerprints. A watch." He put the bowl in the dishwasher. "A watch, for crying out loud."

She laughed.

"If only we'd get so lucky."

She laughed some more. It was positively ridiculous, wasn't it?

At least he didn't pick up on her mention of the ring. That clarified the situation a little, didn't it? It meant either that he was waiting for her to reveal more, or that he didn't want to signal that she'd touched on the truth. Unless he meant to signal that by *not* mentioning it.

In other words, it didn't clarify the situation at all.

Guy moved toward the door and Stacey stood, heading for the sink to tip out the rest of her coffee.

"You keep your ears open," he said. "Tell me if you hear anything else I ought to know about."

"I will."

"Like if somebody left behind their ID bracelet. Or a Social Security card or something."

"Yeah. Really."

"A driver's license." Guy stuck his hands in the pockets of his bathrobe and headed toward the stairs, laughing as he went.

Stacey tipped out her coffee and leaned hard against the sink. She watched the coffee swirl down the drain and she ran some water and watched that swirl down after it. She was no better off than she'd been ten minutes ago, but no worse, either. At least she didn't think so.

She took a few runs with Chip mid-morning, and on one trip up the lift she managed to ask him about sharing that table with Andy.

"If you live in this town long enough," he said, "you'll share a table with pretty much everybody."

"How long is long enough?"

"Not very long." He clacked the tips of his skis together and watched the snow break free and tumble off in clumps.

"So that's it, then? You and Andy Paxton? Just the luck of the draw?" She was thinking about the dark looks that the two men had exchanged toward the end of their conversation. About the way their heads had moved in tandem. About the fierce expression on Andy's face and the threat of his long arthritic finger.

"Pretty much." He caught sight of a couple of college kids careening through a slow-skiing zone on snowboards, and hollered down at them to take it down a notch. He could pull their passes for that kind of thing, and he hoped they knew it.

"Looked kind of serious to me."

"Ahh, you know. Employer-employee stuff. The usual."

"The usual."

"I can't even remember, to tell you the truth."

But even behind his goggles and his neck gaiter, it was clear enough to Stacey that he wasn't. The only question was *why not?*

FIFTEEN

In between skiing and work, if the roads were clear enough, Stacey liked to drive up into the high-end construction projects hidden in the mountains that ringed the town. Half the fun was the thrill of discovery. Basically, you started by looking for tire tracks coming down from some dirt road. As often as not those roads led nowhere special—maybe to a couple of ramshackle house trailers surrounded by piles of wood for burning, or to an abandoned barn with its siding gone a greasy brownish gray and a little cupola getting ready to fall from the ridge of the roofline—and sometimes they just ran past an old graveyard or frozen-over pond and doubled back and dumped you out pretty much where you'd started. But now and then they led to pure pay dirt. Lifestyles of the Rich and Irresponsible.

Upscale log cabins big enough to house Paul Bunyan and Babe the Blue Ox, too.

Massive post-and-beam lodges cantilevered from mountainsides so as to block all views but their own.

Indescribable monstrosities with turrets and domes and balconies and decks and bridges and gables and various other architectural add-ons for which there might not even be names.

All of these ostentatious things standing dark and utterly unused, fifty weeks a year at least.

According to the scuttlebutt, they were owned for the most part by investment bankers from New York and Connecticut. It seemed to Stacey that you'd have to pillage a whole lot of retirement funds to come up with the millions it would take. Which seemed to her, now that she thought about it, just about a perfect aspiration for that unfaithful snake of a former fiancé she'd left behind. She hoped he'd never see one of these disgustingly magnificent houses, because it would be the next thing he'd want. The next thing he'd want and the next thing he'd get and the next thing he'd cast aside when some other conquest came along.

But enough about Brian.

This particular afternoon, in between finishing up at the mountain and beginning her shift at the Binding, she turned the Subaru up an unmarked lane she'd never noticed before. It ran across a little bridge and then turned sharply uphill. Uphill was always a good sign. That's where the money went. The trees along the lane were close in, barely cleared, and in the summer the way up would be pretty nearly choked off with leaves. Invisible. Which was also a good sign. Money liked to hide. The lane was more or less cleared of snow, too, which meant that somebody cared enough to maintain it and no doubt had some use for it even now.

She drove up and up, downshifting past a stack of felled trees and the parked bulldozer that had torn them out of the ground. The road turned abruptly just beyond the dozer, nearly switching back on itself uphill into the trees, and as she rounded the bend she spied a car dead ahead, idling in the middle of the lane. It was a big black Mercedes wagon, four-wheel drive, with Vermont tags that read SKIBUM. Pretty darned ironic, she thought. Like that deadhead sticker in the song, stuck to the bumper of a Cadillac. And it was totally blocking the way.

Until she realized that it wasn't. Not exactly.

The lane ended just where the car was parked, and the reason for the road existing at all turned out to be about twenty yards uphill of that: a huge rectangle cut from the forest, a vast open space stripped entirely of trees. Two people were up there, a man and a woman. They were standing very near to each other with their backs in her direction, and the man was pointing here and there with a gloved hand. The arrival of Stacey's car seemed not to disturb them at all. It was as if they were expecting the arrival of someone else, a surveyor or a contractor or some other tradesman beneath their immediate notice. She swung left and stopped the car and threw it into reverse and began angling through a tight K turn on the cramped pathway. The power steering squealed under the strain, and the two people in the clearing deigned at last to turn around.

She recognized the man as Richie Paxton—SKIBUM, wasn't that just about perfect?—but the woman was unfamiliar. She certainly wasn't Richie's wife. She was slender, nearly as tall as he was, and wrapped in a long elegant coat of hunter green wool bound at the neck with a crimson scarf. Her skin was pale and she had accented her features with makeup applied skillfully enough to make Stacey feel childish and a little poverty-stricken by comparison. Her hair was a brilliant flame against the snowy woods.

As Stacey cranked the wheel and threw the car into gear and gunned it back down the hill, she decided that the woman's hair was the kind of red that could set all kinds of things on fire.

Tina Montero was settling onto her usual stool when Stacey pushed through the door from the kitchen. *Right on time*, Stacey thought. *I could set my watch by her. If I wore a watch.*

Stacey still cleaned up before her shift in the employee locker room. Old habits die hard. Plus the drive back to the sheriff's house had been entirely out of her way. And not only that, but there was always the chance that she'd find her lost engagement ring in some unexpected and unexplored cranny by the showers or the mirrors or someplace. Boy, would *that* ever change a few things.

One thing it wouldn't change, though, was Tina's clockwork appearance at the Binding. Happy Hour, baby. Seven days a week.

"Hey, Tina." Stacey tied on her apron and grabbed a glass for Tina's first chardonnay.

"Hey, Stacey."

Nobody else was in the bar.

"Didn't you used to sell real estate?"

"Yeah. I've still got my license, but—"

"You know that property out on the west side, in between the sugar house and the bait shop?"

"On the left?"

"No." She opened the bottle. "On the right. It's along this little narrow road that runs up the hill."

"Oh, yeah." As if something was dawning on her slowly but surely. "It's been on the market for years."

"Has it?"

"I had the listing myself for a while."

"Really?" Pouring Tina's drink.

"Really. This was in the nineties. Some guy from Montpelier owns it."

"It looks like it finally sold."

"He must have come down a lot. He was asking a fortune on account of the view."

"I didn't get a chance to check that out." She came over with Tina's drink, laid out a coaster, and put it down.

Tina admired the glass. "Now what, pray tell, were you doing over there?"

Stacey told her. It was just something she liked to do. A little exploration. A little curiosity.

"Which is what killed the cat."

Stacey laughed and leaned against the back bar. "I don't think I have much to fear from Richie Paxton."

Tina lost all interest in her drink. She looked at Stacey and cocked her head to one side as if she was stretching out her neck. As if she had water in her ears. As if she couldn't believe the evidence of her own senses. "Richie?"

"Yep."

"Richie Paxton." It wasn't a question.

"Richie Paxton."

"Wow. You saw him up there?"

"Just now. He was scoping out the lot."

"Really?"

"Really."

Tina sat dumbfounded for once.

Stacey opened the register and checked the drawer. Looking at the money gave her an idea. "As mercenary as it sounds," she said, "I guess he's worth more now."

Tina shook her head. "You have no idea."

"Well. With David dead and all."

Tina looked like she saw the light. "With David dead, they've got a two-way split. The parents and Richie."

"So he's worth that much more." She thought for a minute. It was Brian who was good with numbers, but this was easy. "Half again as much," she said. "Half of David's third."

"Bright girl."

A couple of snowmobilers entered the Binding on a gust of wind from the front door. Dressed in Day-Glo yellow, they stomped their boots in the foyer and made their way between the tables for the other end of the bar.

Tina lowered her voice as they came. "Very bright. But there's more to it than that."

Stacey stopped her with a raised finger and went off to take orders from the snowmobile guys, who were busy opening the top halves of their insulated coveralls and peeling them back. They looked like a heavyset pair of fluorescent bananas. She got each of them a Long Trail and filled a couple of bowls with Chex Mix—snowmobilers always went through that Chex Mix like mad—and then she went back to Tina's end of the bar. She got close enough that the older woman didn't have to speak up very loudly, and she leaned there with her elbows on the bar.

Tina gave a thoughtful look. "The thing is, without David around, everything's liquid all of a sudden."

"Liquid." She felt as if she were talking with Brian. He was big on liquidity.

"*Liquid.* As in David was dead set on not selling the mountain."

"*Dead set.* Isn't that a little—"

"Sorry."

Stacey noticed that Tina had drained her glass while she'd been taking care of the snowmobilers. Wow. That was fast, even for Tina. She'd never make it through the whole evening at that rate.

"He was determined not to sell, anyhow. David was. So even though everybody had a third, they weren't worth squat."

"Oh, sure. Those Paxtons really seem to be struggling."

"You know what I mean."

One of the men from the end of the bar looked their way for a moment, and Stacey straightened up. "Can I get you something?"

Like some kind of trained gorilla, the snowmobiler grunted one word—"remote"—and pointed with a big meaty paw to where it lay

alongside the register. Stacey got it for him and he switched the
overhead TV to ESPN. It was always ESPN with these guys. Minus
the sound, they were stuck reading the captions and crawls for
themselves, a feat that seemed to Stacey pretty miraculous in itself.
Unless they were just entranced by the way the pictures moved.

"If you can't sell a thing, what's it worth?"

Stacey understood. "You want another chardonnay?"

Tina looked down at her glass and seemed surprised to find it
drained. "Yes," she said. "Yes I do."

SIXTEEN

She didn't fade the whole night long, although she did keep pretty much to herself and look unusually pensive—if that was a word you could ever use to describe Tina Montero. *Morose* might be the more conventional term. Stacey looked at her and felt as if she was looking into a bleak future. Tina sitting more or less alone at a crowded bar, methodically addressing glass after glass, harboring some sad secret.

It turned out that she was waiting for the crowds to thin a little before asking Stacey another question, which emerged just as a scratchy old rendering of "One Toke Over the Line" burst from the jukebox: "Was he up there all alone?"

"Who?"

"*Who?* Richie, that's *who.*"

"Oh. Sorry. No."

"He must be getting ready to start in the spring, if he's up there with the contractor."

"Oh, they've already started. They've knocked down the trees already. Had a bulldozer and everything."

"He works fast, that Richie."

"But I don't think it was the contractor with him."

"No?"

"Not unless contractors around here do their shopping at Neiman Marcus."

"I hear you." Tina laughed and tipped her glass. "There's money in construction."

"I mean—"

"And I don't blame you for noticing. Like they say, 'Every girl's crazy for a sharp-dressed man.'"

"This was more like a sharp-dressed woman."

"Oh." Tina stopped breathing and started again. "That'd be the broker."

"Probably."

"What'd she look like?"

"Well-preserved. Revlon and Chanel."

"Sounds like Sheri from Mountainside Realty."

"Tall and thin."

"I wouldn't exactly call her tall, but—"

"Red hair."

"Really."

"Oh, yeah. And I'm talking *red*. Like, expensive sports car red."

"Hmm," said Tina. "Then that's not Sheri. She's dumb blonde from the get-go, and that's the way she likes it." Pointing to her own hair, peroxided into near oblivion.

"Maybe she had a change of heart."

"I don't think so." She sat looking puzzled for a minute or two, and then pushed away from the bar without even saying good night.

Pete Hardwick, who owned the place but wasn't on the schedule tonight, came by at closing time to make up a deposit. He stood by the register with his boots draining snowmelt onto the rubber mat, and he asked Stacey how much Tina had had to drink.

"How come?"

"Just curious."

"The usual, I guess."

"Maybe the usual's getting to be too much," he said without looking up from the drawer. "Maybe it's starting to creep up, you think?"

"How come?"

"For one thing, she just about sideswiped me on Main Street a minute ago."

"Ow."

"Had this look in her eye."

"She's always got that look, Pete."

"I'm not so sure. She looked pretty far gone. Glassy and then some."

"I'll keep tabs on her."

"You OK with cutting her off? If you need to?"

"Sure." Stacey gave the bar a few squirts of disinfectant and began to rub at it with a clean white cloth.

"Sometimes it's easier to cut off a stranger than somebody you know."

"I guess." She wondered what on earth Pete Hardwick, with his investment-banking fortune, would know about it.

"I'm just saying."

"I hear you."

"It's a liability issue."

"I'm on it," said Stacey. "Don't worry."

But it was plain that he did worry, even as he was occupied with counting bills and stacking them into neat piles and adding up the totals on a little pocket calculator. "She get started early or something?"

"No. But she kept at it pretty seriously." She squirted a stubborn spot on the bar and rubbed at it again. "Now that you mention it."

"Hmm." He lifted his shoulders and let them fall. "You never know."

"You never know." The jukebox died and she lowered her voice. "I was telling her about Richie Paxton. Looks like he's building."

"He's always building. That house of his'll never be done."

"This is a new one."

Pete stopped counting. "A new one?"

"A new one."

"Really."

"It looks that way. They're up there knocking down trees and all."

Pete shook his head. "You ever meet his wife? You ever meet Jeanette?"

"No. I've seen her, but—"

"She's got no patience for that kind of thing. No patience at all. A year back she threatened to divorce him for adding a third bay to the garage."

"So."

"So there's no way she'd be building a new place. If Richie's out there knocking down trees to put up his dream house, he's not doing it with her."

Stacey thought of the woman with the red hair.

"Where is it, anyhow? Where're they building?"

"Out on the west side, up that little road by the sugar house."

"Nobody tells me anything," he said.

"It must have been in the paper."

"Who reads the paper?"

True enough. The newspaper of record, if you could call it that, was published out of Rutland. The only other thing printed around here was a weekly promotional rag jammed with amateurish advertisements for restaurants and ski shops and firewood. But it was probably more relevant than the Rutland paper. You pretty much had to count on getting all the scuttlebutt you needed at the post office and the hardware store and right here at the Broken Binding. No wonder Pete felt blindsided.

"If there's any justice in the world," he said, "Jeanette'll do pretty well for herself when they split."

"If they split."

"They'll split all right." He stuffed money into a bank bag and zipped it up. "And hey, lucky her: She had the good sense to wait till David was dead. Everything that guy had was in that mountain. And now half of it belongs to his brother."

"Smart girl," said Stacey.

Turned out it was a fine night for near misses with cars.

A little fresh snow had fallen by the time Stacey left the Binding. Not much, maybe an inch or two, that kind of light and powdery stuff that covered up all the grit and sand and made the world look fresh again. It was still coming down, and there was a slight wind blowing it. She didn't bother scraping her car clean but just swept at the side windows a little with a mittened hand. The wipers and the wind would take care of the rest, front and back. She clicked on her headlights and could see by the way they accentuated the falling snow that she'd left the high beams on. Head down the road like that, and the slightest snowfall would turn into a hyperspace jump from *Star Wars*. You'd be half hypnotized before you knew it. So she turned off the high beams and put the car into reverse and heard a troubling thump.

The last thing she needed was a flat tire.

Make that the next-to-last thing she needed. Because the very last thing was the stooped figure of Danny Bowman, his ponytail whipping in the wind and his black eyes squinting against the blowing snow, looming up in her window. She was pretty sure she must have hit him. But if she had, he wouldn't be grinning that awful grin, would he?

Who knew, with Danny.

He kept grinning and made a circling motion with his hand. It meant "roll the window down."

She didn't.

He straightened out his hand and whacked the palm of it, hard, against the side of the car. It made the thumping sound she'd heard. The oldest trick in the book. He laughed like a maniac and made the window motion with his hand again.

Again she ignored it.

He looked her in the eye and rubbed his thumb and forefinger together in the universal sign for money, and then he ran them together across his closed lips. He'd be quiet if she paid up.

Stacey blew the horn to startle him, and when he jumped she backed the Subaru up into the fresh snow. Let him try the Marcel Marceau routine on somebody else. Her headlights raked across Danny's narrow form as she yanked the wheel, and then she found first and made for home as fast as she could go.

SEVENTEEN

Danny Bowman lived nowhere and everywhere, and even though blowing nights like this weren't the worst they were close. Freezing rain, that was the worst. Not because he couldn't get out of the weather at all—he wasn't a moose, for God's sake; he had alternatives—but because he couldn't stay entirely out of the weather *forever*. He could spend most of the daylight hours circulating from Bud's to the pizza joint to Judge Roy Beans and back again, but come nightfall his choices got narrower. Bud's was open all night, and generally stayed empty between nine or ten o'clock and dawn. The convenience store at the Shell station was open twenty-four seven, too, but lately the night clerk had decided to be a pain in the ass. Some pierced and tattooed kid with no respect for his elders. Thank God there was an unlocked men's room at the Citgo. Sometimes it got cold enough in there to freeze the water in the bowl, but it was better than nothing. Better than some unlocked parked car where he could freeze his ass until dawn.

A few bucks would go a long way, if that girl in the yellow jacket and the Subaru weren't so damned stubborn. And here he thought he'd be able to pry enough loose to splurge on a night at the Timberline Motel. Think again, Danny boy.

There had to be another way to make use of what he knew.

He shuffled out of the dark lot and made his way back to Bud's in the accumulating snow. The sidewalks were already drifted pretty full, so he kept to the street and stayed in the tracks of the most recent car. That girl's, he figured. Damn her.

There was no free coffee at Spruce Peak. Not even in the executive suite, such as it was. If you wanted coffee, you went to the cafeteria in the main lodge and flashed your employee badge and got a tall paper cup of absolute rotgut for half price. Unless you were Richie Paxton. Richie kept a private Keurig single-cup machine in his office, plumbed for water and everything. It was one of the few small pleasures he permitted himself in this life, he liked to say, and nobody he told that to knew exactly how to take it.

This morning he was sitting at his desk, fixing to brew himself a second cup of Green Mountain Double Black Diamond, when he smelled the presence of a visitor. He actually smelled him before he saw him. He probably would have smelled him over the hot steamy fragrant goodness of brewing coffee. That's how refined his nose was, and how long it had been since Danny Bowman had had a bath.

"Morning, Mr. Paxton." Danny gave a kind of salute that seemed insolent and pathetic all at once.

Richie imagined him in Vietnam, wondering what kind of failure he'd been at that early stage of his life. At the same time he reminded himself that a company of this size really needed a proper receptionist out front. He could imagine the professional way that SkiAmerica would run things, and he half wished he could be around to see it.

Danny gave him a strangely troubling look of camaraderie, as if they had both signed up for the same exclusive club. "You mind I close this door?"

"To tell you the truth, I do." This kind of close encounter was exactly the reason he never went to Judge Roy Beans or any other place where Danny hung out. Not even the grocery store. Jeanette took care of the shopping, although come to think of it he might be handling that sort of thing on his own for a while.

"Nah," said Danny, pushing the door shut behind him. "You won't mind. Believe you me."

In the closed room he smelled worse. Richie couldn't think of a way to get rid of him that didn't involve escorting him down the hallway and walking him down the stairs and literally showing him the door, so he didn't move. He just sat there at his desk and gritted his teeth, realizing that he wasn't going to get that fresh-brewed Double Black Diamond anytime soon. No way he'd make one for Danny, too. "So," he said, folding his hands on his conspicuously empty desktop, "what brings you here?"

Danny flopped down in the overstuffed chair and wasted no time with small talk. "I know who kilt your brother," he said.

"Oh, come on."

"I do. I seen 'em leave."

Richie fidgeted. "Sure."

"I seen 'em leave the condos. I was there."

"Where?"

"Snowfield. The condos."

Richie blinked once, slowly, like a cat. "I know where my brother lived. Where were *you*?"

"In the lot."

"You were just hanging around, I suppose. Just keeping an eye on things. In the middle of the night."

"I was taking a nap in somebody's car. I don't know who."

Richie sniffed the air. "I'm sure they enjoyed having you stop by."

"They don't want people sleeping in 'em, they shouldn't leave 'em unlocked."

"So you were asleep, and you saw the person who killed my brother."

Danny straightened up in the chair and tugged at his ponytail. "Who're *you* all of a sudden? Perry Goddamn Mason? I come here to tell you something and you don't want to hear it."

"I just want to get the facts straight is what I want."

"I got your facts straight. I was in this car and I saw 'em come out of the condo."

"Fine. The night my brother died."

"It was that night or the other one."

"Wait a minute."

"The night they found him."

Richie's face showed a kind of astonishment. "So let me get this straight. You're not even talking about—"

Danny made his eyebrows jump. "Scene of the crime, man. Scene of the crime. They always come back. It don't make no difference."

"Get out of my office."

"I ain't told nobody yet."

Richie's face began to redden. "Get out, or get to the point."

With the palms of his greasy hands, Danny smoothed back the hair on both sides of his head. He looked up from the low seat of that overstuffed chair and spoke. "I need money, man."

"*You need money.*" The smell of his visitor—a kind of animal stench, dense and penetrating at the same time—suddenly made Richie want to throw up. "Great. So since you need money, I'm supposed to *buy* this worthless information from you? Or am I supposed to pay you to keep quiet?"

"Whichever way. It don't make no difference to me. You give me a little money, the info's yours."

"Aren't I the lucky one. Since it's absolutely worthless."

"Maybe so. But it's all yours. I promise. Do what you want with it. Take it to the police, or go on and bury it under that new house of yours." He showed his teeth in a cunning look.

Richie was thrown for a second but he tried not to show it.

"Like I said, it don't make no difference to me. Long as I get my money."

"For the name of some guy who you *claim* to have seen leaving the condos, in the middle of the night, either on the night my brother was killed or a few days later."

"That's the thing," said Danny, leaning forward in the chair. "It weren't no guy."

A look of relief or at least diminished fury passed over Richie's face.

"It was a woman, see."

"No kidding. I thought it was Bigfoot."

"It was a woman. In a yellow jacket. I give you that much for free." He sat back, satisfied. "Five hundred gets you her name."

"*Five hundred dollars.* Don't insult my intelligence."

"Two."

Richie looked at Danny as if he was calculating how low he'd go and how fast he'd get there.

"I'd settle for a hundred."

"I'll give you a cup of coffee if you'll go away."

"You don't want the info?"

"No. I don't want the info." Somehow, he looked as if he already had all the info he needed.

Danny cocked his head like some kind of predatory bird. "You don't know what I'll do with it, then."

"You're right," said Richie. "I don't have a clue. And I don't exactly care." He pulled his wallet from his pocket and extracted three singles. "Take this to the cafeteria and buy yourself a cup of coffee."

"I can get free coffee a million places."

Richie tucked the bills into his own shirt pocket. "Have it your way," he said. "I wasn't crazy about you walking around with my logo on your cup anyhow. That kind of thing is just plain bad for business."

EIGHTEEN

Stacey's day off came around, and rather than brave the pre-Christmas crowds at the mountain she stuck around the house. She had a little reading to do anyhow. And some laundry. The usual. May as well make a day of it. She had just gone into the basement to start folding when Guy came home for lunch. He didn't usually, and with Megan working today it made just the two of them in the house. He built a sandwich and put it on a plate and went to the basement himself, his heavy boots clomping down the open wooden stairs.

"Hey," he said, about halfway down. "You want some?" Raising the plate toward her and indicating the sandwich.

"No, thanks. I'll grab a sandwich at Mahoney's later."

Guy nodded and went over to the workbench and snapped on the overhead. His chain saw was there on the bench, laid out under the harsh fluorescents like something dead. In point of fact it was. Dead, that is. At least for a while. The spark plug had fouled back in the fall, when he was just about finished cutting wood for winter. He'd brought it down here and left it on the bench with a mixture of frustration and relief, figuring that he'd have all winter to get to it. Alongside it now were a fresh spark plug and a bottle of chain oil and a new air filter, and he put his plate down and took a big bite of his sandwich and set to work.

Stacey finished folding the laundry and sat down on the steps for something to do.

Changing the plug and the filter took about five minutes, tops. His fingers were black with grease right away and he ended up working on the sandwich between the thumb and pinky of his left hand rather than delay or go upstairs for a napkin. He changed the oil while he was at it, dumping the old into a coffee tin. He talked to Stacey as he worked, describing in a kind of offhand monotone the circumstances under which the chain saw had quit and the necessity of taking good care of your tools. She thought he sounded like her father, although her father had never actually had so much as a single hammer of his own. He hired everything out. Still, a platitude was a platitude, and he had never come up short in that department.

When Guy was done with the engine he turned his attention to the chain. He said he might as well sharpen it while he had the opportunity. It had never occurred to Stacey that such a thing was even done, but what did she know? She watched as he picked up a tool that looked like a big wrench, fastened it onto the chain, and strained at it. *Ping*—something popped loose and rang down onto the workbench. A small metal pin. And no sooner had it fallen than the chain, separated now, fell away from the bar like a gleaming black snake.

"Just like that?" said Stacey.

"Just like that. Nothing to it, if you know what you're doing."

Stacey thought of the chain that she'd seen wrapped around David Paxton's neck. How hard and stiff it had looked from the blood. And how the free end of it, lying there on the bloodstained pillow, had been torn and bent, as if it had been cut free and ruined in the process. It would take bolt cutters or something like that, she figured. Apparently, it would also take a person who didn't know much about chain saws.

Guy cranked the chain into a vise and picked up a small flat file, with which he addressed the little cutting edges one by one. Just a couple of zinging passes on each, and then he'd open the vise and move the chain and close the vise again and repeat the process. After a bit he turned and looked at her there on the stairs, a kind of rapid assessment in his eyes that might have suggested anything. Perhaps that he was wondering how long she'd hang around with that basket of laundry. Perhaps that he, like her, had been thinking about what kind of person might mangle a chain open instead of taking the easy way.

Somebody who didn't know any better.

Stacey felt a chill go up her back that didn't have anything to do with the unheated basement. So she gathered up her laundry basket and said good-bye and went back up the stairs to her room, and before Guy surfaced again to wash his hands and rinse his plate in the sink, she was gone.

She couldn't think of it as a date.

It wasn't a date, was it?

It was just Chip running into her at Judge Roy Beans and asking what she was doing for dinner.

That was all it was.

Most definitely not a date.

But Maison Maurice was the nicest place in town all the same—a far cry, people said, from Cinco de Taco and Vinnie's Steak-Out—and that was a perfectly good excuse for taking her second shower of the day and actually drying her hair for a change and putting on her very nicest nonfleece. She used a little makeup, too. Nothing like

Ms. Revlon and Chanel from up on that mountain road, but there it was.

It turned out that the difference between Maison Maurice and the other places in town pretty much came down to white tablecloths. White tablecloths and a list of specials printed in a fancy script font on pale green paper, instead of scribbled on a smeary chalkboard. Those two things, plus a snarky waitress with altogether too much mascara and a spiked black haircut about fifteen years too young for her.

The food was pretty good. But the food was pretty good at the taco place and Vinnie's Steak-Out and the pizza joint, too. Not to mention the Broken Binding. Pretty good just about summed things up around here—if you didn't count dead men with chains around their necks, and wild-eyed lunatics stalking you in your car, and rich guys running around on their wives, and a sheriff who thought you were involved with a murder on account of your engagement ring, which you'd obviously dropped at the scene of the crime and a busted chain saw chain, which a city girl like you was too ignorant to know anything about taking apart properly although everyone around here obviously did.

Maybe it'd be good to think of this as a date after all.

"This place is a little pricey," she said once they had their menus. "Don't you think?"

"Relatively," Chip said. "But that's why we're here."

She looked up. "Meaning . . ."

"The money my dad sends me? I make a point of not touching it for necessities. So every buck is a bonus." He ran his finger along the entrees. "The lobster looks good. But Maine lobster, at this time of year? I don't know."

"How about donating it to the Sierra Club? The Wilderness Society? They could use it."

"They get their share, believe me."

She didn't want to seem ungracious, so she left it at that.

They started with calamari and a bottle of white wine, neither of which seemed to earn the waitress's full approval. She looked like a person who went strictly for red wine and red meat, the bloodier the better. She also looked like she was sizing up Chip for something unmentionable, an idea that bothered Stacey more than she thought it should.

Once their glasses were filled he lifted his in something well short of a toast. "So, how are things at the sheriff's house?"

"Fine. They're perfectly nice."

"I'd hope so." However he might have meant it, he didn't give her the opportunity to decide that he might be taking too much of an interest. "I mean, you don't want some nutcase enforcing the law. Driving around with that gun and all."

"No. I guess not."

"Hope he doesn't bring his work home."

"I don't think anybody'd mind if he did. Something tells me his work isn't all that exciting."

"I can hear it now," Chip said. "Supper-table conversation about how many tickets he racked up today. Fascinating."

"Absolutely."

Chip's face grew serious for a second, although he crinkled up a smile that looked meant to disguise it. "On the other hand," he said, "there *is* the murder and all. You'd think—"

"Honestly," she said, "I don't really eat there. Not with the family. I mean, I've got kitchen privileges and all. But we kind of pass by on different schedules. And then there's the Binding."

"Then there's the Binding."

"I'm kind of occupied at suppertime."

"What's with that, anyhow? You live on hot wings?"

"Sometimes it feels that way."

Chip gave her a level and almost uncomfortably steady look. "How about we see if we can fix that right now? At least for one meal, on my old man."

"Sounds good." She had to admit it.

"Or on Big Oil, if that doesn't spoil your appetite."

Richie Paxton's black Mercedes—SKIBUM plates and all—eased through the dark town like a big fish slowly making its way upstream. Its fat radials whispered on the wet pavement. Danny Bowman sat on a bench outside the pizza joint, lit from behind by lamps hung low over red formica tabletops, and watched the car slip by. He didn't even move his head. He could have been a statue or a dead man, except for his eyes, which watched Richie's car come up the street and stop at the town's one traffic light and move on when the light changed. He couldn't see in. The car had deeply tinted windows and the little bit of light that was still lingering in the western sky was thin and pale as milk. Still he watched, focusing with a furious visual intensity on the car and the place where its driver must be. Like a kid focusing sunlight on an insect through a magnifying glass.

And soon enough, just as if Danny had pressed a button on some remote control, the dome light inside the Mercedes blinked on. He couldn't have been more surprised to see it happen, and as soon as he registered it he had second thoughts about having drawn down this weird mojo upon himself, because in the dim light behind the gray windows of the passing car, swiveling like a piece of artillery mounted on a turret, he saw Richie's head turning and turning as slowly and methodically as death, tracking him where he sat all by himself on that bench, his belly full of leftover pizza and his options running out. It gave him a powerful psychic chill to go along with the physical one, and after holding Richie's gaze for as long as he could—maybe a second, tops—he looked away. When he looked back the car was some distance down the road and he couldn't tell if the dome light was still on or not. Or whether Richie might still be staring him down in the rearview mirror.

NINETEEN

S o how's your friend Andy Paxton doing?" She asked the question after a glass of wine and the calamari and the soup, just as their entrees were arriving. The truth was that she had already run out of other things to talk about.

"My *friend* Andy Paxton?"

"You two've got a connection. Don't start denying it now."

"I know, I know." He scanned the table and saw that he was missing a knife, so in the absence of the spiky-haired waitress he helped himself to one from the next table. "We do have a connection. It's nice."

"So?"

"So he's doing OK, I guess. Considering."

"Considering that his son is dead and they don't have a clue who did it."

"Yeah."

They ate in silence for a few moments. From speakers hidden in a dusty potted fern, Dean Martin sang "That's Amore."

Chip chewed slowly and appreciatively, and as he did there appeared on his face a look almost as guilty as it was thoughtful. "You know," he said, after a swallow of wine, "I wasn't entirely honest with you about Andy and me. At that table in the Binding."

"No?" She said it with just enough emphasis that nobody on earth could have been sure whether or not she was surprised.

"No. Not entirely."

"Tell me more. I'm accustomed to guys who aren't entirely honest with me." She left it at that, just let it slip in there while he was bound for another destination entirely.

"It's just that there was a reason he was coming on so strong."

"There usually is."

"It wasn't an employer-employee thing."

"No?"

He picked up a slice of garlic bread. "He was really pissed at me, is what it was."

"No kidding."

"You want to know why?"

"If you want to tell me."

He put the bread down and leaned forward a little, almost like Andy in the Binding. "I told him I wouldn't put it past Richie."

He couldn't mean what she thought he meant, and she looked at him dumbfounded.

"You know what I mean." Picking up the bread again.

"No. I don't. Put what past?"

"David." Drawing the garlic bread across his neck just like that.

"You can't be serious."

"*You can't be serious.* That's what *he* said."

"I don't blame him."

"But it makes perfect sense, don't you think? One, Richie's a first-class son-of-a-bitch. Two, he's building that giant house that everybody in town knows about but doesn't mention. On account of what, sparing his wife's feelings? As if she doesn't know all about it already? Come on."

"It could be—"

"Three, he's got a little something going on the side. Or is that two B?"

The red-haired woman. Stacey took a bite and said, "Two B or not to be."

"Right. Very funny. Anyway: four, he's stuck with a brother who owns a third of the family business and doesn't want to sell it, and a father who's in between. Which means he's completely SOL until David changes his mind." He bit hard into the garlic bread, which had gone cold. "Or until David doesn't have a mind to change."

"I hope you were more delicate than that with Andy."

"Not really. No."

"Too bad. It might have helped."

"It's a guy thing."

"Andy doesn't look like a guy thing kind of guy."

"You might be surprised."

They ate in silence for a few minutes, until Stacey asked, "So he just sits down at your table and orders his hot toddy—"

"Yeah. A hot toddy. Get that."

"—orders his hot toddy and you strike up this conversation about how you think one of his own sons might have murdered the other one?"

"I didn't exactly say *he might have.* I said I wouldn't put it past him."

"Out of the blue? Just like that?"

"Hey," he said, lifting up the flat of one palm in a pantomime of self-defense, "it's not exactly easy to work up to that kind of thing."

"Still." She gave him a look that she might have been saving up for a sneak thief or a child abuser, a look that must have been terribly discouraging to a guy sitting across the table from an attractive girl just his age in a pretty darned romantic and more or less

French restaurant in a little Vermont ski town with a light snow just blowing up in the streetlights beyond the windows. She gave him a look custom tailored to make him want to explain himself, whether she intended it that way or not.

"We'd been kind of circling the subject all evening."

"All evening."

"All evening."

"You'd been there for like fifteen minutes. Tops."

"No." He put down his fork and folded his napkin on his lap. "We'd been out for a while. Did some night skiing. Just us two."

Stacey squinted at him. "Night skiing? Where?" As far as she knew, you had to go all the way to the Poconos in Pennsylvania for that, although there might have been someplace in New York State where they did it, too. If that was your cup of tea, anyway. Which in her case it wasn't.

"Up on the mountain." He pointed with his thumb.

"Spruce."

"Yeah. We skinned up after the groomers were done."

Now that was a horse of a different color. The look she had given him a minute ago was gone, and in its place was one brighter by about a million watts. "You're kidding."

"I am not."

"Up Spruce. In the dark. And back down."

"Yep."

"In the dark."

"We had headlamps."

"Still."

"There's nothing in the world like it."

"I'll bet."

"Andy's been doing it forever. Since he was a kid. The boys used to go with him, but that was a long time ago."

"The boys."

"Richie and David. He calls them that."

"So you do, too."

"You know. When you spend time with a person . . ." He took a sip of his wine and put the glass back down.

A huge smile broke across Stacey's face. "So you and Andy Paxton have been running around behind people's backs for a while."

"Shhh." With a finger raised to his lips and a look in his eye that said he meant it.

"You've been sneaking around like a couple of—"

"Hey. It's kind of our little secret, OK? I'm not even sure why. It's just, I don't know—private. Personal. It's a thing we do."

"And then—wait a minute—then, when you're done, you meet at someplace like the Binding—"

"Always at the Binding."

"*Always.*"

"Always."

"There's an always."

Chip just grinned.

"You meet up at the Binding like it's just some random thing?"

Chip shrugged. "I know. It seems kind of stupid. Silly."

"You come over in two cars?"

"Uh, yeah."

"So nobody knows what you're up to."

"It's just the way we do it."

"I can't decide whether you're a couple of untrustworthy grownups, or a couple of overgrown boys."

"I'll take B."

"I'll withhold judgment."

"Would it help if I took you up there sometime? Up to the peak? Some night after the groomers are done?"

Stacey saw the waitress approaching with the little dessert menus and a frankly appraising look. She turned back to Chip, definite mischief in her eyes. "It might help," she said. "But don't expect me to do any sneaking around. I've lived through enough of that."

"Meaning what?"

"Never mind."

They had studied the dessert menus for about twelve seconds tops, when Stacey put hers down.

"I don't have another night off until next week this time."

"Are you asking me for a date?"

"Maybe not the way you think," she said. "I'm asking if you want to go ski that mountain right now."

It took practice to get a good night's sleep in a parked car in the dead of winter.

It took experience and a broad base of information, too, along with a certain amount of luck. First, the car had to be unlocked. Although the locals left their cars unlocked all the time, it was different for flatlanders, who'd driven up here from New York or Connecticut and brought their cautious habits with them. And no way was Danny going to get into the business of breaking into parked cars. Second, the passenger seat had to recline, although he'd settle for the driver's seat if he had to and in an absolute pinch he'd curl up in the back. So he had to know which cars either had manual seats (which excluded every single one of those big, comfortable, leather-padded SUVs, foreign and domestic both) or else left the switches live when the key was out of the ignition (which eliminated Subarus and VWs, but put certain Fords and Lincolns back into play). Third, you had to be prepared with some insulation. Newspapers were the best—Danny had owned a blanket for a while and it was plenty useful, but since he couldn't bring himself to be the guy who walked around town all day with a blanket he ended up stowing it on top of the big dryers at Bud's Suds and one day it was just flat-out *gone*, if you can imagine the nerve that *that* would take, stealing a homeless veteran's blanket. At any rate, he needed insulation and newspapers were best, but it took a lot of them because the free tabloids in the boxes by the grocery store were just pathetically small. It took four or five of the things just to insulate him against the cold seeping up from the seats.

Once you had an open car with seats that would recline and plenty of copies of the *Mountaintop Pennypincher,* you still needed a kind of Zen concentration to make it all work. Danny would begin by closing his eyes and lying absolutely still and imagining himself anyplace but here. He'd steady his breathing and envision some nice warm spot, like maybe back in 'Nam, sitting in the hot iron cage of a Rome plow; or on his father's farm, lying still in the warm dreamy sunlight of the hayloft. And soon enough he would drift off to sleep. He was reliable that way.

On this particular night, he was so sound asleep—on the passenger seat of a vintage Volvo 240, a real find—that when someone came along and raked the beam of a flashlight over him through the fogged-over windows, he didn't even stir. He lay there exposed under a thick layer of newsprint, cold and pale, laid out like a cadaver. After a while the intruder's footsteps crunched away into the distance and a snowmobile growled from low burbling idle into full roaring life, and then the world was quiet again.

Through it all Danny Bowman slept on, oblivious.

TWENTY

Chip's apartment was a mess, but from somewhere in it he produced a spare set of skins and an extra headlamp that still sort of worked. He would use that one for himself and let Stacey have the good one.

While he was digging she went back to the Ramseys' place and sneaked her gear out of her room, through the kitchen door, and into the car. Nobody in the living room even stirred.

They met at the mountain and parked alongside the shed that housed the snowmaking compressors—idle now and dead quiet. The whole place was dead quiet. The only light anywhere came from the arc lamps around the base lodge, just up the hill from the parking lot. Falling snow swirled in their cones of light.

"Fresh powder," said Chip as he pulled on his helmet.

Stacey pulled hers on, too, and took the headlamp he offered her. "Man," she said. "Is this what a person has to do to make first tracks around here?"

"It's either this," he said, "or sign up for the patrol. We get first tracks every day of the week."

With that they shouldered their skis and hoisted their boot bags and started toward the snowy benches outside the lodge.

Skinning up the mountain in the snowy dark, Chip discovered that he might need to rethink a couple of things.

First, he realized that doing something this strenuous right after supper may not have been the best plan. He felt like a kid who's disobeyed orders not to swim until an hour after lunch, his stomach cramping a little and his energy diminished and a feeling of wooziness in his head.

Second, gauging his uphill performance by that of a seventy-year-old, even one as fit as Andy Paxton, may have given him a distorted picture of his own abilities.

In other words, he simply could not stay ahead of Stacey. The girl was a beast.

When they reached the first of his usual stopping places, she was skating along so furiously behind him that there was simply no opportunity to slow down. When they reached the second, and he was growing seriously short of breath, he slowed methodically and raised his arm and spun to a stop where he could show off a view of the town, as if that was reason enough to take a break. Through the mask of his gaiter, and shielded from view by the dark, he singled out one or two points of interest sparkling below.

And hoped that she couldn't hear how hard he was panting.

They were both pretty well blown out by the time they reached the top, which suited Chip just fine. They had cut through the trees dividing two of Spruce's most difficult trails, Oh Brother! and Finesse, and emerged into the open from under a patrol rope meant to keep people out. The low squat rectangle of the Peak Lodge was below them by thirty yards or so, and the top of the Peak Chair, a high-speed quad, stood just to their right. It looked like a scaffold in the moonlight. No snow fell up here, and the wind was still.

They clicked out of their skis and stripped the skins from them and put them away, and then side by side on the snowboarders' bench they sat and sucked water from their Camelbacks. The stars overhead were piercingly bright, and a quarter of a mile below them the moonlight shone on a soft bed of cloud. After they'd admired it for a few minutes Stacey rose and walked over to her skis to click back in.

"Hey," Chip said from where he sat, "don't let me hold you back."

"I'm getting a chill," she said, but she didn't really mean anything much by it. And then, from her vantage point at some distance from his, she called, "Hey! How come there's a fire going in the patrol shack?"

"A fire?" He rose and tromped over, his footsteps squeaking in the quiet.

"Yeah. A fire." She pointed down toward where the shack stood, most of it obscured by the Peak Lodge. She could see just the blank surface of one corner of the building, protruding beyond the end of the lodge deck, and above that a fragment of the roofline. Including the chimney, from which smoke and quivering heat unmistakably rose.

"I'll be," Chip said.

She took off in the direction of the shack, but before Chip could click in and follow her she stopped. In the moonlight reflected from the snow he could see her mitten lifted vertically in the general area of her mouth, making a well-insulated version of the universal symbol for "Ssshhhh!"

He slid down after her and stopped where she had, alongside the ski racks just at the edge of the Peak Lodge deck. There was light in the windows of the patrol shack. Dim light dimmed further by frost on the outside of the glass and condensation on the inside, but

light all the same. It looked to Stacey like candles, or maybe a kero-
sene lantern. Plus the flickering of a fire in the hearth.

Instinctively the two of them swung wide around the place, digging in with their poles and skating around to the front where in
addition to the usual clutter of ropes and stakes and the pair of
neatly stowed toboggans there sat a high-end snowmobile, big and
muscular and gleaming in the light from the windows and the stars.

Chip kept his voice low. "Let's go," he said.

"Where?"

"Downhill. Anyplace but here."

"But don't you want to find out who it is?" Her eager posture said
she was about ready to click out of her skis and go creeping up toward the gleaming windows. "It'll be fun. It'll be an adventure."

"I know who it is. And I'd rather he didn't catch me poaching
his mountain in the middle of the night."

She was incredulous. "Andy?"

Chip shook his head slowly. "If it was Andy, I'd go knock on the
door. It's Richie."

TWENTY-ONE

Come morning, Stacey took the lift up and looked around like a criminal visiting the scene of his most notorious crime. She'd gotten a late start on the mountain, late for her anyhow, and there had already been plenty of skiers and riders leaving tracks everywhere by the time she got to the top. Even the broad swath chewed up by that big snowmobile in front of the patrol shack was pretty well tracked over and gone. Like it had never been there at all. She wondered if Richie had left any sign of his having been inside during the night, and she wondered how he could have managed not to, and she wondered above all else what he'd been doing up here. The dim light, like candles. It was a long way to go for a romantic evening, even if you did have kids at home sticking their noses into everything.

Somehow, just one of those things, she never managed to connect with Chip at all no matter how many runs she took and how she varied her speed. She saw him from the lift once, and they waved their arms and hollered at each other as people will do on a blue-sky day in the high and frosty air with three inches of fresh snow on the ground, but that was that. She took off down the trail he'd been on, but he'd already gone someplace else.

No worries, she thought. It wasn't that he was avoiding her. It was like they always said: *No friends on a powder day.* Apparently, that even went for people who'd just taken you out to dinner at Maison Maurice.

Tina sat snarling on her usual stool at the Broken Binding. Her lipsticked mouth was twisted into a kind of a petulant grimace—a far cry from the predatory smile she ordinarily leveled at whatever man sat down alongside her—and she sat like an electrified statue, staring with black eyes into the mirror above the back bar.

Stacey asked what was wrong and got no answer, even early on, when they were the only two present in the room. She asked again during a lull in the Friday night action, bending forward over the bar as solicitous and confidential as a kindergarten teacher or a nurse, and again she got nowhere. That Tina was a stubborn one all right. She looked hurt, wounded, double- or triple-crossed by fate. She looked like she was drinking for a reason other than social lubrication. It just wasn't like her.

By the end of the evening, though, the wine had done its work and she was ready to unburden herself. Stacey turned up the volume on the wide-screen so the snowmobilers at the end of the bar could catch the end of some basketball game, and she came around the bar and took a seat alongside Tina. She even got herself a cup of coffee—decaf—that she could nurse while they talked. Just two girls with nobody else to tell their troubles to, sneaking up on closing time.

Tina shook her head. "You wait long enough," she said, "you see everything."

"Everything?"

"Everything."

That was it for a while.

Stacey drank half of her coffee and wondered how much caffeine was in decaf. Not that she'd ever had any trouble sleeping, but still. You never know.

Tina started up again. "I saw your red-headed stranger today, for example."

"My . . . ?"

"Miss Revlon and Chanel? With the green coat and the red scarf, and the lower back she'd thrown out doing something she shouldn't have?"

Stacey let out a long "Ohhhhhh."

"Yep."

"So it wasn't that Sheri from Mountainside, like maybe you'd thought?"

"Nope."

"Hmm. Where'd you see her?"

Tina swiveled her head in Stacey's direction, slow as could be. "Where do you think? If I saw her in the grocery store I wouldn't know she had a bad back. *Or exactly how she got it, down to the most intimate detail.*"

"Aha! She came in for a massage."

"Two points," said Tina. "You catch on quick."

"I try."

"Turns out she's from someplace in Connecticut, just like you'd think."

"She looks it."

"Stamford, I think she said. But right now she's renting an apartment up in Woodstock."

"That can't be cheap."

"It's not. Little Miss Bad Back gave me all the details."

"Don't you hate that?"

"I do."

"How generous of her."

"Yeah. And me the captive audience."

"I hope she was generous with her tip, too."

"Oh, she was," Tina said. "She gave me a tip that a certain Richie Rich is running around on his wife. Building a big new house that he can share with Little Red Riding Hood. And in the meantime he's banging her not only in the Woodstock apartment but in the patrol hut on top of *his* ski mountain."

"Wow."

"That's how come the bad back, poor thing."

"Yeesh."

"She said she thought I had the right to know."

Stacey drained her coffee cup. "You learned all that in what, an hour?"

"Fifty minutes," said Tina. "And you'd be surprised. People take off all their clothes, sometimes they just can't stop talking."

"I guess."

"It makes 'em nervous."

"I suppose it would." Stacey sat and thought. "Here's a question," she said after a while. "You think Richie's paying for the place in Woodstock, too?"

"I get the feeling he's paying every which way," said Tina. "And I don't think he's halfway done."

The wind whipping his ponytail and a ratty wool gimme hat with a Burton logo peeling away from the front of it jammed down over his eyebrows, Danny was waiting outside the door when Stacey came out. He'd taken up a spot among the four or five big chainsaw grizzly bears that stood alongside the entryway, shielded against the wind and out of anyone's line of sight, and he'd waited there while Pete Hardwick left and Tina left and the two snowmobile guys left, too. When only Stacey's car remained, he emerged into the light and the wind like a shadow peeling itself away from the carved grizzlies. And as Stacey emerged and turned to lock the door behind her, he spoke.

"Seems like nobody's on your side but me, little lady." A sound like the scraping of gravel across pavement, alarming and harsh in the semidark.

"Good God!" She jumped a mile, dropping the keys into a little swirl of snow at her feet and clutching the collar of her jacket around her neck in an instinctively defensive gesture.

"I told the brother about what I seen. I give him a chance to help you out."

"You did *what?*"

"I give him a chance but he weren't interested."

"Who?"

"Richie Paxton. I said he could take it up with you direct, no law involved, and he didn't give a shit."

"You told him you saw me leaving the condo."

"That's right."

"His brother's condo."

"That's right. You and that yellow coat." He took a step toward her and she smelled his approach.

Stacey squatted quickly to retrieve the keys, keeping an eye on her car, considering what she might do to distract him just enough. "Look," she said, "how about I just give you something to tide you over."

"I don't need tiding over."

"Just while I think about my options."

"You had enough time to think."

She took off a glove and dug in her pants pocket and pulled out a clump of bills. Crumpled tip money, beer-damp and limp. Without even examining them—what could they be? singles, a five or two at most?—she thrust them in Danny's direction as if hoping they had some kind of magical power to ward him off.

He lurched back, startled. The touch of her skin against his bare hand was electric, even more shocking than the surprising presence of that fistful of bills. For a brief moment he was completely befuddled, his head and his heart set spinning, and while he was unbalanced Stacey dodged around him and made for the car.

When he came to his senses she was long gone, and in his fist was a measly fourteen bucks. He shoved it into his pocket and kicked at a lump of ice fallen from Stacey's car and cursed his luck. The richest guy in town gets murdered and he's got the inside dope, and the only person he seems to be able to touch for it is almost as down on her luck as he is. It just ain't fair.

TWENTY-TWO

Green Mountain Massage didn't often merit a visit by the sheriff, but Tina didn't mind. Mornings were slow anyhow. Afternoons, on the other hand—afternoons were a madhouse. The trophy wives would show up as soon as they'd finished brunching somewhere, whining to each other about how you simply *could not get a decent hot stone massage anywhere north of Westchester County.* When she was finished working them over, their husbands would come limping in, straight from the mountain, not one actual appointment for a dozen of them. They smelled like animals and they winced no matter how cautiously she went at the knots in their quads and calves. *Flatlanders.* You can't live with them, and you can't make the rent without them. (Although sometimes, if you play your cards right, you might get one to buy you a drink at the Broken Binding.)

When Guy walked in, she had the computer booted up and was going over the accounts. With a name like QuickBooks, you'd think there'd be something quick about it—but that wasn't the way it seemed to Tina. To her it was a royal pain in the ass that no massage would ever relieve. And no matter how many boxes she checked and how many budgets she set up and how many reports she ran, the result was always a variation on the same old bad news. More expenses than income.

The trouble was a direct result of living in a ski town, where anything—a piece of real estate, a fresh-baked apple pie—could have either of two values: the amount it was worth to a local dude struggling to put dinner on the table, and the amount it was worth to a flatlander absolutely rolling in Wall Street dough. Things settled out pretty quickly under those terms. Culture stratified. And now that she was out of the real estate business, it seemed even worse than before. She'd gotten tired of the lousy hours in that line of work, and she'd gotten sick of reporting to a broker who didn't know enough about selling houses to fill up a thimble, but now that she set her own hours and was her own boss it wasn't actually any better. She was every bit as weary of pushing and pulling at the privileged muscles of the out-of-town trade. And now she had her own mortgage to worry about, along with the electric bill and the gas bill and the insurance bill and everything else. The only thing that gave her pleasure was knowing that she kept two different rate schedules: one for locals, in the top drawer, and one for the rest of the world, in a stand on the reception counter. And nobody from New York or Connecticut had to know.

She sat at reception, behind a little open window with artificial violets on the sill, and as he stepped into the waiting room Guy cleared his throat to get her attention. She had seen him coming but she took her time closing down the file and turning his way all the same. One of the guiding principles in her life was that it never paid to betray too much interest.

"Hi, Guy." She said it in a way that acknowledged the rhyme.

He hated that. He'd gotten it from junior high on, and he hated it. He tipped his flat-brimmed hat. "Tina."

"How're you doing? What can I do for you?"

"I've got . . ." He was putting his gloves in his coat pocket with his left hand and fishing in his pants pocket with his right. He pulled them both out empty. "I've got a couple of questions for you is all. You mind?"

"Come back sometime when I'm not so busy." She indicated the empty room.

"I picked a good time, I guess."

She rose from the computer table and came around to a little half-door, which she opened to let him in. "Come on back where we can have some privacy."

Guy shrugged and followed.

In a narrow room hung with pale lavender draperies and smelling of something he took for patchouli, she motioned him to a chair. She sat on the massage table, a bit higher than his level. There was power in it, and he took note but didn't care.

He began with an apology. "The boys from the state police barracks up in Rutland think I know everything," he said, "but I don't."

"Too bad," she said. "That would make your job a lot easier."

"I guess it would." He hung his flat-brimmed hat in his hand and rotated it slowly between his fingers, around and around.

"What do they think you know this time?"

"Nothing all that important." He cleared his throat. "They were wondering if you knew the deceased."

"The deceased."

"David."

"I know who you mean." She fidgeted on the table like a person who wanted a cigarette, which she no doubt was.

"I said of course you knew him."

"Of course."

"But I wanted to find out for sure."

"Sure."

"Who didn't know David, right? And you, you know pretty much everybody in town anyway. Regardless."

"I guess I do."

"So between you and David the chances were pretty good."

"They were."

"So I was right."

"Yes. I knew him. I used to babysit him, in fact."

"No." He stopped rotating the flat-brimmed hat. "You didn't."

"Oh, yes I did."

"You're not that much older—"

"A few years. I'm a year older than Ricky, but Ricky was never one for watching his little brother."

"I see." Guy sat quiet for a moment, like a farmer chewing on a stalk of hay, ruminating, waiting either for some cloud to pass overhead or for some thought to clarify in his mind. "Yeah. You and Richie. I remember."

Tina shifted her weight on the table and asked, "So why'd they want to know?"

"I can't say," he said. And then, placing the hat on the floor, he said, "No. To be truthful with you, I can."

"I guess I have a right."

"You do." He leaned back and reached into his pants pocket and pulled out a little clear plastic envelope. It had a ring in it.

The ring was smeared with something gooey and white and with something else powdery and black, as if it had been put into the envelope with a little bit of Crisco and gunpowder.

"Sorry for the mess," he said as he held it out. "Would this belong to you?"

Tina hesitated. It might have meant anything. Then she took the envelope and held it up to the light. "Yes!" she said, her jaw dropping open. "Yes! Where was it?"

"Well—"

"I've been looking everywhere!" She started to tug at the envelope but Guy stopped her.

"Please. It's. Uh, it's—it's evidence."

"Evidence?"

"Sorry." He took the envelope back and pocketed it.

"But I can prove it's mine. I've got a receipt for it somewhere at home."

"I don't think you'll have to do that." He picked up his hat again. "They were pretty sure it belonged to you."

"Good."

"I just wanted to find out for sure."

"Thank you."

"This was lots easier than asking you for fingerprints and everything."

Either she was very cool or she hadn't heard him accurately.

"That's what that black powder was. The white stuff is—"

She finished his sentence. "Massage cream. I know."

"Right. Massage cream."

Tina stood up and walked to the head of the massage table and turned on a CD player. The music that came out sounded like enormous church bells mixed with sound effects from *George of the Jungle*, overlaid on a steadily babbling creek in an endless loop. The water noises made Guy want to use the bathroom. She came back and sat down and said, "So here's the sixty-four-thousand dollar question: Where was it?"

"In David's condo."

"Of course!" She slapped her knee. "I take it off when I work."

"When you work?"

"I went to his place to give him a massage."

"He didn't come here?"

"Never." She pointed to the hinged portable table, folded up in the corner. "I use that one for shut-ins and like that. Elderly people."

"And David."

"David was funny."

"How do you mean?"

"He was self-conscious," she said.

"Really?"

"I guess you wouldn't think it."

"Because he was . . ." he searched for the word.

"Gay?"

"I was thinking *flamboyant*," the sheriff said.

"OK. Granted. Maybe a little. But he liked his privacy."

"I understand," Guy said. "So you went to him. Just like the mountain and Mohammed."

"That's right."

"Folded that table and went." He tugged at his lower lip. "That's pretty slick. That's a very nice service."

"It meets a need."

"Oh, sure. And I bet it's steady. For you, I mean. Which would be nice. Some of these folks probably need you once or twice a week."

"David was Mondays."

"Every Monday? Just like that?"

"Yeah."

"Monday morning at ten."

"And it would explain the ring, too." He patted the pocket where he'd stored it away. "It sure would."

"I didn't know it needed explaining."

"Those guys in Rutland," he said with an uncomfortable little smile, "they like everything tied up with a bow."

"I understand."

"I'm just here to give 'em a little hand."

"Lucky you," she said. "But I guess you've got this one worked out."

"I guess I do," he said, rising to his feet, that New Age jungle brook still running and running. He looked around and asked, "Before I go, which way to the restroom?"

TWENTY-THREE

s executive vice president for SkiAmerica, Buckminster "Buck" Bradley had bought more mountains than you could shake a stick at. Devil's Creek in Idaho and Big Burn in Utah. Topmount in Montana and Dingman's Notch in New Hampshire. Not to mention Snowdrift in Maine, where even in the high summer it still got cold enough to freeze your feet to the ground. And those were just the high-profile transactions. He could do the deal for a little nothing mountain like Spruce with his eyes closed. And when he was finished, the development boys would step in and convert the place from a recreational facility into a real-estate venture, at which point the money would rush in as if you'd broken down a dam. It all began with the mountain, though, and it usually ended with the Forest Service. But in between those two, the pathway most often led through an entrenched family that had owned the place for two or three generations, led by an old-time sunburnt hardass like Andy Paxton. Some clean-jawed ramrod type who actually loved the sport and loved the land, too, and acted as if the world hadn't gone on to bigger things while he was studying his own Choate- and Amherst-educated belly button.

The plane from Denver had been late and the little twin-engine commuter that flew between Albany and Rutland had taken off without him and he'd had a devil of a time getting a car. Plus he'd gotten lost. He'd overshot Troy altogether and ended up somewhere at the ass-end of civilization with no GPS and a map he couldn't make heads or tails of and an iPhone that was useless in these woods. Back home in the Rockies they had a cell tower on every peak. What the hell was wrong with the East Coast? Wasn't everything supposed to be all sophisticated here? All liberal and civilized? Christ. It was worse in Vermont than in Dingman's Notch.

Bottom line: This was no way to impress somebody whose mountain you were angling to buy. Screw that twerp David Paxton anyhow, the goddamned tree-hugging fairy. Not to speak ill of the dead, but Buck Bradley was just as content not to have him around mucking up the deal anymore. With him gone, there was nobody left to handle but his father, Robert A. "Andy" Paxton the third and the last. The end of the line. Why the old man hadn't passed on his name to one of the boys Buck would never know, but he did know this: If he'd done it, and if he'd had his choice between the two of them as grown men, he'd have picked the fairy, sure as shit. What a world. It was perverse.

Whether the old man liked it or not, Richie was the only family member with a shot at carrying Spruce Peak forward—since he was the only one with the sense to unload the place before it went bust and the Forest Service agreements turned null and void and Mother Nature yanked one more income opportunity back underneath her goddamned wing.

These days it took deep pockets, a long view, and world-class cojones to make a dollar on a ski mountain, and Buck Bradley had them all in spades. Right now he also had a Saturn Vue with a busted windshield wiper and next to no washer fluid, both courtesy of the rental agency in Albany, and a brand-new vow to himself that he would never, ever, come here again without a driver. If he had to come here at all. Isn't that why God invented FedEx?

He stood out in the Broken Binding, that was for sure.

It hadn't taken Stacey long to learn that there would be only a certain number of types in the bar or the dining room on any given night. Local businesspeople and day laborers and ski moms, dressed in the Vermont uniform of faded jeans and a Lands' End turtleneck and a fleece vest. Snowmobile guys with their bulky insulated overalls and Mad Bomber hats. The out-of-town L. L. Bean and Eddie Bauer crowd, mostly couples with the occasional squalling baby dressed for adventure just like its parents. Snowboarders in baggy jackets and baggier pants, and their older and sadder incarnations, those handfuls of late-middle-aged men in hideous ski sweaters, stinking of mothballs.

This guy was different. He had a sunburnt face, all angles and crags just beginning to slip toward fat, shaded by a broad cowboy hat as white as snow. A soft leather duster that was probably worth what most of the customers here earned in a month, shaken off and hung on a peg by the door as if it were the most useless old castoff in the world. And a sharply cut flannel shirt with the look of an expensive horse blanket, tucked with military precision into deep indigo jeans of the same brand that Brian was always throwing money away on. He lifted the cowboy hat and screwed it down over that gorgeous duster and strode in tall handmade cowboy boots to the bar. Without even stamping off the snow. *Nerve*, personified.

"Hey, sweet thing." As if he owned the place. As if he owned her. He settled onto a barstool as far from Tina as possible, which Stacey took for an accident of fate.

Tina slid a glance his way and went back to studying her drink.

"What'll it be?" Stacey loved saying *What'll it be?* She recognized it as a formula, one of those things that people find to say instead of actually communicating, but that didn't diminish her love for it.

"Glenfiddich."

"Rocks or up?"

The look that he gave her was sufficient for her to understand that he didn't want his expensive scotch diluted. She put out a napkin and set down the glass and poured. "You're not from around here."

"And neither are you," said Buck Bradley.

"Correct."

"Until I heard that Boston accent, I took you for one of those seasonal imports. The Aussie crowd."

"Nope." She crossed her arms and leaned against the back bar.

"Too bad. I sure could see you in a bikini on Bondi Beach."

"Not if I saw you first." It was either a game or something else, and either way it was what you did in this job.

Buck raised his glass and sipped his whiskey and eyeballed her through it. "Too bad."

She left him alone with his sunburn and his Glenfiddich, because down at the other end of the bar Tina was rolling her eyes like a vaudevillian. But before she could get down there, the space between them filled up with a couple of snowmobilers and a handful of guys from one of the ski shops, probably MountainWerks, smelling like heat and grease and melted wax. Everybody needed something different, and by the time she had served them all the cowboy down at the other end was lifting both his glass and his eyebrows and she had to refill him, too. He'd ostentatiously laid a hundred-dollar bill on the bar and she was hoping he didn't intend to drink all of it.

Tina tossed her head toward him and hissed at Stacey when she finally made her way down to where she sat. "That one at the end? He's the one with the money."

Stacey just furrowed her brow.

"Mr. Expensive Scotch. Ragtime Cowboy Buck. He's the guy who holds the checkbook at SkiAmerica."

"Aha! That would explain the hundred on the bar."

Tina grimaced. "It would explain where it comes from. But not what he's hoping to buy with it."

Stacey's jaw dropped in a kind of mock awe. Down at the other end of the bar, Buck was grinning boldly at her.

Tina said, "Don't say I didn't warn you."

Stacey just shook her head. "So you're telling me that money really *is* the root of all evil?"

"Just like they said in Sunday School, babe."

Stacey stepped away and filled a couple of glasses and came back. "So how do you know this guy?"

"I just do. He likes the idea of being known."

"I guess he does."

"Otherwise why the hat. Why the whole outfit."

"Why the hundred."

"Exactly."

"But he doesn't know *you*."

Something that might have been a wince passed over Tina's eyes, and she raised her glass and swallowed some of her chardonnay. "Oh," she said, "he knows me all right."

The wind blew Andy and Marie through the door into the Binding, and it was all they could do to latch the door behind them. Andy put his back into it while his wife stood shivering, craning her neck to see if there were any empty tables in the dining room. Andy smiled and shook his head, astonished even after a lifetime in the Green Mountain State at how much power the wind had, even at night, and as he finally stood upright and took Marie's coat he realized that the gust they'd rode in on had scattered some things hung on the pegs in the foyer. A big white cowboy hat in particular, which he picked up from the floor without any particular enthusiasm. He flicked away some grit that had gotten onto the brim and hung it back up where it had come from, knowing without a moment's reflection that it belonged with that long and luxurious leather duster. Richie hadn't told him that Bradley was coming to town, and he was in no mood to run into him here. He took off his own coat and hung it up and took Marie by the elbow, the two of them stepping into the dining room like a pair of sneak thieves. Nope. No Buck Bradley in sight. So far, so good.

The Australian girl behind the hostess station looked for their name on the chart, as if Andy Paxton had ever once in all his life made a dinner reservation in this town. The surprise was that she found it. Or she almost found it, since Andy shook his gray head and vehemently denied that he had called.

"But look right here," she said. "Paxton." As if the scribbles on that photocopied chart had the power of holy writ. "Party of two. Nine o'clock." She bounced the eraser of her pencil on the words. "You're early."

"We're not early."

"Oh dear me," said Marie, "we never eat any later than seven." She unwrapped a smile that never failed to charm. "Any later than that, and Andy would never get to sleep."

Her husband put a finger on the offending square, pushing the bouncing eraser aside. "This must be Richie," he said. "Richie and Jeanette." He turned to his wife. "Although who they've found to sit for the kids on a school night, I'll never know."

The Australian girl gave up and showed them to a table back toward the kitchen, and even before Jamal the busboy arrived to fill their water glasses Andy had looked back into the foyer and realized his mistake. The problem was habitual thinking, which made your mind run in the same old circles even in the presence of new information. New information like Buck Bradley's big white cowboy hat. "*Well*," as his grandchildren said, "*duh*." Things got tougher as you got older, that's all he knew. Blame it on becoming an old-timer.

They ordered and stood to help themselves to what passed for a salad bar at the Binding. A big shallow bowl of romaine and spinach accompanied by some cut radishes and shredded carrots and picked-over cauliflower, all of it surrounded by ten or twelve big ceramic crocks of wilt-proof premade potato salad and three-bean salad and pasta salad and runny Harvard beets and onion-flecked red beans and soggy chickpeas. He remembered bringing the boys here after church on Sundays when this place had been called the Broken Binding for the first time, way back when. The salad bar hadn't changed much since those days. The Plexiglas sneeze guard was cloudier and a whole lot more scratched up, but that was about it. Even those Harvard beets looked suspiciously familiar. He always kept his distance from the stuff in the crocks.

TWENTY-FOUR

On a run to the cooler, Stacey peeked through the kitchen door's porthole-shaped window and saw the Paxtons standing pensive in front of the salad bar. Andy with some romaine and a slab of bread with butter, Marie with just the romaine, both of them looking through the cloudy sneeze guard as if they expected something down there to have changed after all these years. Evolution at work. Stacey put their presence together with Bradley's and added it up.

"I get it," she said to Tina when she came back through the kitchen door, lugging a cold half case of Sutter Home pinot grigio. She bent her head toward the dining room. "The Paxtons."

"Richie and Jeanette."

"No. Andy and Marie. The Paxtons Senior."

"So?"

She bent her head in the other direction, toward Cowboy Buck. "Does he always fortify himself before a meeting with management?"

"Not with Andy," Tina said. "Andy, you'd want to be stone-cold sober. There's no mixing business and pleasure as far as he's concerned."

"You don't think?" She was remembering the old man's late-night adventures—*transgressions,* you might even say—on Spruce Peak with Chip. If that wasn't mixing business with pleasure, then she didn't know what was.

"Believe me, no. Besides, she doesn't have any power in this."

"She."

"Marie."

"Oh. Right." And then: "Are you positive? 'Behind every success-ful man,' like they say."

"They don't say it about that generation."

Which was true enough. Women of Marie's vintage had learned to keep their ideas to themselves. They may have seethed inwardly, but they never told their husbands about it. Or spoke their minds on anything, for that matter. Why risk it? Why bother? Stacey's mother, back in Boston, was the exception that proved the rule. Either that or the missing link between the so-called greatest gen-eration and Stacey's own. As long as Stacey could remember, she'd met the world on its own terms and bent it—sooner or later—to suit her own iron will. No challenge was too great. No circum-stance was good enough. No achievement was entirely satisfactory. And now, as senior partner in the Bay State's third-oldest and second-largest law firm, she lived on a severe diet of nothing but fresh radicchio, shredded wheat, and raw ahi tuna, while those in her wake subsisted mainly on aspirin and Maalox. Stacey owed her a call.

"I guess not," Stacey said. Then she went off to pour another round for the snowmobilers. Apparently, tearing around the country-side at the helm of an Arctic Cat really worked up a thirst. She won-dered if it would be the same for the motorcycle dudes in the summertime. She wondered if these guys would turn into motorcycle dudes come summertime. She wondered if she would still be around to find out, and she wasn't sure how she felt about it either way.

Tina looked from Buck to Stacey. "Trust me," she said. "He's not here to talk with Andy."

And sure enough: In an hour or so who should come blowing in through the front door—on the same gust of wind that blew his parents out—but Richie. He shot an imperious and appraising glance into the bar, stepped forward to speak quietly with the girl at the hostess station, then stepped back again and sent a reiteration of that first look into the bar again. Like a fisherman throwing out a second cast. And Buck bit on this one. He winked at Stacey and slid that hundred-dollar bill forward across the bar.

She came down. "You need change?" Just playing.

"That depends on how much your Glenfiddich is going for these days."

"Let me see." She turned and rang him up. But before she could finish and turn back around with his check in her hand the cowboy was gone. Because if there was one thing that everybody in town knew, it was that you didn't keep Richie Paxton waiting. Not if you wanted something from him, anyhow.

The two of them were huddled together over the table when she arrived with the cowboy's change. They grinned and gleamed red-faced—Richie from the cold and Buck from the Glenfiddich— like a couple of jolly pirates hatching a plot.

"No, no, no," Richie was saying. "I'm upgrading."

"Really?"

"It's just as well you keep your mouth shut about it."

"*You're upgrading?* I've got to say I don't blame you."

"Excuse me," said Stacey, sliding a check folio between them.

The cowboy told her that she had nothing to apologize for and asked if she had kept herself out a tip.

"No, sir."

The cowboy looked from her to Richie. "No, sir," he said. "You know you've crossed some frontier when you start hearing, 'No, sir.' "

"I'm . . ." Stacey had to get back to the bar.

The cowboy slid the folio back toward her, unconsulted. "You just go on and keep that for yourself, honey."

There was a time when Stacey would have rejected an offer like that as overgenerous or pitying or just plain creepy, but that time was long gone. It had ended the night she'd found David in that bed with the chain around his neck, when her expenses had gone through the roof and her sense of what was normal had started teetering on the edge of some precipice. She looked Buck Bradley square in the eye and took his folio and the sixty-seven dollars inside it and she said, "Thank you. Thank you very much."

She turned and headed back toward the bar, and Buck followed her with his eyes. He made some remark to Richie about whatever upgrade he'd been talking about, and Richie said, "No, no, not that one," and that was all she heard before the sounds of silverware and conversation and awful 1940s Muzak drowned them out.

Back in the bar at closing time, drinking slowly and seriously and all by himself, Buck hunched forward in that expensive horse blanket of a shirt and asked if he couldn't please arrange for one more.

"Sorry," said Stacey, with a practiced look that said she would like nothing better than to accommodate him when she really wanted nothing more than to be home in bed. She'd have been an easier mark a month ago, back when closing time was just the last stop before snuggling up in the icy Subaru.

"Aww," said the drunken cowboy. "Come on. Have a heart. Who'd know?"

"Her landlord the sheriff, for one," said Tina, from over the lip of a wineglass refilled at the last possible second.

"He sits up waiting for me," Stacey put in, "with an alarm clock on the table and a shotgun on his lap."

"You're kidding me."

"I'm kidding you about the shotgun," said Stacey.

Tina snapped shut her purse. "But not about the sheriff."

"That was my father," said Stacey.

"The sheriff?"

"The shotgun."

"You lost me."

This was altogether too easy. "Never mind," Stacey said. And she tipped a little scotch into the cowboy's glass anyhow, on the house.

TWENTY-FIVE

Morning dawned blue and white, one of those crystal New England days that could rival anything the West had up its sleeve. A surprise two inches of snow had fallen at the Ramsey place, and it turned into four or five on the mountain. Every bit of it untracked, and underneath it a smooth underlayment of fresh corduroy that the groomers had laid down overnight. It was, in other words, the best of all possible worlds as far as Stacey was concerned.

Something about the bright sunshine had awakened her even earlier than usual, and she made the first chair without even trying. She took the Thunder Bowl straight down, not even stopping to catch her breath or take in the blue-sky views, and she let out at least three involuntary whoops as the waves of silky snow rose up over her skis, over her boots, over her knees. Rule One: You didn't stop when it was this good. Rule Two: Review Rule One.

At the bottom she turned sharp into the lift entrance, and in the process she bathed a certain cowboy head-to-foot in white powder. He was actually wearing the hat. Like Billy Kidd out in Steamboat,

but without the medals and the everlasting cred. They guy was actually skiing in a giant white cowboy hat. Amazing.

But a bigger surprise, now that she thought about it, was that he
was skiing at all. Or that he was even upright, after all the whiskey
he'd put away the night before. Maybe, Stacey thought, he was a
little closer to the genuine article than she'd given him credit for.
Then again, there was the hat. So you couldn't be too sure.

He was slow on the draw and she was still carrying a lot of momentum so she made the next chair before he did, turning as she
lifted off to call over her shoulder and apologize for the snow he was
just now beating out of his hat. "Sorry!" she hollered over the roar of
the machinery. He had a sour look on his face, and she couldn't
blame him.

Fucking teenagers. At least the kid had had the sense to apologize for
soaking him head to foot. But still. It was a good thing he hadn't
come out in that custom-made duster. One dousing like that and
two grand worth of calfskin would have been shot to shit. What was
it with this place, anyhow? Was Vermont such a goddamned back-
water that the kids hadn't heard of snowboards yet? Everywhere else,
you could tell the little bastards at half a mile by their choice of
equipment. Jesus H. Christ. What was the world coming to?

Imagine Buck Bradley's surprise when the juvenile delinquent
who'd gotten off the chair ahead of his lifted her goggles.

He kept pace with her all the way down, but it wasn't easy. He told
himself that it was his first run, and he told himself that she had a
dozen years on him, but neither of these excuses made him feel any
better. The second one made him feel worse. Nonetheless he was
right on her tail when she skidded to the end of the liftline. She
was panting hard and he was panting harder, despite the low eleva-

tion that made him scowl every time he looked at this little eastern mountain on a topo map.

There was a narrow lane marked for single skiers but the traffic on the slopes was too light to bother using it, so Stacey lined up behind a couple of young guys with Canadian accents. Buck came up alongside her. "You get around," he said, removing his pole straps from his wrists.

"Hey," she said. "I know you."

"The pleasure is all mine," he said. Bradley's hat was held on by a rawhide thong that snugged under his chin with a fat turquoise bead traced in silver. It was the silliest thing that Stacey had ever seen in her life, but it explained why the thing didn't fly away when they got on the lift and they gained a little elevation and the wind picked up. He held the brim down anyhow, and he squinted at her underneath it— from behind three-hundred-dollars' worth of streamlined polarized sunglasses—like some kind of genuine cowpoke. "It's all mine, honey."

"I won't argue with that."

"I'd advise against it." He let his hat brim go and surveyed the landscape. "And thanks for that extra little pop last night, too."

She thought his sunburned face had crinkled up a little bit in a wink, but she couldn't tell for sure. "Hey," she said. "No problem."

"It's still appreciated. People treat you kindly, you feel less like a stranger."

"You don't seem much of a stranger around here."

"I don't?"

"No."

"What makes you say that?"

Stacey didn't answer for a minute. Off to her left, on the trail called Blowdown—a narrow strip of tall pines in between two broad groomers, only recently named and opened up for the use of skiers and riders who liked dodging trees—she had seen a familiar flicker of red. It could have been any patroller. It could have been anybody with a red jacket. But she was thinking maybe it was Chip Walsh, and she was hoping she'd see him emerge onto the open slope.

"What makes you say I don't seem like much of a stranger?"

Damn. It wasn't Chip.

"That old gal down the end of the bar wasn't telling stories on me, was she?"

"Tina," she said.

"That's right. Tina. She wasn't telling stories on me, was she?"

Buck was a guy who jammed his poles under his leg on the chairlift. It made a person a pain in the neck to ride with, the next worst thing to going up with a snowboarder. Stacey absolutely hated guys who sat on their poles. Why couldn't they hold onto them like everybody else? It wasn't as if they needed their hands free to get at their cell phones, the way the service was around here. Besides, a guy who ruined a perfectly good lift ride by talking on a cell phone was even worse than a pole-sitter.

"What kind of stories would she have?" Stacey asked it just to fill the time.

"You tell me."

"Look," Stacey said, "she didn't say a word."

"That's good."

"Not a word."

He chewed on his lower lip, nodding. He probably thought it made him look a little like Bill Clinton, which a guy like him would figure was a plus around younger women. Yecch. "That's *real* good," he went on, releasing his lip but still nodding and looking thoughtful. "Discretion is a fine quality in a little old gal."

The lift station was approaching, but nowhere near fast enough.

Then, twenty feet from the ramp, the chair stalled out. It happened. Usually, in Stacey's experience, it happened when you least wanted it to. Like when the guns were pumping snow at you a mile a minute, when the wind was brutal and you were on the very last run you could stand, or when you had to go to the bathroom really bad. Or like right now, when the sky was blue and the snow was white and you were trapped next to a moron with a cowboy hat as big as his ego.

"Damn," she said.

"Damn right," he said.

Stacey jumped up and down in the chair a little bit as if she could urge it on. As if she could shake Buck with his poles and his shades and his hat right off, like a bug. It didn't help. She resigned herself to staying put. "How often does this happen out where you come from?" She was careful not to let show that she knew anything about who he was, other than what a person could tell from the outfit and the occasional cowboyism.

He didn't seem to feel the need to be so careful. "About as often as it'll happen here when our boys get through with the place," he said. "Which I wager'll be less than you're used to."

"Your boys?"

"There's no need to be coy," Buck said. "It's not becoming."

"Really. I mean it. You have *boys?* That sounds like the *Sopranos.*"

"More like *Bonanza.* Or maybe *Dirty Jobs.*"

The chair lurched forward a little and Stacey's heart took flight but they both went nowhere in the end.

Buck went on. "Our people know how to run a place like this."

"Now you've got people."

"Six or eight thousand of them, last time I checked." He stuck his right hand toward her.

Stacey now doubly wished he hadn't sat on his damned poles. She had to wrangle hers in order to take his hand and shake it.

"Buckminster Bradley," he said. "From SkiAmerica in Denver."

"SkiAmerica. You're the people who—"

"Exactly. My friends call me Buck."

"Stacey Curtis." She said it as if she was giving up something crucial.

He let go of her hand, a little slowly. "Stacey," he said. "I know. I saw your nametag. Made a mental note."

She consulted the season pass that hung from her pocket clip.

"No, no, no. At the bar, I mean. I saw it at the bar. A place I'll personally make sure we have nicer alternatives to once we take over this place. It'd be a shame for a gal like you to spend her life at the Broken Binding."

Stacey looked down at the lift station where a couple of men were moving around, opening panels and peering inside. One of them noticed her and shrugged, his hands out flat. Her shoulders slumped. "The Broken Binding isn't exactly my life," she said.

"I wouldn't think so. There's a great big world out there." He gestured like he owned it. "A world of opportunity for a gal like you."

The lifties were banging on something with a length of iron pipe, and the hammering sent a shudder all the way up through the pylons and along the cables and into the chairs. At one particular blow their noise coincided with a slamming of the front door of the Peak Lodge, from which a pair of little kids came tumbling out like bad news. Richie Paxton's son and daughter, Cameron and Mackenzie, followed at some distance by their mother, Jeanette. She looked long-suffering even from where Stacey sat. Jeanette was round-faced and heavyset, not fat by any means but solid. If she had been dressed like Stacey was, in generic Columbia stuff all puffed up square, she'd have been easy to take for a hefty teenage boy. But as usual she was dressed in the best and best-fitting of everything. The kind of gear not sold much of anywhere in town, much less at the ski shop on the mountain: Cloudveil, Helly Hansen, Mammut. But even outfitted in the finest and the most expensive, and even with her chestnut hair pulled back into a luxurious ponytail that peeked from beneath a helmet of a brand Stacey had seen only once before, locked behind glass in a Boston shop and lit by a dozen tiny museum spotlights, and even on this glorious bluebird day, Jeanette Paxton followed those tussling kids as if her feet were made of lead.

Stacey could see why. They were punching each other and screaming like lunatics and whacking one another over the head with their poles. If not for their goggles, somebody was going to lose an eye. At the very least there'd be tears—and not all of them would belong to their mother, with any luck. She looked like a person who'd suffered enough.

Or maybe not *quite* enough.

"Do you know Jeanette Paxton?" Stacey asked Buck. She bobbed her helmeted head in Jeanette's direction.

"I do, I do," he said.

Perfect.

He lifted his shades and hollered down to her. Jeanette's face brightened a little at the sound of her name, and she even showed a smile for a second or two. Once she identified Bradley, though, that smile turned brittle in an instant. "Wait up," he called. "Let's do a couple of runs together."

The lift bumped and chugged into motion, and Stacey beamed from ear to ear.

TWENTY-SIX

The sheriff's office was in the township building, tucked behind the records room, across from the little provisional kitchen that Guy shared with the town clerk and the volunteer fire department. The town clerk was a sawed-off little Scotsman named Archie MacGregor, allegedly retired from the maple sugar business but still up to his knees in it every spring. He came in only two or three mornings a week, even less when the sap was running, and when he wasn't around his duties fell to his long-suffering secretary and sister-in-law, Mildred Furlong, who knew where all the skeletons were buried and didn't mind telling you. She put in eight hours a day, two of which were supposed to go to the sheriff's office, but it was a hard thing to keep track of. Mildred meant well.

She was manning the desk out front all by herself when Danny Bowman breezed in. *Breezed* was the operative word, since the wind outside the double door was strong and it carried with it Danny's unmistakable scent even before the man himself showed his face around the corner. Mildred twisted her features into a grimace and sniffed. Then she sniffed again, and regretted it. As the door opened and closed she turned her attention to her typewriter and hoped for the best.

"Howdy," said Danny Bowman. She heard his feet on the lino-leum but didn't need to. The smell of him in the closed room was overwhelming.

It wasn't in Mildred's nature to delay taking care of a visitor. She wasn't the hard-edged and uncooperative Department of Motor Vehicles type by any means. And besides, most of the folks who came into the office were people she knew from church or the PTA or whatever. Still, it was with mixed emotions—reluctance to deal with Danny and eagerness to get rid of him—that she turned and looked up and asked, "What can I do for you?"

"I come to see Ramsey."

"Sheriff Ramsey?"

"There some other Ramsey I don't know about?"

Mildred let his attitude lie there, and turned back to her type-writer to pull out the form she'd been working on. She folded it patiently in thirds—doing her best to hold her breath the whole time—and slid it into a number-ten window envelope. Then she dampened the flap with a sponge mounted on a little bottle of water and sealed the envelope shut and turned to Danny. "No," she said. "I don't believe we have another individual by that name around here."

Danny grinned, satisfied as all get-out. His teeth, visible between his wind-cracked lips, were little brown stumps. "Then lemme see him."

She poked a button on the phone and lifted the receiver. "First," she said, "let me check if he's in."

"Oh, he's in all right," he said. "I seen his car around back."

Mildred ignored his crafty and self-satisfied look. She punched Guy's extension and pushed her chins down into the folds of the bulky turtleneck sweater she wore against the cold. The sweater had evergreens and snowflakes and a couple of moose worked into it, and it smelled of the cedar chest where she kept it during the summer. The cedar chest smelled a whole lot better than Danny, that was for sure.

When Danny stepped into Guy Ramsey's office he left behind a roomful of his smell, but he still managed to bring a roomful of it with him. It was a miracle like the loaves and fishes. There was no limit to his stink.

"Hey, Danny," said Guy. "What can I do for you?"

"Got a cup of coffee?"

"I think we can part with a little." Guy stood and went to the kitchen, dragging Danny in his wake. "You can't stay in there all by yourself," he said, indicating his office. "Policy."

Danny laughed to himself, kind of a wheezing chuckle that set Guy's nerves on edge. "I guess not," he said. "You got sensitive law-enforcement stuff in there. Evidence and like that."

"Like that," Guy said, fetching down a long tube of foam cups from a high cabinet and pulling one of them loose for Danny.

"I understand."

"I appreciate it." He poured two cups of pale coffee and set one on the counter and pointed Danny toward the sugar and cream.

"No, thanks, man. I take it black."

"Suit yourself."

"I drunk it that way ever since 'Nam."

"A person learns to do without, I guess."

"That's one lesson the army'll teach you for sure," said Danny, shaking his head. *"Do without.* No two ways about it."

Guy pulled a folding chair away from the table and sat down. Better to handle Danny here in the kitchen than in his office. Most of the surfaces here were hard, and Mildred scrubbed the whole place with bleach and Bon Ami every Friday afternoon. "So what's up?"

Danny slid into a chair and sniffed his coffee. Then he looked up and spoke very distinctly: "I happen to be in possession of some very sensitive information."

Guy figured he must have rehearsed that one for a while. "Oh," he said. "Is that so?"

"Yeah."

"About what?"

Danny leaned back and threw one arm over the back of his folding chair, making himself distressingly at home. He poked at his coffee cup with one finger of the other hand, pushing it around on the tabletop. "About David Paxton."

"Paxton. All right," said Guy. "I'll be interested to hear it." He reached into his pocket and pulled out a notebook and flipped it open, even though he had absolutely zero expectation that Danny would have anything useful to report. He found a pencil and licked the tip of it and said, "Go."

"I seen somebody leave the Snowfield. That night."

"The night Danny died?"

"The night Danny died. Sure." He'd begun to wonder exactly what night it was when he'd seen that girl leaving the Snowfield in her yellow coat, but what difference did it make? He was sick of trying to pin it down. So far, pinning it down had netted him a frustrating fourteen bucks, and that had come hard. Christ, the girl had nearly run him over.

Guy put the pencil down. "Then you're one step ahead of me," he said.

"I know. That's why I come."

"No," said Guy. "I mean you're one step ahead of me if you know exactly what night David was killed. And you're one step ahead of the state troopers and the BCI and the coroner, too. They may never be one hundred percent sure."

"Lucky me," said Danny.

Stacey was in her car with the heater going full blast, midway between the mountain and the Binding, when her cell phone rang. The ringtone was one she hadn't heard in a while, one she'd paid money for—two bucks she wished she could get back these days.

It was Stevie Wonder, singing "I Just Called to Say I Love You." And it meant Brian.

She almost didn't answer.

To tell the truth, on the very first ring she jumped for it just like old times. It was pure reflex. On the second ring, she came to her senses. On the third she hollered back at Stevie, calling him a series of names he did not deserve. And on the fourth, stopped dead at the only traffic light in town, she gave in and picked it up.

Guy leveled his eyes at Danny like a man sighting down the barrel of a gun. "Maybe you're not so lucky," he said.

"What do you mean? I know something nobody else knows. That's got to be worth something."

Guy looked down between his shoes and gave his head a shake. "Danny, Danny, Danny," he said, looking up, "think about it. Nobody knows when David was killed. Nobody. So whatever you saw doesn't exactly count."

"I'm pretty sure—"

"No." He drained his coffee mug. "You're not pretty sure. Nobody knows what night it was. And I don't care if you saw somebody leaving the condo with blood on his hands—"

"*Her* hands."

"Huh?"

"Her hands. It was a her. A she."

"Huh?"

"A woman." Now that he had Guy's attention again, he smiled and ran his tongue over the ugly brown stumps of his teeth. "You know. A lady." He jumped his hands in front of his chest as if he were hefting a pair of cantaloupes, making the universal symbol for absolute doofus pig.

That wasn't a crime, but it was enough for Guy. He leaned forward with a steadiness in his look that made Danny drop his hands. "I don't care if it was the queen of England," he said. "We don't know the time and date of Danny's death. Not yet. So what you know and what you think you know may be two different things. Can you get that through your head?"

"Yes sir, I can."

"Good." He picked up his pencil again. "Now. I need you to tell me exactly what you saw, and I need you to tell me exactly when you saw it."

"It was Tuesday. Or else maybe Wednesday. Late."

Guy threw down the pencil.

"Wednesday."

"Wednesday's the night we got the call. That's the night they found him, for God's sake."

"So maybe it was Tuesday."

"Maybe it was. But how about we stick with Wednesday for a while, just to be on the safe side, huh?"

"You're the doctor."

"Wednesday, then." He folded the notebook and put it back in his pocket. "And who'd you see on Wednesday night, leaving the Snowfield condos, suspicious as they come?"

"I seen your new roomer."

"It wasn't the queen of England."

"Nope."

"You're sure."

"I am. I'm sure."

"It was my new roomer. Stacey Curtis."

"Yep."

"The twenty-something art historian and bartender from Boston, up for the winter."

"That's the one. She had on that yellow coat."

"I appreciate the information."

"You gonna write it down?"

"You think I need to write it down to remember it?"

"Seems more official that way, is all."

"Don't tell me how to do my job, and I won't tell you how to do yours."

Danny showed his teeth. "Joke's on you," he said. "I ain't got a job."

How do you even answer a call like that?

Stacey tried "Hello?"

"*Stace.*"

"Brian?" As if she didn't know. But flatly and without a trace of enthusiasm. Keeping *that* out of her voice wasn't exactly difficult.

"Stace. How're you doing?"

"Fine. I'm doing fine."

"Where are you?"

After all this time. What had it been, a month? Six weeks? She didn't bother answering.

"Where'd you run off to?"

"I didn't run. I was driven."

"Now, Stace."

"Don't *now* me."

"It was a mistake."

"Tell me about it."

"It was a huge mistake."

"You're getting warmer."

The light changed and she pressed the gas pedal and moved slowly through the intersection. There was no hurry. The street was empty of other moving cars, and for a change Danny Bowman was nowhere in sight. Once she got past the post office there were plenty of empty parking spaces she could pull into, if she wanted to keep talking. Otherwise she'd just keep going toward the Binding, and let the cell signal die wherever it might.

"Look. I'm sorry."

"That doesn't cut it."

"Where are you? I mean it. Where'd you go?"

"Vermont. You'd hate it here."

"Not if I could be with you."

Blecchh. "Correction," she said. "You'd hate it *even more* with me."

"No."

"I'd make sure."

"No. You wouldn't."

"Trust me."

"Look, Stace. I don't want to be there anyhow."

"No shit."

"I want you to come home."

She braked to let a car pull out from in front of the phone company.

"Home. That's a funny word for it."

"Home to me. My home. Our home."

"No way, José. We don't have a home, you and me."

"We did. We could."

"No."

"We could again."

"Sorry. It doesn't work that way. You blew it."

"I want us to try again."

"Us? Us? You're the one who didn't try in the first place."

"I know. I know that. And I'm sorry."

"Good."

"Stacey."

She hit the gas and the line crackled. "I'm losing you," she said, which was more true than he could have imagined.

"Call me back."

"Don't hold your breath."

"You're breaking my heart."

She held her tongue.

"Stace?"

And she clicked the phone shut. Before driving the rest of the way to the Binding she doubled back into the center of town where she could get a solid signal. Then she gave Stevie Wonder the boot and splurged two bucks on something more appropriate: An old Warren Zevon tune, "Poor Poor Pitiful Me." Just the thought of it cheered her up. She could hardly wait for Brian to call again.

TWENTY-SEVEN

"Did I tell you what that landlord of yours did to me a couple days ago?"

Stacey looked hard at Tina and thought. There was that close call that Pete had had with her near closing time. She could certainly imagine Guy catching sight of her Saab convertible weaving home through the snow and pulling her over, but it wasn't likely. Guy didn't work nights much. At night, whatever happened in this little town was pretty much between you and the lamppost.

"Did I?" Tina and Stacey were the only ones in the bar.

"No. I don't think so. I don't think you did."

"Well." She tossed her perm and leaned forward on her elbows. "He as good as accused me of murdering David Paxton."

"He didn't."

"He did."

"I don't believe it."

"Neither did I."

"What'd he think? It sure wasn't a lovers' quarrel."

Tina looked hurt. "If you're talking about the difference in our ages—"

"You said yourself the guy was gay."

"Oh. That."

"Yeah. That."

"I reminded your landlord of that little fact."

"I bet you did."

Tina sipped at her chardonnay. "Anyhow, he shows up in my waiting room with an evidence bag."

It made Stacey wonder. He'd been pretty clear with her that he wasn't involved in the investigation, hadn't he? So what was with the evidence bag?

Tina went on. " 'He makes small talk for a while, like he thinks he's Columbo or something, and then when he thinks he's got my guard down—which he *does*, for Christ's sake, since I didn't have anything to be defensive about in the first place—when he thinks he's got my guard down he pulls out this evidence bag and starts asking me about David."

"Ewww."

"I know!"

"What was in it? In the bag?" She pictured tissue samples, bits of hair, a length of bloody chain.

"My own goddamned ring." Tina held up her right hand, the back toward Stacey, to show the empty spot where it belonged. "It wasn't anything special. I bought it on the beach in St. Thomas, from a guy who was selling jewelry and palm-leaf hats and I think cocaine."

Tina kept going, rattling off some story that went more or less nowhere, but she may have been speaking Urdu for all that Stacey cared about the St. Thomas stuff. Back behind the bar, her knees had actually gone weak. She'd heard the expression used a million times, but other than one high-speed near-miss on the Mass Pike she'd never had the feeling for herself. *The ring*, she thought. The ring that she'd overheard Guy and Megan talking about had belonged to Tina after all. Which meant her own engagement ring was still at large somewhere—but she was perfectly happy leaving that for another day.

"So wait a minute." She broke into the St. Thomas story after a while, once she'd recovered the presence of mind to make sure she acted as if the whole deal were news to her. "What's your ring got to do with David?"

"They found it. In the condo."

"Who found it?"

"The troopers. Guy said it was the state troopers. He was only—"

"In the condo? They found it in David's condo?"

"Yeah."

"Your ring."

"Yeah. Guy said—"

"I don't get it."

Tina finished her glass and ate a little Chex Mix. "It was under the bed."

Stacey smacked her forehead with the flat of her hand. "Sorry, but—"

"I was there giving David a massage. I took the ring off and it rolled under the bed and there you go."

"Right."

"So Guy comes to me and dangles my own ring under my nose and acts all innocent and everything, but it's obvious he thinks I did it."

"Did it."

"You know. David."

"I know. But—"

"Or *somebody* thinks I did it, and he's checking."

Stacey poured her another drink without even asking, and Tina didn't object. "Wow."

"I wouldn't mind if it weren't such a stupid idea." She held up both her hands. "I mean, these are my livelihood. Such as it is."

"Such as it is."

"Why would I risk my own two hands—on the chain from a chain saw, no less—to strangle a guy who's been a friend of mine forever?"

"You've got me."

"A gay guy at that."

"It doesn't figure."

"What's in it for me?"

"You'd have to ask the sheriff."

"I guess."

Stacey had a thought. "Did you ask the sheriff?"

"Why they thought I'd do it?"

"Yeah."

Tina shook her head. "Not exactly, no. Then again he didn't exactly say anybody was *accusing* me. He made it seem like they were just tracking down the ring."

"But *really*—"

"Yeah. Really. Really they wouldn't have asked if they hadn't thought."

"Right. But you know how when somebody asks you a really stupid or annoying question, and you can't come up with the snappy answer until you're in the car driving home?"

"It was like that."

"It was just like that."

"I can't blame you," said Stacey. "You were caught off guard."

"I sure was."

At which point a couple of over-the-hill snowboarders came stamping into the bar—guys probably thirty-five or forty years old, dressed wrong for their age but right for the sport in that baggy-pants, hip-hop style affected by teenagers and college kids; whether they looked sillier to Tina or to Stacey was anybody's guess—and the time for talking about David Paxton's murder and Tina Montero's ring and Guy Ramsey's suspicions about any connection between the two was suddenly over.

Guy was sitting up when Stacey got home. He'd had a beer while watching some cop show on TV and another one after Megan had gone to bed, and they hadn't helped him stay awake any, that was for sure. He sat in the recliner with the TV on and the sound all but shut off rather than disturb the kids upstairs. He had the three-way bulb in the floor lamp switched low. He wondered if he was the only person in town watching CNN at this hour. The only person in town watching anything at this hour, come to that. Because by now the bars were closed and their big screens were shut off and everybody and his brother was heading for bed.

Stacey came quietly in the back door. Having seen the light of the TV dancing in the living room when she pulled in, she put down her bag and went on through the kitchen to see who was still awake. "Hey, Guy," she whispered. "You're up late."

"I am." He stretched and yawned and she yawned, too. "I wanted to ask you something."

"Sure. Shoot."

"Thanks."

"I'm available in the daylight, you know."

"I know." He rubbed one eye with a knuckle. "Sit."

She did.

"You ever seen that homeless guy in town?" he asked. "Long greasy ponytail, hangs around the laundromat and the pizza joint and like that?"

"Danny, right? Danny something."

"Danny Bowman. That's him."

"I've seen him around." Stacey was perched on the edge of the chair and the mention of Danny did nothing to make her want to settle back and make herself comfortable.

"It's hard not to notice the guy, sad to say." He aimed the remote and switched off the TV. "He's not exactly the best this town has to offer."

Stacey smiled.

"Danny was born and raised here. Went to school with my uncle."

"Oh."

"Anyway." He set the remote down on the coffee table. "That was a long time ago."

"You didn't wait up half the night to ask me if I'd ever seen him."

"No. No. Right."

"So?"

"So. Danny came into my office today, and after he drank my coffee and stank up the place he told me something."

"He told you I was at the Snowfield the night they found David Paxton's body." She slumped a little, out of relief or something like it.

"Sort of. He was confused about the timing, though. I don't think he looks at a calendar much."

"No. Probably not. I can't imagine."

"He might have thought it was before."

"Before?"

"Before they found the body. A night or two before."

"No. It wasn't."

"So are you telling me you were there?"

"I was. The night—"

"The night they found him."

"Yeah. The night I found him."

"You called 911. That was you."

"I needed someplace to sleep." Stacey told him about how she found the master keys and how she'd used them to cadge a bed in one condo or another and how she'd stumbled on David Paxton's body on the bloody bed. "You aren't going to press charges, are you?"

"For what? Squatting? Something like that?"

"Maybe." She sat very still on the edge of the chair, looking smaller than usual. "Breaking and entering? I don't know."

"You didn't break anything, did you?"

"No."

"Breaking and entering requires breaking."

"I guess."

"I haven't heard word one from any of the owners. Or the management or whatever. So no harm, no foul."

"Thank God."

"But you're on the record that that *was* you on the phone. The 911 call."

"Yeah."

"You did the right thing."

"You mean it?"

"Absolutely. Given the circumstances."

"Given the circumstances."

"Anything else you want to tell me?"

"No."

"Anything you noticed, or—"

"No. Honest."

"That's too bad. I sure would like to get this mess over with."

She brightened a little. "I'm sure you would."

"And I've got to tell you, I've had my fill of innocent women."

She didn't know if it was her place to mention it, but she didn't care. "Tina told me."

He cocked his head.

"About the ring."

"Oh. The ring." He shrugged. "That didn't amount to a hill of beans. I knew there wasn't anything to it. But other than that one little bit of nothing, the troopers have kept me pretty much in the dark. Between them and Danny, all I get is hot leads on innocent women. I'm sick of innocent women."

"That's funny."

"It is. But I've had 'em up to here. Give me a guy with good rea-son to want David out of the picture, and enough strength to yank that chain—"

"Please."

"Sorry. Give me those things, though, and I'll be happy." He looked tired.

"I'll let you know if I remember anything."

"Thanks. Or if anybody says something. Down at the Binding. You know." Rising to climb the stairs, reaching for the switch on the floor lamp.

"I know. I will."

"I'd appreciate it."

TWENTY-EIGHT

Between getting turned in to the sheriff by that spooky Danny Bowman and hearing Tina's story about getting questioned, between Guy's mention of that bloody chain being yanked tight and her ongoing curiosity about what might have happened to her engagement ring now that it wasn't in an evidence bag in Rutland, Stacey didn't exactly sleep like a baby. And on top of everything else there was the call from Brian. Brian. Jeez. She sure did hate that horny little conniving skunk. But he was kind of cute. And right now he seemed like just about the only person she knew—aside from Guy—who didn't stand a chance of being The Chain Saw Killer.

What if Danny had turned her in to direct blame away from himself? He might have gotten into the condo looking for money or something—that made sense—and found David there or been surprised by him and gone ahead and done the stupidest thing imaginable. Which would have been just like Danny Bowman. Heck, maybe his old army training had kicked in and he'd gone all Rambo. Maybe he was a victim of post-traumatic stress disorder. Maybe he was having an acid flashback or something. Who knew?

Or what if Richie had done it? That would make sense. He certainly got half again richer as a result, and he got his tree-hugging brother out of SkiAmerica's way in the bargain. Plus he probably needed money for that house he was building with the red-haired woman whose apartment in Woodstock he was paying for.

Or so Tina said.

But what if she was lying? Either about that, which meant one set of possibilities, or about how the ring got into David's condo, which meant another. Then again, didn't Richie say something to that cowboy about how he was upgrading? If that wasn't a reference to the new house, it could have meant Miss Woodstock. And given the way Tina focused on Richie, couldn't he have been upgrading from a little fling with her? It would explain a lot. And it would also be plenty creepy.

Which—the creepiness—brought her right back to Danny Bowman. And the cycle began again.

She wasn't sure she'd slept at all when the clock finally turned over to 5:30, and at that point she gave up. She went out into the living room and turned on the floor lamp and sat in Guy's chair reading one old *Yankee* magazine after another. Even an hour later there still wasn't much light coming in the windows. The weather, what she could see of it, had closed in overnight. Beyond the trees was a high overcast that didn't look like snow and didn't look like much of anything except a day on the mountain when the light would be lousy. She sat reading an article about lobster pots—there seemed to be an article about lobster pots in every single issue of *Yankee* magazine; maybe it was a regular feature—and wondering if Guy would suspect anything when he found her up so early. Like maybe she had a guilty conscience and couldn't sleep. She wondered if he'd sprung that business with Danny on her in the middle of the night for just that reason.

The sky brightened after a while without turning less gray, and right on schedule Guy came down the stairs to start his oatmeal. When he saw Stacey there in his recliner he allowed himself a crooked little smile. "I didn't sleep much, either," he confessed, and for a while that made her feel a little better.

Chip was at Judge Roy Beans early, sitting in a window booth with a large cup of coffee in front of him and his gloves and hat and keys scattered around the table and the bench, looking out at the day with undisguised dread. The cloud-draped top of the mountain was visible now and then from where he sat, and he studied it as if it were a weapon pointed right in his direction—as if it were something untrustworthy, something a person ought to keep an eye on. Below the cloud cover the day outside looked frigid but had turned out to be weirdly warm, and thanks to a temperature inversion it would get even warmer as you got higher on the mountain. The whole deal just didn't feel normal.

His face lit up, though, when Stacey's Subaru turned into the parking lot.

She parked and climbed out and walked to the door, her mind elsewhere and the gray and white world reflected in the glass front of Judge Roy Beans. When Chip rapped on the window with his knuckles, she jumped a mile.

She came in through the entryway with its newspaper racks and bulletin boards—ski gear and firewood for sale, snowplowing and housecleaning services available—taking off her hat and gloves as she went. She'd hardly gotten through the second door when Chip leaned out of his booth and said, "A little jumpy today, are we?"

"I didn't see you." She went over to him and put her stuff down.

"I was right here."

"The reflection."

"Go get your double espresso." The way he looked at her, it was clear that he thought she could use it. More to the point, it was clear that he thought she looked tired—but was too nice to put it that way.

"You scared me half to death," she said as she stood running fingers through her hair. But it wasn't one hundred percent true. The Claw had scared her half to death—The Claw with his threatening passage around the windows of her poor defenseless '87 Subaru—and compared to that this was nothing. Still, she *was* ready for that shot of caffeine. She left her stuff and went.

The counterman had it half ready when she walked up, and she was surprised to learn that Chip had already paid for it. She tipped the guy double and loaded the coffee up with Sweet'N Low. As she returned to the booth she stirred it with a wooden stick that looked kind of like a tongue depressor for Doctor Barbie.

"Thanks for the double shot, Chip."

"No prob."

"You shouldn't have."

"Let me live a little."

She sat down. "Okay. But your next one's on me."

"You got it. Tomorrow morning. It's a date."

She cocked her head forward and to the left about half a degree, and he was smart enough to let it go. "So," she said, checking her watch and seeing that they were both as early as she'd thought. Something about this weather, maybe. It wouldn't let you rest easy. She looked around the room and made sure that the booths on either side were empty, and then she went on. "I've been thinking about Richie Paxton."

"That's not my idea of a good time."

She blew over the coffee in her little cup. "About how you wouldn't put it past him. The thing with David. About what you said to his father."

"Hey, maybe I ought to write a book about how to win friends and influence people."

"Tact aside—which is probably a good thing in your case, considering—it's still an interesting idea. Richie, I mean." She drew a finger quickly across her throat.

"You think so?"

"I do."

"How come?"

"I don't know. I guess I just think he's got reasons."

Chip set his paper cup on edge and knocked it on the tabletop a couple of times, watching the surface of the coffee ripple. "He's got a *ton* of reasons. He's got nothing *but* reasons."

"Still, people can want things—a bigger house, a different relationship, whatever—without going that far."

"People, sure. That doesn't include Richie. Richie's a rat."

"What about his kids?"

"I don't think he'd strangle his kids. They don't have much money." He jumped his eyebrows and raised his cup. "Wouldn't be worth the trouble."

"Chip."

"I mean it. Sort of. I mean the guy's a pig. A rotten apple that fell too close to the tree."

"You didn't say all this to Andy."

"Andy doesn't need me to tell him what kind of a son he raised. He just needed me to put it into perspective."

Stacey sat quiet for a moment, then raised her cup and emptied it in two swallows. "So what do you think put him over the edge? If he went. Hypothetically."

"The woman."

"The woman. You mean the woman from Connecticut. Not Jeanette."

"God no." Then: "She's from Connecticut?"

"Yeah."

"Figures. How'd you know?"

"Tina told me. Do you know Tina? Tina Montero?"

"Yeah."

"She knows everything."

"Knows all, tells all." He finished his coffee. "Anyhow, the woman from Connecticut's the cause of it."

"Don't blame her. That's not right."

"I'm not."

"It'd be sexist if you did." The look she gave him indicated that it would also mean he wouldn't be getting that cup of coffee tomorrow morning.

"I don't blame her," he said. "It's just that everything needs a catalyst."

"I guess."

"And he didn't kill his brother last year."

"And he wasn't building that big house last year either, was he?"

"Exactly."

He reached for his gloves. Stacey dropped her squat little espresso cup inside his empty one and stuffed napkins and stir sticks after it and took everything to the trash. Then they headed out together into the gray light.

Buck Bradley would have probably earned points by staying somewhere right on the mountain, but he didn't give a damn about earning points. The condos were crap and he wasn't going to go slumming in them just to ring the Paxtons' bell. Once SkiAmerica got hold of the place they'd build some proper high-end spots set up for all kinds of fractional ownership—shares by the quarter, by the week, by less than that if that's what it took to elevate the level of accommodations around here.

The motels in town were crap, too, by the way. So as usual he ended up seven or eight miles away, in the honeymoon suite at the Chateau, an elegant old resort that didn't get much use outside of weddings in the summer and leaf-peepers in the fall. Even this place didn't come close to his standards—the worn-thin sheets could have come from the hospital, for Christ's sake, and the television had a fricking picture tube, if you could believe that—but it would have to do until he got this deal finished and the development guys arrived.

He ate his breakfast over a complimentary copy of the Rutland *Herald* and left a lousy tip in keeping with his overall level of satisfaction and left. The locks on the Saturn had frozen up overnight and he had to go back inside the hotel to get a book of matches so that he could heat up the key. It meant he'd be late for his meeting with the Paxtons elder and younger, but he didn't care. He stood under the gray sky with one glove on and one glove off, holding fire to the key and jamming it into the lock and failing and trying again. The air went blue with his curses.

"You *do* know that we've got some underground parking at the Last Run," Andy advised him later on—pretty damned paternally, he thought—once he'd told the story of the frozen locks. "If you'd get off your high horse and quit staying at the Chateau, you wouldn't have those problems."

"I don't like to let my personal experiences color my understanding of a business proposition," he lied.

"Understood." Andy rose from behind his desk. "Coffee? I'm buying. Let's walk."

When they came into his office with their paper Spruce Peak cups steaming, Richie was pretty sure he saw Buck cast a sorrowful look at that private Keurig coffeemaker of his. "Cheers!" he said as they made themselves comfortable at the conference table. He lifted his mug, lording it over Buck. Screw him.

That particular sentiment turned out to be a two-way street.

Buck set down his coffee and opened his briefcase. What he drew out was three copies of a document that Richie had been looking forward to for six or eight weeks, something he'd been anticipating with the eagerness of a kid waiting for Christmas morning. SkiAmerica's final offer, the culmination of two years and more of negotiations. The presentation was flawless and, to Richie's flattery-prone heart, breathtaking. It was just shy of embossed.

Andy opened his copy and started at the beginning. Richie went straight to the end.

"This doesn't add up," he said.

"I assure you," said Buck, "it adds up."

"I mean . . ." He went speechless, running his index finger along a tall column of figures.

Andy drew from somewhere a copy of the prior proposal, and squared it up on the tabletop alongside the new one. "Let's give Buck, here, a chance to go through things," he said.

"Appreciate it," said Buck.

"I've gone through what I need to go through," said Richie. He reached across the table to snatch the prior document from in front of his father, and then he opened both versions to the same page. "I've gone through plenty," he said. "I've seen what there is to see."

"Now, Richard."

"Andy, Richie," said the cowboy, looking from each to each in turn. "I promised we'd do what we could. We've run the projections six ways to Sunday. We've dug deep. We've ground this all just as fine as we can, believe me. And in the end, the facts are the facts."

"The offer went down, Pop. It actually went *down*." He pressed both copies open and pushed them together across the table toward his father, bumping his mug in the process and spilling coffee.

Buck, helpful and solicitous as he could be, given the circumstances, grabbed a handful of napkins and mopped up after him.

TWENTY-NINE

"You can't do this to me, and I'll tell you why."

"I'm not doing anything to you, Richie."

"Oh, yes, you are. Let me show you." Richie spun the wheel of the big Mercedes and sent it careening up the hill between the bait shop and the sugar house, one building shuttered for the season and the other decked out for the holiday trade.

"Whoa!" Buck reached for the granny handle as the car changed directions and shot upward. "I thought we were going to lunch."

"We were. We've got somebody to pick up on the way, is all."

The downed logs were covered over with snow and the bulldozer was covered over with snow and the evergreens ringed all about were thick with it, but the scar on the landscape that was Richie's building lot was still obvious. Another car was parked up there already, right on the edge of a precipice that would become the foundation. A racing green BMW roadster, as ill-suited to this terrain and this season as a car could possibly be. It had Connecticut tags.

They pulled up behind it and stopped, a little too abruptly for Buck's taste. He winced, imagining Richie's two-ton wagon skidding into the little convertible and sending it to the bottom of that excavation. No fun. A powerful argument against driving angry.

The BMW was running, and whoever was behind the wheel wasn't in a hurry to get out. Richie and Buck sat for a moment, too.

"So what's this?" Buck asked. As if he didn't know.

"This is the reason I need a better offer from you."

Buck grinned and craned his neck. Here in the big cabin of the Mercedes, he was able to ride with his cowboy hat intact. "Nice location, I'll grant you that."

"It is."

"That's a hell of a big hole, too."

"I know."

Buck wasn't much good at playing dumb, but he gave it a shot for Richie's sake. "Gonna be a nice place. How many units?"

Richie just snorted.

"This wasn't on any of the site plans, though. How come?"

"Because it's mine, that's why."

Ahead of them the BMW's engine cut out and the driver's side door swung open. Buck couldn't see it from where he sat, but the woman inside put out two long legs wrapped knee-high in glove-soft leather. The boots were to die for, but the heels were a little precarious for these conditions. She was obviously a person accustomed to being taken care of.

"Actually," said Richie, as she stepped out and stood facing the Mercedes, "it's ours."

Buck whistled between his teeth. "Talk about an upgrade," he said.

The woman's name was Lisa MacDonald. Formerly Lisa Santangelo. Even more formerly Lisa Boatwright. And now, at long last, she was right back where she started. Lisa MacDonald again. Just like thirty-seven years ago, thank God. She wouldn't be changing her name again, that was for sure. It was too much trouble and it was way too temporary.

Still, she wouldn't mind changing a few other things. Like the floor plan of this house that Richie said he was building for her. She'd change it every which way, and she'd alter the siding and move the roofline and rework the façade and everything else, too, if only so that when she was done her handprints would be on every inch of the place. If Richie Paxton ever decided to show her the door, he'd be looking at her handiwork when he latched it shut behind her. And that's just the way she wanted it.

Unforgettable. That's what Lisa MacDonald aspired to be.

She could tell by the look in his eyes that Buck Bradley thought she was pretty close already.

"Howdy, miss," he said with a wink and an outthrust hand.

He wasn't bad-looking, she thought, if you liked the Marlboro Man. And if you were old enough to sort of remember the Marlboro Man. Which she was. Just. He was rugged, in a kind of over-the-hill way that she didn't mind.

"Richie's told me all about you," he went on. "But I don't think he had words enough to do you justice."

"Flattery will get you everywhere." She turned toward the excavation and gave her long green coat a spin. Even over the high pervasive scent of the pine trees that flanked the scene, the two men couldn't help but be transported by whatever expensive perfume she'd put on this morning. It meant different things to them. To Richie it was soothing and intimate and thrilling all at once, while to Buck it was a wild card: It might distract Richie and put him in a better mood, or it might set him off into some kind of territorial macho display. He'd just have to wait and see.

Stacey's cell phone was all charged up, and she was by herself in the mid-mountain lodge where there was a pretty reliable signal, so she had absolutely no excuse not to call her mother. No excuse, that is, other than the ones she always kept handy. They'd served her well enough, that was for sure. All the way through college and grad school and beyond. But it had been what, a week since the two of them had talked? Maybe more than that. It was definitely before she'd moved into the Ramsey place. So she fixed her brought-from-home tea and peeled open an energy bar and keyed in her mother's office number. She'd known it by heart since grade school. Since before she could remember much of anything else. Since before the Tooth Fairy and the Easter Bunny and Santa Claus.

"Hiya, doll." It was Penny, her mother's secretary and long-suffering factotum. Over the years, Penny had seen more of Stacey's class plays and band concerts and piano recitals than her own mother had. And she'd enjoyed them more, too. "Your mom's tied up. Discovery."

"You'd think she could have found the Northwest Passage by now."

"You would."

"So what is it today? A deposition?"

"Yep. Video. Nothing's as simple as it used to be."

"I guess not."

"They should put it on MyTube."

"YouTube."

"Whatever."

"When's she coming back?"

"Are you all right, sweetie?"

Oh, that Penny. "Fine. When'll she be back?"

"Are you sure?"

"Penny, I'm fine. Really."

"All right. She'll be back late."

"How late is late?"

"I'm thinking *tomorrow morning* late." Which was something.

Giselle Owen-Curtis thought nothing of breezing into the office at nine or ten at night, and keeping her whole staff waiting there until she did.

"Yow," said Stacey.

An audible ringing came over the line—two or three different rings, actually, each one of them more urgent than the others—and Penny said she had to go. "Can I tell her you called?"

"You've put it in the log already," Stacey said.

"You know me."

"Bye."

"She'll be sorry she missed you."

"Good to talk with you, Penny."

"Same here."

The lunch place was picturesque, anyhow. It was an out-of-the-way general store somewhere in the woods near Woodstock, with a lunch counter in the back. To get there, they had to wind past shelves where stovebolts and mousetraps and cleaning products shared space with racks of postcards and tins of maple syrup and jars of more or less local salsa. There were coolers along one wall filled with bait and soft drinks and beer, the last of which never failed to surprise a Colorado native like Buck. There wasn't a Coors in sight, he noticed. Just Harpoon and Magic Hat and Long Trail. Beer was everywhere in this state—wine, too, although hard liquor was nowhere to be seen—and the whole place was nuts about the locally made stuff. Like you tapped a pine tree to make it or something.

The air back where they served lunch was hot and dry in the extreme, thanks to a Franklin stove that blazed at one end of the room and a brick oven that smoked at the other. The old-timers along the counter had their coats on anyhow. They were a severely local and hard-bitten group, not a full set of teeth among them, and over their coffee cups they sized up Richie and Lisa and Buck as if they were visitors from an alien world. They drank their coffee and watched one of the fires or the other and sat wordless as stumps, as if they'd already told each other everything that needed to be said. They probably had.

Richie raised three fingers to the girl behind the counter, who motioned toward a couple of picnic tables and said, "Sit anywhere that ain't taken."

"You got it."

They all got the special. By the looks of the men at the counter, everybody got the special. By the looks of the disused menus that drooped between the salt shakers and the napkin holders, everybody always got the special. Ordering meant walking over to the counter and explaining yourself to the girl there who'd give you a slip of paper with a scribble of magic marker on it and then walking back out into the front of the store for something from the cooler and a bag of chips. When they returned to the picnic table Buck raised his eyebrows to Lisa and said, "Richie's told me all about you."

"That's a nice change." She reached and took Richie's hand.

"Mmm. Yeah. I guess it would be." He ran a finger around the collar of his shirt.

"I mean, so far our relationship is the kind where going *out* to lunch means going *out of town* to lunch. To someplace like, well . . ." She shrugged and left it at that.

"I know what you mean."

"You do?"

"Well. Not firsthand. But."

"Right."

Richie sat with his hand in hers and looked at the men at the counter, checking their faces one after the next just to be sure.

Lisa tilted her head his way and said to Buck, "See?"

Buck elbowed Richie. "What'd you see, pardner? Those sandwiches ready?"

Startled, Richie looked back. "Huh?"

"He's not looking at the sandwiches, Buck."

"Right."

"Hey," Richie put in as his attention wandered back into their general vicinity. "I've got a lot on my mind." He turned his attention fully upon Lisa and cocked his head toward Buck, saying, "This guy right here, for example—this *bandito* who sits before you even now—has decided to lower his offer."

Well, well, well. Buck had not expected this.

"Really," she said. Flat as that.

"Really."

"Hey," Buck began. "You know it wasn't entirely my . . ." He certainly had not anticipated having this discussion in front of the woman.

"Are you the money man or what? Richie's said all along that you're the money man."

It sure was hot in that back room. "I am," he said. "I am. But that doesn't mean I'm the only party involved."

Lisa gave Richie a cockeyed look. "So what are the numbers? How far down did they go?"

Richie opened his mouth but Buck got there first. "Richie," he said, "this is all strictly confidential. I don't think it's wise—"

Richie gave him a look that suggested he'd better not try questioning his intelligence and picking his pocket on the same day.

"Fine," said Buck. "You guys talk about what you need to talk about, and I'll go fetch the sandwiches."

They were almost ready but not quite, and he took his sweet time bringing them back.

THIRTY

"I told Lisa you want her to lower her sights a little," is how Richie greeted Buck when he returned with a laden tray.

"None of this was my idea." He distributed the sandwiches on their paper plates. There was no trick to it, since all three of them were having the special. It looked pretty good, actually. At least you got good cheese up here. "The numbers are the numbers. The economy's tight. The real estate market sucks, if you'll excuse my French."

"Excused."

"And then there's the Forest Service."

"Bullshit," said Richie. "My father might believe you on that, but I don't. There's no uncertainty about it. They'll kowtow just like they always have."

Buck popped open a bag of chips and dug his hand in. "Still," he said, through a mouthful of them. "We can't be sure. So we've got to make allowances." He set the bag down. "Like I said, though: If you want to wait a year until they've gotten off their fannies and made a decision, I'm sure that'll be fine with the boys in Denver."

Lisa cut her sandwich in half and picked up part of it with her pinky fingers extended. She took a delicate bite and chewed for a moment.

"They can wait," Buck said. "That's a promise. You, on the other hand, seemed to feel some urgency about the deal."

Lisa swallowed.

So did Richie.

After lunch she went her way while the two men headed back to town. Buck sat in the passenger seat of the big Mercedes, blowing warm breath white into the cold cabin, while Richie put her in her own car. For a nicely put-together woman she looked hard as nails and sharp as a pickax. But she hadn't made a dent in Buck Bradley.

"I'm surprised you wanted to let her in on so much of your business," he said to Richie when they were moving.

"It's my business."

"I know that."

"It's my business how much of my business—"

"I know. I was surprised, is all."

Richie drove.

"Usually, these things—"

"This isn't *usually*. This isn't one of the usual things."

"I can see that." Buck leaned back in the seat and picked at a bit of potato chip that had gotten lodged between his back teeth. "Which is why I didn't mention the other thing."

"The other thing."

"The other thing I didn't mention with your father, either."

"What other thing?"

"David." He turned a little and watched the fog of his breath bloom on the side window. "I've got to level with you. A murder in the family makes some people nervous."

Richie drove.

"I'm just saying."

Richie was quiet for a while. He switched on the radio and switched it off again. "I don't like it any better than you do."

"Way I see it, you ought to like it less."

"Well. Yeah." His hands unclenched the wheel and clenched it again.

"People talk."

"It's not like we're the Wild West here."

"I know that," said Buck. "I'm *from* the Wild West, for crying out loud."

"Good."

"It's more like . . ." He sat for a minute. He reached up and fingered his cowboy hat. "It's more like people think it's . . . I don't know . . ."

"People think it's what? What do they think?"

"Like there's something dirty going on or something."

Richie touched his brakes at the speed limit sign that marked the edge of town. "Then you can keep your goddamned money," he said.

But Buck knew he didn't mean it. Because how would he explain it to Lisa?

It was the run-up to Christmas, and the ski patrol was doing some last-minute first-aid drills. You never knew what Christmas week would bring. Actually, you did—and that was the trouble. It brought the same thing that Presidents' Week and Martin Luther King Day always brought: amateur hour. Middle-aged men who skied once a year and thought they were experts. Twelve-year-olds who'd just unwrapped their first snowboards and thought they were bulletproof. College kids who dared their pals to take treacherous black-diamond runs where they didn't in a million years belong. And dumb-ass fathers who dragged little tiny kids onto those same slopes—screaming and kicking and wailing like banshees—just so they could have a chance to ski them themselves. That last crowd was the worst, as far as Chip could see. He and his own dad had struggled with their differences, but they'd been nothing compared to the wreckage he foresaw in these kids' future. Christmas week for them was a lesson in Why I Hate My Dad.

Chip was on his knees in the snow at the top of Spruce Peak's longest bump run, strapping another patroller down onto a toboggan. The other guy had a bandage wrapped around his head and a splint bound to his leg and he was about to enjoy the singular pleasure of taking an involuntary toboggan ride down the bumps. Chip had better go easy, he was telling him, and not only because at some time in the future there would be actual life and limb at stake. What was at stake right now was Chip's immediate comfort and health, since he'd be the next one to take a ride on the sled.

The run—appropriately named Watch This!—was underneath a lift. A trip up that lift was at least two kinds of nonstop fun for Stacey. First, there was the chance you'd see somebody coming down who really knew what he was doing. There was nothing like seeing somebody take a long and demanding bump run at high speed, angling from one trough to the next as if the decisions were automatic, poles planted like signposts and knees hammering up and down like well-oiled pistons. It was something to aspire to, and watching it done well always gave her a thrill. The other kind of fun was a little more cruel, she had to admit. It was seeing some dopey high school kid or middle-aged wannabe get his butt handed to him about twenty feet down the first face, when he realized he'd bitten off a whole lot more than he'd like to be caught chewing in public. Half of these doofuses didn't know there was a bailout lane on the left, and the other half were too proud to use it. Good skiers or bad, Watch This! made for better theater than you could find in a year in Boston. The thrill of victory or the agony of defeat—you never knew what you might get.

The run was pretty much empty today, though, and when she saw the rescue scene underway at the top—a patroller in his red jacket, two poles X'd to mark the spot and ward off other skiers, and a toboggan, for God's sake—her spirits fell. Whenever you saw the patrol at work it was a bad sign. Just thinking about it made Stacey's stomach do a flip. Unconsciously, she took a better grip on the chair with her leather mitten, as if to keep herself from falling off. Then the chair drew nearer and she realized that what she was watching wasn't a real accident but a drill—both guys had patrol jackets—and she relaxed again. Until she noticed that the guy retrieving the poles and lashing them to the toboggan was Chip, and her spirits fell once more. Not too much, but enough so she'd notice. She'd lost track of him on the way over to the mountain and she hadn't seen him again on the slopes until right this minute, when her day was three-quarters gone. And now here he was in the middle of some drill that was sure to take forever. Dang. It looked like she'd spend the rest of her day skiing alone.

Not that *that* was the worst fate in the world.

It beat the heck out of finding your fiancé—what was his name, anyhow? Brian? she tilted her head from side to side and pretended that she couldn't quite remember—finding that loser in bed with somebody else. It beat the heck out of looking for a regular job in Boston now that she was finally done with grad school. It beat the heck out of almost anything she could think of, if you wanted to know the truth. Even though the clouds were still low and the sky was still pearl gray and the light on the slopes was so flat that you could hardly make out a thing. Didn't matter.

She watched Chip finish lashing down the poles, and as the chair passed over him she called down. He had just come to his feet and was tramping over to where he'd left his skis, and when he saw her he waved back with his whole body and gave a smile that brightened up the gloomy day considerably.

Brian who?

Chip cupped his mittens around his mouth and called up that he'd see Stacey later on at the Binding, which was better than nothing.

Richie said he needed something from home, so they kept going past the Spruce Peak access road and around the edge of the village and up into what was once the better part of town. Andy lived up here, in a house that his own father had built. The place was modest by today's standards—modest in fact by the standards of twenty or thirty years ago, when the boys grew up surrounded by far fancier places occupied only two or three weeks out of the year—but the views from the promontory of rock on which it sat were absolutely beyond compare. Richie had built his own place on the same road once he'd come of age, no more than three-quarters of a mile past his parents', but on a plan that was two or three times as big as the house of his youth. And now there was the new construction up the side road by the sugar house, but nobody talked about that.

Richie pressed the remote halfway up the drive, and they slid into the garage with only an inch and a second to spare.

"Hey," said Buck. "Don't wreck the car on my account."

The garage was a disaster area. Richie could hardly get his door open, and Buck's side was no better. He'd have stayed put if he hadn't seen Jeanette's van in the other bay. Since she was home, he ought to pay his respects. Regardless of what Richie thought.

"You can stay put," Richie said as he pushed the door open. As if he'd read his mind. "I won't be a second."

"Just thought I'd say hi to Jeanette." Buck pushed at the door with his shoulder and took off his hat and slid out into the narrow gap permitted him by the drifts of junk everywhere. By the looks of it, most of it belonged to the kids. Skis and snowboards and sleds and snowshoes and everything else that too much money could buy.

Richie was pushing junk around on his workbench. Tools and broken toys and envelopes stuffed with paperwork. A busted chain saw and a hatchet gone to rust. Orphaned mittens and broken crampons and warranty cards that would never get sent in because the things that they covered were already used up or ruined. Buck left him to it and knocked at the back door and went in when Richie told him to go ahead.

Jeanette was in the kitchen, past the mudroom with the washer and the dryer and the utility tub, and Buck's knock—coming after the car had pulled into the garage—threw her off. "Who is it?" She sounded a little alarmed.

"Hey, Jeanette. It's me. It's Buck. Richie told me I should—"

"Come in."

"Right. I did."

"No, I mean come on in."

"Oh. Sure." He eased the door closed behind him and scraped his boots on the mat.

Jeanette clacked a wooden spoon down on the countertop and headed toward the mudroom, moving across the marble floor of the kitchen, her feet making hard sounds.

They met on the threshold. Jeanette was a good-looking woman, there was no doubt about that, but she was built solid. Even in the middle of whatever work she was doing in the kitchen she managed to look polished and satisfied and settled, as if she'd achieved and acquired everything she'd ever wanted in this life. Lisa was different. Lisa, on the other hand, looked as if Jeanette had been eating her rightful lunch for years, and her breakfast and dinner, too. By comparison to Richie's satisfied wife she looked like the very picture of want—which was a different thing from desire—and Buck wondered how it was that Richie had been drawn, at one time or another, to the both of them. Maybe he was just unlucky.

"I didn't know you were still in town," she said.

"We had a few last-minute details to clean up."

"Richie doesn't tell me anything."

"Oh, now." He rolled the brim of his cowboy hat in his hand. "He doesn't."

Buck looked toward the family room with its three-story fireplace and its high arched windows and its wood, wood, wood. Cherry and poplar and ash. He sniffed and thought that the carpeting smelled new. "He seems to take pretty good care of you all the same."

"We didn't have you to dinner."

"That's all right."

"If you're buying in to the mountain, we ought to treat you more like family."

Buck didn't correct that "buying in" business. Jeanette had lived in this town all her life, and in spite of Richie and in spite of her spoiled children she was genuine enough for anybody, and he didn't want to think about what fates the outright sale of the mountain and Richie's plans with Lisa might have in store for her. He thought for a second that she was just uninformed and maybe a little selfish about the business deal—hard to imagine that the mountain might pass entirely out of family ownership—but then he wondered if maybe Richie was just keeping her in the dark. "You've done your part already," he said. "We took those runs together, didn't we?"

"We did," she said. "You're right." She seemed satisfied.

She seemed, now that Buck thought about it, like a woman who'd made it her life's work to capitalize on whatever bits of satisfaction presented themselves. The physical comforts, naturally. She'd had plenty of them. But he was thinking now about the personal stuff. She was a woman who settled.

The idea hit Buck like a fist. That was it. Richie was smarter than he'd given him credit for. He'd made up some bullshit line about the scope of the sale, knowing that when he got around to asking Jeanette for a divorce she'd never question his finances. She'd never know the truth. Up here in the woods she'd hire some small-time bumpkin of a lawyer, and the two of them wouldn't bother digging. She probably wouldn't let him if he wanted to.

Was it possible that she was that stupid? Probably not entirely.

Was it possible that she was that naïve? That her world was that small?

You bet it was.

He felt an uncharacteristic little pang of sympathy for her. Then he felt another one for Richie, who probably didn't know what he was getting into with that new woman. You could bet she'd have a team of tax accountants on his ass night and day.

Richie opened the door and hollered to him from the garage, so he put his arms around Jeanette and told her that they'd all have a nice dinner out the next time he came East. She and Richie and the kids and everybody. Just like family. Andy and Marie, too, if they could swing it.

They didn't stand together that way for long. But by the time he let her go, Richie was in the car and blowing the horn like mad.

THIRTY-ONE

Chip didn't leave his coat on the pegs in the foyer, but stamped in wearing it and sat at the bar shivering. He still had on his hat, too. And it was all he could do to take his gloves off.

Jack the bartender ducked into the kitchen and brought him out a cup of coffee without being asked. "Hey, buddy," he said, "you look like you just had a fight with the abominable snowman. And lost."

"Some days I hate this job." He gripped the coffee cup in both hands like it was a life preserver or something.

"What happened?"

"Tell you what. Go stand in the cooler for about eight hours, and you'll get an idea. No moving around. Just stand there." He took a sip of coffee. "OK. You can sit a little. Or maybe get down on your hands and knees. But that's it."

"First aid drills, huh?"

"Absofrickinlutely. First aid. It's the worst. And whose job is it to do first aid on us, when we've frozen ourselves half to death out there?"

Jack smiled and reached over and tapped the coffee cup. "That's why I'm here," he said.

"Thanks, buddy." He drank some more. "I'll let you know when I'm warmed up enough for something cold."

"I could put a little brandy in there."

"And spoil perfectly good coffee?"

Jack leaned against the back bar and scratched his silver head. The Starbucks generation. Go figure. They didn't know what they were missing. Then again, maybe *he* didn't know what *he* was missing. Back when he was Chip's age, booze was booze and coffee was something that a white-aproned waitress sloshed into a china cup at the donut shop. It was weak and pale and full of grounds. Maybe these kids were onto something after all. Who knew. Things changed. And if you hung around this world long enough, you could see everything.

Once he'd thawed out, Chip had two questions. *Could he get a cheeseburger?* and *Where was Stacey, anyhow?*

Jack's answer threw him. "Sure thing. In the dining room."

"You don't serve at the bar anymore?"

"No. I mean yeah. Sure. I can get you a burger." He took out a little multiform pad from his apron pocket. "How do you want it?"

"Medium."

"You want American, Swiss, cheddar, or provolone? You'd be nuts not to go with the cheddar, seeing as they make it just up the road."

"Wouldn't that make it American?"

"What a kidder." He marked the pad and turned away, stepping toward the kitchen door. "One medium burger with cheddar. Coming up."

"Where's Stacey?"

"Like I said. She's in the dining room."

"Oh." Now he got it.

Jack pushed the door open with his shoulder and light spilled out from the kitchen into the bar. "Bev's coming in late. Do you know Bev? Nice gal. Her kid's sick. Once her husband gets home she'll come in, but until then somebody's got to cover her tables."

"How about I have my burger out there?"

"You can have it anywhere you want," said Jack.

Here's the way it was, apparently: Everything that Danny Bowman touched turned to crap.

He sat by the window at Bud's Suds, listening to the machines go around and watching the windows sweat.

Every single goddamn thing he touched turned to crap.

Agitated, he flipped through a dog-eared copy of *Redbook* and thought it over. His bad luck wasn't exactly a new realization, but what bugged him most about it right now was that for once in his life he actually had something valuable to his name—he'd seen that girl leaving the Snowfield right around the time that rich queer had turned up dead—and nobody cared. The guy's high-and-mighty brother didn't give a shit. The girl coughed up a lousy fourteen bucks after two tries. That's like what—seven dollars a try? A person couldn't get very far on that. And then when he took the facts to the sheriff, the sheriff wouldn't even write them down. It was *evidence*, for Christ's sake. It was *eyewitness testimony*. And because it came from Danny Bowman, it wasn't even worth the sheriff's time to scribble it into his goddamn flip-top notepad.

If this was the start of the dinner hour in the days just before Christmas, Stacey thought maybe she'd applied for the wrong job. Sure, it was only five-thirty. But the dining room was a ghost town. On the other hand, unless things picked up soon, the tips would be lousy. Either way, food service wasn't exactly turning out to be her idea of a productive career option.

She was behind a screened partition folding napkins and keeping an eye on her one occupied table when Chip came in, accompanied by the Australian girl from the hostess station. She tried to seat him up front but he asked if this was Stacey's table and she said no, so they kept going. He was carrying his coffee cup and he finally had his coat off, although he still looked beat.

The Australian girl tried to give him a menu but he turned it down. Jamal the busboy fetched him a glass of ice water from out of nowhere and disappeared. Once he was gone Stacey put down the napkins and came over, looking delighted enough for the both of them. "Hi," she said, pulling the pad from her apron pocket. "My name is Stacey and I'll be your server this evening."

"God, I hate that," he said, shaking his head. "Who in the world ever came up with a word like that. *Server.*"

"It's non-gender-specific. And I guess it beats *servant.*"

"Maybe. If a word that's not even a word to begin with can be better than a real word."

Stacey shrugged and tapped on the pad with her pencil. "Hey. I've got to say it. It's in the employee manual."

"I already ordered, just so you know. Jack's sending a burger around."

"I'll keep an eye out." She surveyed the dim and nearly empty room. "It'll be tough, with these crowds and all. I can't promise anything."

"He said you were out here."

"So you came to keep me company. How sweet."

"It beats looking at Jack." He put his hand on the glass of ice water and drew it back. "Can you sit down? For a minute maybe?"

She shot a glance at the family at the other table and pulled up a chair, feigning weariness, although nobody but Chip was watching. "My feet are killing me."

"I don't believe it."

"Good. They're not."

"How does anybody make a living in this place?"

"It'll pick up. Anyway, Pete's loaded. This is just a hobby."

"But the tips."

"I know. That's why people end up living in their cars."

"They don't. Not really. Really?" Having grown up in the muggy postmalarial swamps of Washington, D.C., where people lived not only in cars but under bridge overpasses and inside shipping crates and pretty much everywhere else they could squeeze themselves to get out of the rain and the heat, Chip was blind to the same basic thing when it happened up here in the frozen North. Probably because it seemed impossible. It was too cold, wasn't it? The only exception he could think of was that gray-haired vet, so he corrected himself. "Unless you mean Danny, I guess. And he doesn't work, so that would make it kind of hard to pay rent."

"Working people live in their cars everywhere, Mr. Middle Class. I did, for a while."

"You did? Not here."

"Here."

"In the winter?"

"You bet. And all I had for company was The Claw."

"The Claw?" He was thinking it was some kind of safety product sold on infomercials or the Home Shopping Network. Like the Club.

"*The Claw.* You know. Like The Hook. Didn't you ever listen to stories around a campfire?"

THIRTY-TWO

The family at the occupied table looked like they needed re-fills on their drinks, and they were probably going to want a look at the dessert menu, so Stacey tried to get it all over with at once. "Jeez," said the guy, a burly lump up from Jersey by the sound of him. Either he didn't shave while he was on a ski vacation or else he was the kind of gorilla who had a five o'clock shadow by ten in the morning. "Cabernet don't go so good with ice cream. Give us a break, huh?"

So much for *that* tip.

Stacey went to log the order with Jack, and as the kitchen door swung behind her she heard the guy say, "If I wanted a pushy wait-ress, I would have stayed in Bayonne."

So much for being elevated to *server*, too.

Chip's burger was ready so she brought it back along with the tray of drinks for the crowd from Jersey. Plus a Long Trail that she fig-ured he wouldn't mind.

"Thanks," he said. "And now we're going to have to go back to your campfire story," he said.

"Oh, that." She leaned against the wall and told him about The Night of The Claw. How she'd been living in the car behind Bud's Suds, how that awful scraping had gone all the way around her car windows in the middle of the night, and she was pretty sure that it was Danny Bowman—who'd freaked her out a time or two, anyhow. She didn't go into specifics. She didn't mention how Danny had tried to extort money from her (if that was the word; it seemed kind of strong, given his weakness and how little it had come to) or how he claimed to have seen her leaving the Snowfield somewhere around the night of David's murder.

Like a little kid, Chip poured ketchup all over everything. He dug into his burger and shook his head. "What a loser."

"Tell me about it." She slid down the wall a little.

"Stay away from that guy, OK?"

"He's everywhere."

"You know what I mean. Just—"

"I know."

He lifted a french fry dripping with ketchup and held it up to her in offering.

"No, thanks. I ate."

"Did you ever tell Guy?"

"About what? The Claw?"

"Sure."

"Why would I do that?"

"Why wouldn't you?"

"What's he supposed to do about it? It's history now. Besides, at the time, I didn't want him to know I'd been—"

"What? Loitering? What's the word for it?"

"Squatting. I don't know."

"I think squatting calls for some kind of building."

"Maybe so."

"Yeah. I think you squat in an empty house or a condemned apartment complex or like that."

"Could be."

"I don't know what it's called when you do it in a car."

Stacey was getting exasperated. "Anyhow—"

"What about vagrancy?"

"Anyhow—"

"Right. So where'd you tell him you'd been staying?"

"He didn't ask."

"Great. The guy lets in a tenant with no former address. You've got to love small-town law enforcement."

"Hey," she said, unthinking. "He didn't need to investigate me. Look at this face."

Chip looked but he didn't say anything. He just smiled and dabbed at his lips with his napkin.

The gorilla from Jersey was signaling for his check. Stacey waved the dessert menu at him again but he held up a big meaty hand to stop her. Said they'd probably swing by the Whippi Dip instead. Just the check, OK?

The Whippi Dip had put up its shutters back in October, but that wasn't any of Stacey's business. Sonny Bayonne could drop by the gas station and pick up a few tubs of Ben & Jerry's, take the wife and kids back to the condo, and think they were getting the honest-to-Pete Vermont experience. Good riddance.

Bev arrived at last, full of overlapping stories about her kid's case of the flu and her husband's apparent inability to get home from work on time, and after she got done making sure everybody in the place knew about the whole ordeal Chip and Stacey headed for the bar. They cut through the kitchen, Chip carrying his own plate and some of the stuff from the Jersey family's table. He slid everything into the bins and waited while Stacey did the same. "You're handy enough to have around," she said.

"It beats leaving a tip."

"I'd just have to split it with Bev and Jamal anyway."

They went out through the swinging doors on the other side. The bar was lots busier than the dining room, and if Jack weren't such a trooper he would have given Stacey a look for taking her sweet time getting back. And for having Chip with her in the kitchen, as far as that went. But Chip looked a whole lot more upbeat than he had before, which was nice, and the crowd wasn't out of control, which was also nice, so no harm done. Kids. It was good to see them happy.

Just one stool was left at the bar and Jack gave Chip dibs on it, shooing away some slow-moving flatlander who was drifting toward it from the jukebox. "There's plenty of tables," he said. "That seat's taken." And the guy bounced away as if he were made of rubber.

Chip slid into the spot and pointed to the Long Trail tap, and Jack gave him a thumbs-up look. Just two more nonverbal guys, exchanging necessary information in the time-honored way. He settled in, nodding to the snowmobile guy at his right elbow. He was pretty sure the guy ran a groomer up on the mountain, and he hoped that he wouldn't be working tonight. In the end, though, it was none of his business. So rather than risk finding out more than he wanted to know he fiddled with his coaster and looked over to his left, where Tina Montero sat with her back turned to him, completely oblivious. Past her and suffering her attention—no, wait, make that *basking in* her attention—was that Colorado cowboy, Buck Bradley. He wore that big white hat tilted back on his head and he had a damp hundred-dollar bill thrown casually onto the bar in front of him and he was tossing back a double Glenfiddich that gleamed like a tiger's eye. Despite the close quarters Chip couldn't hear what they were saying—Tina's voice was pitched low

and Buck was laughing in a way that sounded dirty, like sand passing over an iron grate—but he didn't need much in the way of detail
to figure out what was going on. He quarter-turned on the stool and
saw Stacey, who was looking past him at Tina and Buck and shaking her head, visibly clucking to herself like a schoolmarm in some
old Western movie.

If you hung around a place like this long enough, you could see
everything.

THIRTY-THREE

" wasn't sure you two had ever met," Stacey said to Tina and Buck.

"Oh, darlin'," said Tina, reaching over and taking Stacey's hand in a kind of creepily maternal way. "I told you we were acquainted." With her other hand she raised her glass. "Old Buck and me. Didn't I?"

Stacey tidied the napkins. "Maybe you did."

The two of them sat there smug as cats, both of them knowing that Stacey had seen them ignoring each other from opposite ends of the bar just a few nights back. Who did they think they were kidding?

She pointed to Buck's drained glass. "That's Glenfiddich, right?"

"You know me."

"Another?"

"You know me."

"And I'll have another chardonnay," said Tina, "as long as my cowpoke here's running the tab."

Danny Bowman was revved up on free coffee. He'd hung around Judge Roy Beans until the last customers had gone, and now the counterman was letting him sit in the back to eat a couple of left-over bagels and drink his fill from the Green Mountain Coffee mega thermos while he closed up. The sign had said decaf but now Danny wasn't so sure. You couldn't trust these hourly employees. What did they care? Decaf in the regular, regular in the decaf, it was all the same to them.

As usual this time of night, Danny was navigating a fine network of variables between warmth and insomnia and the disastrous eventual need to get up and piss in the middle of the night. A mix-up in the coffee supply didn't help matters.

"You wouldn't have any whiskey to go with this, would you?" he croaked at the counterman—the counterkid, really—as he staggered past with his arms full of cleaning supplies.

"All I got's Clorox."

"You sure this is the unleaded?"

"What'd the sign say?"

"Decaf."

"Then it's decaf."

"It don't seem like decaf to me."

"'Beggars can't be choosers,' my mom says."

"What would your mother know about it?"

But the kid was gone. Off cleaning the bathroom or something.

Danny finished up and let himself out. The lot was empty except for a handful of cars and a couple of snowmobiles parked down by Vinnie's Steak-Out. The counterkid must have walked. Danny figured on walking, too, up the hill and into the condo parking lots until he found suitable accommodations. He opened the newsbox and helped himself to a dozen copies of the *Mountaintop Pennysaver* and set out. As he walked across the dimly lit parking lot, his hands drummed in his pockets and he told himself that that was no goddamn decaf he'd been drinking. No way.

An hour or so later, every glass in the room was full and Stacey had a moment to herself. She was leaning against the back bar, rewinding back to the night when Tina and Buck had sat as far apart from each other as possible. It had been Buck's doing, right? Tina had been there all along as usual, and Buck had shown up and sat himself clear over at the other end of the bar. Which had put some extra miles on Stacey, which she hadn't appreciated. She remembered that very clearly.

And now this.

A new table full of Eddie Bauer types caught her attention and she went off to take care of them. When she came back with their order Buck was gone from his stool and she pulled a fresh Long Trail for Chip and gave it to him, whispering, "Find out what's up with those two. A few nights ago they were strangers, and now they've been all over each other for years."

"He hit the head."

"Go."

"Really?"

"*Go.* I'm not kidding."

So he went.

He found Buck in front of the mirror, adjusting the angle of his cowboy hat. Not since he'd gone with his grandmother to church as a little boy had Chip seen so much fussing over the exact positioning of headgear. It was as if there were some kind of magic to it, possible only when the angle was one hundred percent right. He slipped past the partition to the urinal and looked in the mirror and said, "Nice hat," just as sincerely as you please.

"Thanks, pal. Appreciate it."

"We don't see many hats like that around here."

"No. I guess you wouldn't." Buck's expression was stony, the face of a gambler, and Chip couldn't tell if he had taken offense or not.

"A traveling man like you, on the other hand—you'd see a little of everything."

Buck turned on the tap and worked up a lather. "I guess I would."

"I guess you'd have a girl in every town, too, huh?"

"If I did, it wouldn't be any of your business."

"No."

"If I did, I wouldn't go around bragging on it."

"Not even a little?"

"Not even a little."

"Good man," said Chip, finishing up and backing away.

Buck turned to him with surprising suddenness and speed for such a big man, and he drew his face near to Chip's and asked in a low and penetrating voice, "She send you in here?"

It took a moment for Chip to realize that he was talking about Tina, not Stacey. Either way, though, the answer was going to be the same: "Huh?"

"Tina. She send you in here to talk to me? To size things up?"

Chip pushed past him to the sink. "Heck no."

"'Cause she and I used to have a thing, and then we didn't have it anymore, and then now we're maybe getting it started again."

"Huh?"

"You know. She had this other thing I didn't want to infringe on."

"Oh," said Chip.

"A steady thing. A relationship."

"Ahh," said Chip, working the towel dispenser.

"With a regular guy. A local guy. Not one of those girl-in-every-town cowboys like me."

"Sure," said Chip. "I get it." Although he didn't. Not quite. Not yet.

Buck took him by the shoulders. "We're square, then? She didn't send you in here to feel me out?"

"No."

"Because that would be just weird. Just too small-town. You know?"

"Sure."

"Good," said Buck. And he let him go.

"He's nuttier than he looks," Chip told Stacey on her break. "And I think he's kind of in love."

They were in the cooler with their jackets on, perched on piled cases of beer.

"Really?"

"Really."

"No."

"Yes."

"Tell me. How'd you get him to open up?"

"By not asking. By him thinking I was going to ask, and then him getting angry at me for maybe planning on asking, and then by just standing there while he spilled his guts. I can't explain it."

"Men," said Stacey. "And they say women talk."

"I *know*. It was weird."

She swung her legs. "So what'd he say?"

Chip zipped up his jacket. "He said he had a thing with Tina once, and then he didn't for a while, and now he thinks he's working on having it again."

"I take back what I said. That's the lamest non-gut-spilling I've ever heard."

"No. It's perfectly clear."

"OK, then. Explain it. And remember I don't have all night."

When he was through, Stacey understood that Tina and Buck had been involved for a while, probably back when Buck was first sizing up the mountain, but that it had ended when she threw him over for somebody else. Richie, she figured. Who else could it have been? Who else would Buck have shown that kind of deference to? And why else would Tina have taken Richie's new romance with the red-haired woman so personally? Everything about it made

sense, right down to Buck's avoiding Tina a couple of nights ago—
before he knew what was up with Richie and Miss Woodstock.

She explained it all back to Chip, just like that.

"Sure," he agreed. "They had a thing and then for a while they
didn't have it and now they kind of have it all over again. That's
what I said."

THIRTY-FOUR

The two of them left together, Tina and Buck.

Chip rolled his eyes. "Tina and Buck," he said. "Sounds like a couple of old-time country singers."

Jack laughed and pushed the cash drawer shut with his narrow stomach. "I believe they recorded 'Stand by Your Man,' did they not? About 1964."

Some middle-aged flatlander in a sweater with a pattern that looked like a psychedelic hopscotch course put his nose in. "That was Tammy Wynette," he said, as if anybody actually cared. "It was 1968."

"I'm picturing a soul-country mash-up," Stacey said. "Like with Tina Turner and that Buck what's his name. The one from *Hee Haw.*"

"Buck Rogers," Chip suggested.

The sweater guy pursed his lips and shook his head. "Kids," he said, and set his beer down hard. "It was Buck Owens. The Bakersfield Sound." If he meant to be participating, he was losing ground in a hurry. "Buck Owens and the Buckaroos."

Stacey teased him a little. "You sure it wasn't the Buccaneers?"

The guy with the sweater put his head down on the bar. "Sheesh," he said.

Pete came in at closing time. Jack was already half done counting receipts, so closing out the registers didn't take long, and Stacey signed out while they were finishing up. Chip waited for her in the foyer. They stepped out into the night together and they stood in the shoveled walkway for a minute, four cars in the near-empty lot under clear skies and a high canopy of stars precise as snowflakes. Chip kicked at a clump of snow. "So Tina and Buck have a thing."

"Apparently."

"I guess we could take their exit as confirmation."

"I guess we could."

"Just goes to show," he said. "There's no telling."

"Yeah. Well." She fished out keys and took a step toward her car.

"You want to talk a little more?"

How stupid was she? "About what?" Maybe it was just that everybody she saw lately seemed to have some big secret on his mind, but there it was. *About what?* As if he needed to give her an agenda.

"I don't know. I just thought maybe."

"You don't want to wake the sheriff, do you?"

He watched the hand where she held the keys as if it could give him some clue as to whether she would stay or go. "There's nobody to bother at my place," he said. "And it's in town. Not way out there in the boonies."

Stacey shivered. "You got any hot chocolate?"

"We could stop at the gas station. Get a quart of milk. I think I've got some Hershey's in the fridge."

"You're on," she said, making a break for her car.

She let Chip back out first. He drove an old army-green Wrangler, faded down and caked with grit and fanned all over with a crust of road salt blown up from the wheel wells. The thing had a sagging soft top that would have let in all kinds of air if it had been able to get up to highway speeds, which didn't look likely. Chip four-wheeled across the lot and stopped at the entrance to wait for Stacey.

The road back into town was empty at this hour—and the local law enforcement was pretty much known to be in bed—but Chip drove like an old woman going to church. Probably because he didn't want to splash. Stacey hung back and he slowed down even more. *This was some big change from Brian,* she caught herself thinking. Brian was always in a hurry. And that had never been more true than in their early days together, when they'd happened to be headed for her place or his.

Look where it had gotten him.

Look where it had gotten *her.*

So much for being in a hurry.

The night was brutally cold, and the snow and ice that had melted during the day had refrozen solid. Stacey looked up on the mountain and saw through the dense trees the gleam of the arc lights around the base lodge, that pool of white light that was always shining away up there. The eternal flame. It burned on and on, as if energy were unlimited. As if there were something up there to be guarded against by brilliant and constant light—thieves, maybe, or werewolves. Elsewhere in the woods and fields she saw single lights gleaming in the windows of houses and cottages and condos, more of them now than usual since Christmas was coming. Temporary people. There were no headlights, though, other than her own lighting on the back of Chip's Jeep and a couple of pinpoints in a pasture to the left where some lunatic was riding a snowmobile at this time of night. He must have been freezing himself half to death. The snowmobile seemed to be keeping pace with them—at least it was going in the same direction, paralleling their travel down the main road into town—but it was really hard to say on account of the distance. She heard the high hard buzzing of its engine, that was for sure.

A few houses began to appear and Chip signaled to turn left down a little lane winding toward the back side of the village, away from the commercial district. These little Vermont towns had a way of ending abruptly, and you were never more aware of it than in the dark of the night. On one side, the blank-looking library building with its single arc lamp and a row of houses with maybe one lit window apiece; on the other side, nothing. Nothing but that pasture with the snowmobile tearing around in it, coming closer toward them on its course and turning now to run parallel again. The pasture was twenty or thirty acres of flat land pressed out smooth and running straight on until the next ridge of mountain rose up. A stream ran through the middle of it, now frozen over and probably making no more than a slight indentation in the white landscape. Signs along the road called it a river, although Stacey couldn't figure out why, it was so small. She got the idea that the snowmobiler might be following its course through the hummocks of snow out in the field. He might have even been down in it—did they do that? did they ride down there in the riverbed? was it more dangerous, or less?—she thought he might have been down in it, anyhow, since he was invisible all of a sudden, either down past the line of her vision or else behind something. She couldn't make out anything but the gleam of his headlights hitting a tree or a fence-post or a high drift of snow now and then.

She drove along thinking how much she hated snowmobiles. They were like powerboats on a mountain lake. Worse than that. They were like Jet Skis. What was the use of them? If you couldn't snowshoe or ski or toboggan or something, if you couldn't get close to nature without making a racket and ruining it for everybody else, you should just stay home.

The lights of the snowmobile appeared again, airborne this time and angled toward her. She'd have thought the machine was riding up and down an invisible hill or an ocean wave, pretty much like its offensive equivalent the Jet Ski, judging by how the lights rose up above the contour of the pasture and peaked for a second and then swung down again. Judging by how the headlights and the machine behind them hesitated in midair and then plummeted back toward the ground.

She turned on the radio for a little Sheryl Crow.

The snowmobile was pointed toward her now, humping over drifts and boulders and probably even fence lines in the field.

Chip kept driving at that painfully slow pace, and she stayed close behind. She wondered if he was a Sheryl Crow fan.

The guy on the snowmobile must have been drunk. Otherwise he couldn't have tolerated the cold. Otherwise he would have slowed down a little. He disappeared behind a snowbank and the pasture went dark again. If not for the dopplering of his engine, she'd have thought he'd hit something and come to a stop.

Stacey asked herself if all she really wanted to do was have some fun.

And the snowmobile appeared again from out of nowhere, leaping over the drift that divided the pasture from the road, slamming into her front fender as if possessed by a death wish.

The crash stopped the snowmobile cold and killed its engine, but one headlight was still on, pointing straight up into the night like a Hollywood searchlight. Stacey's Subaru was stopped dead, too. Chip steered his Wrangler into a snowbank and jumped out just in time to see the snowmobile guy peel himself off the road, give himself a shake, and take off like a bat out of hell.

It was either chase him or see about Stacey, which meant he had no actual choice.

The snowmobile's fuel tank had split open and gas was creeping

in a narrow stream down the road. He stepped over it and pulled
Stacey's door open to find her perfectly fine, a little shaken up,
more worried about the guy who'd hit her than about herself. She
put one leg out of the car and started coming to her feet, and he
half embraced her to help.

"I guess he's OK," she said.

"Apparently. He ran off like a crazy person."

Absent the sounds of their engines, the night was dead quiet.
There wasn't even any breeze. The two of them stood together
in the half dark, making for themselves a small spot of warmth between the empty pasture on one side and the dimly lit town on the
other and the stars overhead, and after a while Chip suggested that
they really ought to call the sheriff.

"Dang it," said Guy Ramsey to nobody in particular.

He came stamping back from the library parking lot where the
snowmobile guy's trail had run out. Whoever it was had left no
tracks in the icy hardpack around the machine he'd plowed into
Stacey's car, but in his hurry to get away he'd dropped a flask between there and the library. It still sparkled in the starlight and had
caught the sheriff's eye right off. From there the fugitive had left
tracks in a dusting of fresh snow that had blown over the banks
along the driveway, but the tracks had given out in the lot that the
library shared with the phone company and the chiropractor's office. It'd been no use to keep looking.

"Dang it." Guy stooped to pick up the flask. The cap was off and
a little whiskey had run out onto the snow. It was a steel flask with
a leather covering that looked as if it had been through the war. He
picked it up in a gloved hand and sniffed it as if there might be any
doubt. "These guys," he said. And then, walking over, "How's the
car?"

"Won't start," said Chip.

"It won't start," said Stacey. She could handle this.

Guy set the flask down on a smooth place on the ice at his feet. "Sometimes there's a fuel shutoff, kicks in when you're in an accident. You got a manual in the glove box?"

"Not that I know of."

He checked and she was right. He lay down in the front seat and shined his flashlight under the dashboard and didn't find what he was looking for. So much for that. He shivered and got out of the car. "We'll get somebody to look it over in the morning. Meanwhile how about you put it in neutral and steer her over to the side of the road, while Chip and I give her a push."

The slick surface underfoot made pushing the Subaru a challenge, but after a few tries they managed to wrangle it over to the roadside. As they struggled and rested and put their backs into it and occasionally fell down cursing, Guy asked Chip if he'd gotten a look at the guy on the snowmobile.

"Nope. It happened pretty quick."

"I guess."

"It was just headlights pointing everywhere, and then *bang.* That and the engine, you know. Loud one second and dead the next. Then he was gone."

"You get a look at what he had on?"

"I didn't see *a thing.* Not a thing."

They got the car up against the snowbank and he asked Stacey the same questions. She hadn't seen all that much more than Chip had, thanks to the height of the snowmobile when it was on the ground against the car. The guy had fallen off the other side of it, she thought, but he was up and gone before she got much of a look.

"I guess the bright side is that nobody was hurt," Guy said.

"He seemed to be in good shape," Stacey said.

"Sometimes it's just adrenaline."

"I guess."

Guy and Chip pushed the wrecked snowmobile to the side of the road. All three of them stood together in the cold for a few minutes, and then Guy asked Stacey if she needed a ride home. She said she did, and they took her skis out of the back of the Subaru and went.

THIRTY-FIVE

Guy drove to work early and he dropped Stacey at the mountain on the way. She had the number of the garage keyed into her cell, and when she located some cell service in the parking lot and made the call, the guy on the other end wasn't surprised to hear from her. "I seen that Subie on the way in this morning," he said. "What happened?"

"I was attacked by an unidentified flying snowmobile."

"I seen that, too. Tough luck. Key in it?"

This struck Stacey instantly as a dumb question, but as it turned out she had an appropriately dumb answer. "Yeah," she said. "I guess it is."

The mechanic said he'd go check it out, which left Stacey with nothing to do but ski.

Guy didn't have to work hard to find out who owned the snowmobile, although finding out who'd been driving it was going to be a different job altogether. The phone was ringing when he unlocked the office at a quarter after eight—Mildred didn't start until nine, although she usually showed up fifteen minutes early to start the coffee and crank up the radiators—and he caught it just before it ticked over to the service.

"I want to report a stolen snowmobile." Just like that.

"Is it yours?" asked Guy. He hadn't slept well and it was cold in the office and there wasn't any coffee, and the guy on the other end didn't even have the manners to introduce himself.

"Of course it's mine. That's how come I know it's stolen."

"Maybe you ought to get into law enforcement." Guy considered telling him that the stolen vehicle was already found, but decided not to.

The caller was imperturbable—or else so perturbed already that he couldn't be pushed any further. He started ticking off the specifics, like he'd written them down on a piece of paper. He probably had. "It's a Polaris Switchback, 2006 model year."

"That'd be a blue one, right?"

"Blue and white. Yeah."

Guy took down the information as if he didn't know it already, and then got the guy's name and address and phone. His name was Larry Van Horn—*capital V, space, capital H*—and he owned a gas station in Rutland. He'd come down last night cross lots, one trail after another, to meet some friends for dinner. His sled—lots of people around here called them sleds, as if a hundred-horse snowmobile were something a little kid would coast down a hill on after a good snowfall—was gone when they came out.

"How'd you get home?"

"Friend give me a lift."

"Good for you," said Guy.

"That's what friends are for."

"So why'd you wait until now to make the report?" Guy wasn't suspicious and he didn't really wonder why Van Horn had waited—he was glad he'd waited, come to that—but it was good form.

"Because I figured you wouldn't be around in the middle of the night."

"You figured right. I appreciate it."

"So," said Van Horn. "You want me to come in? Fill something out? Do I need to sign something?"

"No. That shouldn't be necessary."

"Because I'm working all day."

"Like I said. Won't be necessary."

"Good. Because I'm working."

"I know you're working," said Guy.

"What do you think my chances are?"

"Of recovery?"

"Yeah."

"I'd say they're pretty good."

"Really?"

"Yeah. Pretty good. We get 'em back a lot of times."

"Honest?"

"Honest." His stomach was rumbling for coffee.

"They don't take 'em somewhere, wholesale 'em? Sell 'em for parts?"

"You're thinking of BMWs in big cities."

"Maybe."

"Sleds get taken by teenagers, usually. They ride 'em and wreck 'em."

"I was hoping—"

"I know you were. Anybody would. Get used to the idea, though. You're probably not going to like the looks of it when we get it back. If we get it back."

"You find anything, call me," Van Horn said.

"Absolutely," said Guy. And then, after a second: "One more question. You ride much?"

"Enough. At least I used to. Till now."

"You carry a flask?"

"I do. It's for emergency use only."

"I'm sure it is," said Guy.

On the lift Stacey asked Chip how the hot chocolate had been, and it took him a minute to figure out what she was talking about.

"Dang!" he said. "We didn't even stop for the milk."

"If we had remembered and gone that way . . ." She bounced her head from side to side.

"Everything would have turned out different."

"Yeah. It would."

"Man, oh, man. A minute one way or another, and the whole world changes."

"Maybe not the whole world. But a few things." She might have been thinking of the car and she might have been thinking of the hot chocolate and she might have been thinking of something else entirely, but she wasn't about to let on. Not to Chip.

Guy made the coffee and opened the valves on the radiators and caught up on some paperwork. He gave the mechanic a call just in case Stacey had forgotten. He told himself he wasn't taking a paternal interest or anything, just looking after his own obligation to keep the streets clear. Mildred came in right on time and admired his coffee out loud and helped him to another cup. That was Mildred all over, old-fashioned as she could be. A relic of his own parents' generation, really. Any time a man got anywhere near something that looked like kitchen equipment and didn't either kill himself or burn down the house, she seemed to think it was worth a presidential commendation.

He thought about dragging out the chains and fetching the wrecked snowmobile himself, and he thought about calling the mechanic again and having him bring it back to the township building, but in the end he waited until he had about two swallows of coffee left and called Larry Van Horn back with the bad news. The guy had a gas station. Probably a tow truck, too. Let him take care of it.

Since Stacey didn't have a car, Chip told her she could leave her gear in the patrol shack. The building was empty when she finished for the day, except for a first-aid volunteer who sat at the desk with his feet up and a copy of some real estate directory open on his lap. Once it was obvious that Stacey wasn't limping, he didn't give her a second look.

Minus her skis and boots, she started hiking down the access road. As usual at this time of day, she was surprised by how many cars were still arriving at the mountain. The best skiing happened first thing in the morning, no question about it. Her instinct was to consider anybody starting this late a pretender at worst and a dilettante at best. On the other hand, she supposed you had to give them the benefit of the doubt. Especially the flatlanders, who advertised themselves by their out-of-state plates. They were probably just getting here, and they wanted to get a few runs in before tomorrow. Still, she couldn't help but feel a little bit superior.

The road was narrow with snowdrifts and she kept to the right because traffic was usually lighter going down than coming up and she'd get splashed less that way. It was a pain enough to have to walk all the way to the Binding, without getting drenched right at the start. Then again, maybe she wouldn't have to walk the whole distance. She'd stop at the garage to see about the car, and if it was drivable she'd take it and make do.

Midway down, near the entrance to the lower parking lot, a car pulled up alongside her and honked its horn. She didn't lift her head. They were probably honking at somebody coming up. But the car slowed and kept pace with her and the passenger side window slid down, so she had no choice but to look.

It was Richie Paxton, in what passed for a generous mood. "You need a lift?"

She wondered if he'd ask the same of one of his own employees, especially one of the foreigners whose low-paid muscle made the place go. She didn't bother wondering for long.

"I'm going right past the Binding," he said, "if you could use a lift?"

"Sure," she said. And he stopped the car and she got in. "Thanks."

It smelled like Brian in there. That is, it smelled like the leather-lined luxury of a new and very expensive German car. It didn't smell bad.

She told him about her car and about how he could just drop her at the garage, which wasn't really that far. Still, she appreciated the ride.

"So it's fixed?"

"I doubt it. But if it'll run, I'll take it."

"You've got insurance." He said it as if everybody did.

Insurance, in fact, was a whole different kettle of fish, and Stacey hadn't wanted to think about it. Just paying the deductible would be impossible without hitting up her folks, which she didn't want to do. And as for the policy itself, well, that whole business smelled like Brian, too. She'd rather not go there. So she just sighed and looked out the window. "We'll see how it goes," she said. "Wish me luck."

They turned and motored into town. The car was quieter inside than the peak of the mountain on a bright and empty day. A person could get used to this kind of thing all over again.

The garage was up a side street past Bud's and the pizza joint. As they turned the corner Stacey and Richie both swiveled their heads to see Danny bump open the pizza joint's door with his back and stumble out, a slice in his hand and his head bent over it wolfishly.

He turned and squinted at the Mercedes's tinted glass, and then gave up and shuffled over toward Bud's.

"There goes trouble," said Richie. "Trouble with a limp."

"Did he get that in Vietnam?"

"Even if he didn't, he'd tell you he did. Vietnam is the cause of every problem that son of a bitch ever had."

As obvious as it was that Richie had no time for Danny Bowman, Stacey didn't know if it was something personal or just part of his habitual way of looking at the world. So in spite of her loathing for the guy, she took a sympathetic tone rather than pile on. "It's a shame, you know? To end up like that."

"He's been that way from the word go."

"But he's a lot older than you." Let him take that for a compliment if he wanted to. It was true. And Richie couldn't have known him forever.

"People around here don't have many secrets."

Which Stacey knew to be something other than true.

"Besides," he went on, "defending that one is a loser's game." He slowed the car to a crawl as they neared the garage, and he began to tell her about Danny's unannounced visit to his office. How he claimed to know something about his brother's murder. How he wanted money for the information. Money. Could she believe that?

Stacey laughed a nervous laugh and shook her head. "Right here'll be fine," she said. Her Subaru, looking a little more forlorn than usual, was parked at the edge of the lot ahead. But Richie wouldn't stop the car. So she couldn't get out and she couldn't stay. It was like water torture.

"No prob," he said, not raising his foot from the pedal. "Door-to-door service is our specialty."

She unlatched her seat belt and the car complained with the dignified Teutonic sounding of a bell.

He told her how Danny had claimed to see somebody leave the

scene of the crime. What did she think of that? Danny wanted money for information about some cleaning woman leaving the scene of the crime.

"Is that what he said?"

"Oh, he was clear about the money."

"I mean the cleaning woman?"

"*Some woman,* he said. I don't know." He eased off on the gas but the car had so much weight and momentum that it didn't slow down any. "I didn't ask."

"That's my car right there," said Stacey, reaching for the door handle.

"Hmm." He nodded. "That's either a good sign or a bad one. Either it's out there ready to go, or it's out there waiting for parts."

"Let's hope for the first. And thanks for the lift." The car was drifting now, just inching along slowly enough that she could probably get out, its big tires crunching over ice and grit and gravel.

"My pleasure," said Richie. "You want me to wait? I'm going right past the Binding, like I said." Finally hitting the brakes.

"Thanks," she said. "Thanks a lot. But I'll take my chances."

THIRTY-SIX

The car started, and that was good enough for her. The collision had bashed the front fender in against the tire, but the mechanic had been able to bend it back with a crowbar so that it didn't cut the rubber and the wheel spun free. She was good to go, as long as she didn't care how it looked. Which she didn't.

She showered in the employee locker room—mein Gott, *those Germans knew a thing or two about sanitation*—and clocked in early. Pete didn't mind. There was always something to do. Jack set her to work inventorying stock in the liquor closet behind the kitchen, and when she was done with that she cut lemons and limes and oranges. All the while she thought about Danny. Danny who'd been doing his best to get her in trouble, first with Guy and then with Richie. Guy hadn't bitten, but she wondered if one day Richie might. Or if in fact he already had. What if he'd been playing dumb about the cleaning lady business? What if he'd meant it just as a hint of what he really knew—that is, what if Danny had identified her? It could mean that Richie thought she was involved—unless Richie'd killed his brother himself, in which case she might make a very nice distraction.

And then there was Danny's limp.

Somewhere around her third lemon Guy showed up. "I see she runs," he said. "The car."

"She does."

"Good for you." Guy stood at the bar with his hat in his hands. "Very good. The fellow who owns that snowmobile can't say the same thing."

"You found him?" So much for Danny's limp.

"Yes and no. He found us."

She put down the knife.

"Turns out he's a solid citizen from up in Rutland. Got his sled stolen out from under him last night, right in front of Vinnie's."

Jack came through the kitchen door and suggested that maybe the guy from Rutland ought to start frequenting a better class of restaurant, and Guy laughed along with him for a moment.

"So it was stolen," Stacey said. Here came a vision of Danny Bowman again, limping right back into the picture.

"Stolen."

"Which means nothing's solved. Not really."

Jack grinned. "Hey," he said, "don't go making the sheriff's job any harder than it already is."

"She's right. Now we've got theft. On top of reckless endangerment and God knows what else."

"Assault with a deadly weapon," Stacey said.

"I don't know that I'd go that far."

"You never know."

Richie Paxton swung by the Binding after he'd run his errand. He locked his car up tight and went in, leaving his coat in the foyer and not bothering to stamp the snow from his boots. The very picture of blasé entitlement, he didn't even wipe them on the mat. Stacey took note of the omission, and wondered how in the world his wife could put up with him. She figured if the price was right, some people could put up with almost anything.

"So," he said as he picked out one of the two or three empty stools, "I see they got you running?"

Stacey pushed away from the back bar.

"Your car," he said. "They got it running, by the look of it."

"Oh, the car. Yeah."

"Great."

"Uh-huh. Can I get you a Corona"—she paused ever so slightly, just half a beat, barely enough to remind him if he was remindable, and then finished—"Light?"

"Got to watch those carbs." Richie patted himself on the belly, which was probably fifteen pounds less flat than he thought.

"You know it."

Some real estate agency had a Christmas party going on in the dining room, and they seemed to be drinking more than they were eating. The orders came flying in without interruption—almost no beer to speak of, though, and only a slow trickle of wine by the bottle. Very little of the straight stuff, either. The bulk of the orders— maybe it was a holiday thing, Stacey didn't know, but it struck her as weird anyhow—were for mixed drinks of exceptional complexity and towering alcohol content. Things that glistened and sparkled like the Swarovski crystals that half of the agents were draped in. Things in colors that were just plain unnatural. Things that kept Stacey digging through the *Old Mr. Boston's* book like some kind of gin-soaked Talmudic scholar.

She was in front of Richie, running her finger along a recipe for something that called for champagne and grappa, when he reached out and held the book open for her. "Thanks," she said.

"They've got you on your toes tonight."

"Me and my car. Running like crazy."

Richie laughed and showed his teeth. "You and your car. That's right."

She measured something viscous and red that neither she nor Richie had seen before and that didn't look especially drinkable, and then she measured it again to make sure. Like it was nitro or something.

"Tell me," he said, "when's your night off?"

Tina Montero heard it. Above the clatter of the jukebox, above the steady hum of conversation in the bar, above the raucous laughter of the real estate crowd in the dining room, Tina heard it all the way down at the other end of the bar. She lowered her glass and said, low in pitch but with penetrating volume, "You've got to be kidding me."

"No, no, no, no, no, no, no." Richie rapped *Old Mr. Boston's* with his knuckles. "That's not it at all. Give me a little credit."

"Nobody gets credit around here," said Jack. "House rules."

What a bunch of kidders.

Richie clarified. "We need a *babysitter* in a couple nights." He looked at Tina and lifted his eyebrows. Times had changed. Everybody was all grown up and then some. "Rotary Club Christmas party, over at the golf club. And all the little high school girls are tied up during the week."

Stacey stayed out of it, but Jack spilled the beans. "Sounds good," he said. "She's off in a couple nights, right Stace?"

"Right."

"You want the job?" Richie asked. "The pay's lousy but the tips are good."

"Then it's just like here," she said. "Except for the tips." And then, wondering if maybe Richie was up to something but figuring that even if he was he apparently didn't mind everybody in the whole world knowing about it, she said, "Sure. Why not? What else have I got to do?"

. . .

"Damn," Chip said when he got the word. He hadn't come in for a drink, but just to check on Stacey and find out how the car was. See if there'd been any news about the snowmobile or the guy driving it. He ended up having two beers that he hadn't meant to drink. "Damn. I thought maybe we might do something."

A Patriots game had started on the widescreen overhead, and although the sound was down it may as well have been blasting for all the attention that anybody was paying to him and Stacey. "Do something?" she said. It was a question.

"I don't know." He sat on the stool with his thatch of yellow hair all squashed from his hat, and his nose and cheeks still ruddy from a very full day on the slopes. "Something."

"Like you and me, you mean? The two of us?"

Chip squirmed a little. "With your night off and all. I was thinking."

"You were going to ask me out?"

Chip was doing his best to cover it, but his pained look explained everything that he couldn't bring himself to say about the way things were between men and women these days. When was it a date and when wasn't it? Who got to make the decision? Who was in charge? What was expected of him? He nodded a couple of times and shrugged and made some noises that sounded like "Yeah, well, I guess, uh-huh," and then he hid behind a sip of his Long Trail.

"You snooze," said Stacey, "you lose."

"I guess you do. I guess I did. Sorry."

Stacey put her hand flat on the bar not far from his. Far enough that it didn't count, but close enough that he might interpret it any way he liked. "Don't worry about it. Next time."

"Next time."

"Hey, it's coming on Christmas anyhow. Everyplace'd be mobbed."

. . .

A little freezing rain had fallen, and when Stacey went to her car something seemed to be scratched into buildup on the driver's side window. Just her car, she was pretty sure, and just the driver's side. Nobody else's. She checked. Jack's car was still there and Jamal the busboys', too, and their windows seemed untouched. Pete Hardwick's car was alongside Jack's but since it hadn't been there more than half an hour it was still warm and pretty much free of ice.

What was scratched into the window looked like words but maybe not. It could have been just a raw and sharp-edged squiggle. It looked angry, but it also looked kind of offhand. Accidental or incidental. Like a person had just walked by and done it with his keys for laughs. Plus it was half gone under new rainfall, so you couldn't really tell much. Maybe a couple of guys had stopped here on their way to their cars and gotten into an argument about the football game, and one of them had diagrammed something to make a point. Yeah. It was probably that. She couldn't make heads or tails of those football diagrams anyhow.

Still, just in case, she hesitated before she got in. She looked around the lot, expecting to see somebody lurking somewhere. Danny, or The Claw—or Danny The Claw—hiding out among the chain saw grizzly bears like he'd done that time before. But there was nothing. Nobody. She put the edge of her mittened hand on the glass and peered into the car thinking that maybe somebody was hiding in the backseat; but as far as she could see it was empty.

All the same she didn't trust herself. And she sure as hell didn't trust The Claw. So she went back inside and used the bathroom, and then she stood with the ladies' room door propped open, prepared to kill time until Jack or Pete or the busboy was ready to leave.

Jamal was nowhere to be seen—maybe he'd gotten a lift home with somebody else and left his car, who knew?—but as it turned out

Jack didn't take more than a minute or two finishing up. He snapped a little salute at Pete and asked if they were square and when Pete told him they were he left, hesitating only to refold a towel that Stacey had left bunched up on the bar. He was surprised to meet her coming into the foyer from the other direction. "I thought you knocked off a while ago," he said.

"Time flies." She opened the front door for both of them and stood in it while he buttoned up his coat.

Once they were in the lot she didn't waste any time. Before Jack had his keys out she had flung open all four of the Subaru's doors and the trunk, too, which caused him to give her a curious look.

"They always freeze shut in this kind of weather," she said. "I'm just making sure."

"Oh. Got it." He shook his head and got in and started up his car, then came back out with a scraper.

Stacey started her engine and raced around slamming everything shut again, and when the car was closed up she began scraping, too. She started on the driver's side window. Now that a few more minutes had passed, she discovered that she was less sure that there'd been anything scratched into the ice. Either way, she put her back into it and scraped the whole thing clean.

A few miles away, in the cranked-back front seat of a Lincoln Town Car sitting in the unlit parking lot behind the Winter Park Condos, Danny Bowman groaned in his sleep as if a goose had just walked over his grave.

THIRTY-SEVEN

Stacey scraped as fast as she could, because Jack drove a little two-door with tiny windows and he'd have it cleaned off in no time. He'd be done and gone, and she'd be here in the dark with just her little plastic ice scraper for company. As it turned out he hung around until she was all set to go and had given him a little wave for confirmation. A gentleman of the old school. What had happened to guys like that, anyway?

The drive home to the Ramsey place had never felt longer, and not only because the roads were treacherously slick with frozen rain. Even the drive to the center of town, such as it was, was desolate and endless. Jack had gone the other way out of the lot—he lived in the woods on this side of town with his longtime girlfriend, an RN on night shifts at the hospital two counties away—and she limped alone into the village center with the road slick beneath her and that crushed fender threatening her left front tire and one of her headlights out of whack. Apparently the mechanic hadn't noticed it. It pointed up a little bit and slightly off to the left, which she could see would be trouble if she ran into oncoming traffic. *That* wasn't going to happen anytime soon. Certainly not tonight.

The pasture where the snowmobile had been tearing around the night before was empty and still and covered with a gleaming film of frozen rain. The library on the side street was dark except for its arc lamp, and the houses around it were dark, too. She turned her head and looked down the street as if she knew which house Chip's apartment was in, but her ignorance didn't matter since they were all utterly black and shut down tight. Other than the lamp over the library steps, the sole light from down there was a brief reflection of her cockeyed headlamp in the taillights of a parked car. Only that and nothing more.

She crept on.

The gas station in the middle of town was lit up as usual, and as she came near she could see the night clerk behind the counter, leaning wearily on his forearms, his eyes fastened on a wall-mounted TV above her line of sight. His hair was slicked back and his eyes were sinking into big dark half circles and his skin was the color of wax. A pack of cigarettes hung in the pocket of his shirt. One of those underemployed guys who never came out in the daylight and lived on cigarettes and coffee, in the sickly yellow fluorescent light he looked like a corpse, propped up to worship the TV.

She turned on Sheryl Crow and shook off a case of the fantods. And just then, in the light from over the pumps, she picked out something—just the smallest sparkling glint of a hint of something—on the passenger side floor mat. A crystal of rock salt, maybe. Or a chip of ice that had fallen in when the door was open and hadn't melted yet. Yes. Probably that. Definitely that. She considered turning into the station lot and stopping beneath the lights to check, but she told herself that it was a stupid idea. It wasn't her engagement ring down there. She'd searched the car a million times. There was just no way. So she kept her hands on the wheel and her eyes on the road—not daring to break her concentration even to switch on the dome light and check—and she slid on thin ice through the village and out the other side, toward home.

The idea of it was still troubling her when she skated the Subaru down the narrow and tree-lined alleyway that passed for Ramsey Road, and once she'd drawn the car to a slow stop alongside the house she hit the dome light. Not even killing the engine first. Not even waiting for the light to come on automatically when she opened the door. And sure enough. It was the ring. Her engagement ring. A year's pay, at least—tips included—lying there on that grimy mat like something from a gum ball machine.

She snatched it up and ran into the house.

In the morning she'd find a penny and a nickel and part of a linty orange Tic Tac on the floor mat, too, and she'd realize that the accident with the snowmobile had knocked them all loose from someplace. She'd look further and discover the crack in the bottom of the cup holder down which they'd all vanished like Alice down the rabbit hole.

But in the meantime, she was satisfied with a miracle.

The day dawned brilliant, with wide hot blades of white sunlight streaking in through Stacey's uncurtained window to rouse her up. The freezing rain that had blown through overnight was over, and it had left the world to sparkle like the diamond she'd recovered from the passenger side floor mat. Maybe more. *Yes*, she thought as she sat up in bed and looked out the window and watched the ice-coated branches of trees sway and shimmer in the morning light. *Maybe more.*

That bright world out there was all she needed. It was going to be cold on the mountain today, and the conditions would suck, but who cared. It was gorgeous. It wouldn't last forever. So she jumped out of bed and got going.

There was a Christmas tree up in the family room, and the whole house smelled green. Lovely. She found the switch and turned it on and sat for a moment on the couch in front of it, missing home a little but not too much. There were packages underneath it already. One was bigger than the rest and wrapped more formally— gold and silver instead of green and red, a stiff bow instead of none at all—and she recognized the signs instantly. She unfolded herself from the couch and walked to it. Sure enough, it said TO STACEY, FROM MOM AND DAD. Who knows how long ago they'd sent it. Her mother was usually ready for the holidays months in advance. Good for Megan and Guy for keeping it a secret until now. She permitted herself a little pang of guilt over having sent her folks as little as she had, but you didn't get much choice here in the woods. And she couldn't have afforded much anyhow. Still.

Enough of that. She rid herself of whatever sentimentality was starting to creep up by picturing Brian giving some extravagant gift to somebody else. Anybody else. Whoever happened to be available at the moment. And then she went into the kitchen and helped herself to a cup of coffee.

When Guy came down they talked about the tree for a minute. Stacey's parents had gone artificial when she was in second or third grade, and it had been forever since she'd smelled the real thing indoors. Guy said he'd cut it himself the afternoon before. He'd picked Jim up after school and they'd gone out in the woods behind the house with the chain saw and a rope and a sled that the kids had outgrown years before. All very Norman Rockwell, except maybe for the detail of the chain saw. They'd gotten it inside just before the freezing rain hit, which was good.

Guy stood there in his bathrobe watching his oatmeal come to a boil. He crossed his arms and asked her if she had any plans for Christmas. Not if she was going home, on account of he knew about the package. She told him no, not exactly. She'd be working.

Skiing. The usual. He said they'd be going to church on Christmas Eve at eleven, and that Megan figured she might want to come along if she weren't working; but he understood. If she wanted, she could join them to open gifts in the morning—that is, if she wasn't in too big a hurry to get on the slopes. She thanked him and said she'd like that.

He left it there and said once more that he was glad to see that her car was running. She said she was glad, too, because she didn't know how she'd have paid for it if the damage had been much worse. Or how she could have gotten along without it. In Boston a car was a liability, but up here it was a necessity. Funny, she said. You associate cars with the city, but you can't live in the country without one. Once they were on the subject of the car, it wasn't a reach to get back to the snowmobile.

"I've got a funny feeling about that guy Danny Bowman," she said.

"That's his specialty."

"More than that."

"Oh?" Lifting the lid of his oatmeal to check that it wasn't simmering too high or too low. "How's that?"

"I think he's got some kind of weird vendetta against me."

"You?" Guy cocked his neck and twisted his mouth, and sent her a look that said she was as nuts as Danny was.

She told him how far back it went. All the way back to the days when she used to sleep in her car behind Bud's.

"When you *what?*"

"Tell me you didn't know."

"I didn't know. I didn't ask. I didn't care."

"Well," said Stacey, "that's where I was coming from when I showed up in your driveway with everything I owned in the back of the car." It had looked like a rat's nest, as she remembered it, but apparently Megan hadn't said word one to her husband.

Guy shook his head. "I thought you were smarter than that."

"Smart's got nothing to do with it."

"So I see. It is dangerous, though. You've got to admit. Even around here. God knows what kind of trouble you could have gotten into."

"Right."

"Plus, it's cold."

"I noticed."

He laughed. "It's hard not to."

"It's hard not to notice the trouble I could have gotten into, too. Like how Danny's been stalking me. Ever since."

Stalking. That's what it was. At least it was as good a way as any to describe it.

She told him how everything got started, with The Night of The Claw. She told him how Danny had shaken her down for money just because he'd seen her leaving the Snowfield Condos. She told him how she'd brushed him off at first and then how later on she'd given him just a little bit, purely out of panic. She told him she was pretty sure he'd told the same story or some variation of it to Richie Paxton.

"This thing with the scratching. Was it before or after you started sleeping in the condos?"

"It must have been after."

"Then why were you in the car?"

"When you see what I found in that condo, it makes you kind of swear off poking your nose in where it doesn't belong."

"And get a room at the sheriff's house instead."

She drained her coffee cup. "Absolutely. It's like protective custody."

"Or sleeping in the jailhouse." He watched the lid of his oatmeal pot bounce with the steam underneath it.

Unfortunately, even protective custody wasn't perfect. Even sleeping in the jailhouse had its limits. Stacey went on to describe the limp she'd seen Danny walking around with on the morning after the snowmobile accident—and the scratching that she'd seen on her car window again the night before.

Guy shrugged. "I don't know. You might be pushing it a little hard now, don't you think?"

"Frankly," she said, "I'm not sure that I'm pushing it hard enough."

THIRTY-EIGHT

Stacey rinsed her cup and put it in the dishwasher. "I think he's trying to draw attention to me, because I think he's got something to hide."

"Something to hide? Where would he put it?" Guy raised his shoulders and laughed. "Just kidding," he said when he got a load of Stacey's serious look. "I mean, you know, the guy's homeless."

"I know."

"So where would he put *anything*."

"You know what I mean."

"Yeah. I do. Sorry. It's just—"

Stacey let it out. "I think he might have something to do with David's murder."

"I don't," said Guy. Just like that. He pulled out a chair and sat down at the table. "Look," he said. "Just because a person's crazy or off-balance or peculiar or whatever you want to call it, it doesn't mean he's dangerous. It doesn't mean he'd kill somebody."

Stacey didn't answer.

"It doesn't mean he'd help *somebody else* kill somebody, either. Or keep it a secret if he knew."

Stacey still didn't answer.

"I've known Danny forever."

"I don't doubt that."

"Really. For my whole life."

"Just don't tell me he's harmless."

"I'm not telling you that. I'm not saying he's harmless. What I *am* saying is that there are things I don't believe he's got in him."

"I don't think anybody knows what he's got in him."

Guy looked up at the clock on the wall, clearly wondering if he had time to grab his shower and stay on schedule before the oatmeal was ready. The idea that he might be putting his morning routine above the questions she was asking raised Stacey's blood pressure, but she resolved not to let it show.

"I just want you to consider it, is all. Just consider it."

"I'll consider it."

"You will."

"I will. I promise."

"Thanks," said Stacey. "I appreciate it."

Guy stood, and went on up to take his shower.

"I got you a Christmas present," Chip said.

Stacey was tossing her gloves and hat in the usual pile at the far end of the bench—even she realized that it had somehow become the usual thing, a routine, and she wondered how much of it was convenience and how much of it was human nature and how much of it was the simple habitual business of going about your life in a mountain town during ski season. Also how much of it was this growing—was it growing? she couldn't say or else she didn't want to—this growing sense of connection with Chip.

And now he said he'd gotten her a Christmas present. What next?

He ran one hand through his hair and reached his other hand

into his pocket and pulled it out. A crumpled and coffee-stained
Customer Appreciation Card from right here at Judge Roy Beans,
with all ten circles stamped. It was good for a free cup of coffee.
"Ladies' choice," he said. "Don't say I never did anything for you."

"Wow. Thanks."

"I bet they'll even make it a double, if you ask nice."

The place was jumping and the lines were long. The counterman was doing his best to keep up—a counterman and a couple of
counterkids, too, on account of the holiday rush—but the situation
looked hopeless. Stacey shrugged out of her jacket and Chip checked
his watch. Couldn't she get anybody's complete attention today?

She got in line behind a woman probably her age or maybe a
year or two older at most, a mother from Long Island by the sound
of her, a high-gloss individual with two kids in tow and a fur jacket
that was both appalling and appealing at the same time. Stacey
realized that every single thing about the woman struck her that
way. The impossibly perfect hair and makeup. The healthy but ob-
noxious kids. The gorgeous but ruinously expensive pocketbook
that hung from her shoulder. Its certain contents. The life she
doubtlessly led.

She looked at the Customer Appreciation Card and decided that
it was a pretty nice present after all. She decided in fact that it was a
much nicer present than anything Chip might have gotten her with
his father's money. By a million miles. And when she finally got to
the front of the line and the counterman did indeed let her have her
usual double—and stamped her own card, too, even though he
wasn't supposed to—she splurged on a scratch-off lottery ticket and
brought it back for Chip.

Merry Christmas, Baby.

The lottery ticket had some kind of a quasifestive reindeer theme
going on, and Chip took his time scratching away the squares one at

a time. You had to reveal the same dollar amount three times, or else twice plus a little line drawing of a wrapped package that functioned as a wild card. Chip called out the figures as if he were hosting a game show, and it took a while to work all the way through the grid, and when he was through he'd gotten nothing out of it but a few minutes of fun. Which was enough. More than enough, really.

While Chip was amusing himself and her, too, Stacey doctored her double espresso and drank it off like medicine. A pack of one-ski-trip-a-year flatlanders in puffy rainbow-colored jackets and outlandish fleece hats that made them look like court jesters and crested dinosaurs and moose—*wow*, Stacey thought, *it really must be getting close to Christmas*—had ganged up near their booth and were eyeing it without much in the way of subtlety. Two of them had their ski boots on already, in naked defiance of the sign on the door. Stacey had seen that sign a hundred times and never believed that it could be necessary until now.

"Hey." She tilted her head toward them and whispered to Chip. "Where do you think they parked the clown car?"

He clamped his lips into a thin line. "Right next to the ambulance."

One of the flatlanders, an over-the-hill frat boy with shades and a two-day growth of beard, bumped the table and asked if they were through. If they didn't mind, he said, those black diamonds over at Spruce weren't going to ski themselves.

"Well, no," said Stacey, standing and gathering her gear.

Chip stood, shrugged into his patroller jacket, and told the guy that he'd see him out there.

Outside the door Chip asked her if she wanted to do the night-skiing thing again—skin up the hill and shoot back down like they'd done before. He was thinking tomorrow night, after she was through at the Paxtons'.

They stood side by side under the eave, the low morning sun falling brilliant on them, and they shaded their eyes with their mittened hands as they looked out into the lot and beyond. The access road was dead ahead and cars were already climbing it in a pretty steady line. As much as she had liked sitting in the booth with Chip and their coffee cups and the lottery ticket, in her heart she was grateful to the bright-colored flatlanders for sending them on their way. The mountain wouldn't wait. Not on a day like this. "I don't know," she said, thinking of the Paxtons. "It might be late."

"How long can they stay out?" He had a point. It wasn't as if the Rotary Club Christmas party would go on forever.

There were safety cones up on the main road and a guy in an orange vest directing traffic. This was serious. Stacey wanted to get on the mountain but at the same time she didn't want to brave the crowds. She pictured Spruce by night as she had seen it that once, with the snow a fresh blanket and the stars twinkling overhead and the little town spread out below.

With all of these annoying people tucked into their beds somewhere.

The more she thought about it, the more she realized that if she was going to get any decent skiing in at all this week—never mind a run with Chip, who'd be hauling toboggans and splinting legs from now until New Year's Day—she'd better take him up on the offer.

"Sure," she said, stepping off into the lot after a Hummer with Jersey tags had roared past, sending up spray. "Let's give it a shot."

THIRTY-NINE

The rest of the day was going to be an ugly blur, and the day after that would be, too. Between the early vacationers and the busloads of high school ski clubs up from New York and Pennsylvania, standing in the lodge was like standing in an airport on the day before Thanksgiving. Never mind finding a place to sit down and boot up. The whole thing made Stacey more glad than ever to have that season pass. By the look of things, it would have taken half the morning just to buy a ticket. Where was the fun in that?

Now and then, she'd thought about applying for a second job as a ski instructor—she was out there all day every day, so why not?—but right now that notion collapsed under the assault of a thousand screaming six-year-olds. A thousand screaming six-year-olds and their two thousand whining parents. She could have used the pay, that was for sure. Especially the tips, which were probably the key to the benefits package. But spending the day babysitting a bunch of spoiled and needy kids—and that's what it would be, make no mistake; wrangling them on and off the lifts, wiping their noses and buckling their helmets, helping them into and out of their snow pants when it was time to use the bathroom (which would be *all the time*) would drain the fun straight out of her favorite thing on earth. There wasn't enough money in the world for that.

She finished booting up and grabbed the rest of her gear and jammed her bag into a crevice where one of the exposed ceiling beams met an upright, and without even taking the time to pull on her glove liners or her helmet she stepped outside. She thought she'd finish up out there, in relative peace and quiet, but she was wrong. The walkways were jammed. Families at picnic tables fought over Tupperware trays of cupcakes and cookies brought from home. Immortal college kids and older unrepentant nicotine fiends gathered in stubborn little clots near railings and trash cans, smoking furiously. The ski racks were plainly overwhelmed, every slot stuffed two and three pairs deep, the whole business chained and wired together by people who had good reason not to trust strangers around their expensive gear. She found her skis and threaded them free of the confusion like a pair of pickup sticks, and then she walked to the end of a very long lift line.

Skinning up with Chip tomorrow night was looking better and better. It might take less time.

In the end, even the most remote and little-used runs on the mountain were crowded. Skiing them called for infinite patience, nerves of steel, and a sense of geometry in motion that would have done Isaac Newton or Minnesota Fats proud. After one trip down Oh Brother! (where a couple of Chip's patrol buddies were already splinting some guy's leg) and a halfhearted stab at the semiconcealed glades on Blowdown (where it turned out there were more panicking little kids than there were trees), she broke her own personal rule and went off-piste, under the patrol ropes, beyond the boundaries of the resort, where there was a little solitude and a lot of very nice untracked snow.

"You didn't," Chip said when she confessed to him that night at the Binding.

"I did."

"Not all by yourself."

"You bet I did. They *made* me. These . . ." She indicated the crowds with a toss of her head. "These people made me do it."

Chip had fastened a grim and professionally judgmental look on his face, but it was a storm cloud that lasted only a second or two more. He finally gave up and let out the smile that had been working away in there all along. "Atta girl," he said, raising his glass. "Way to go. I knew you had it in you."

Come morning, Stacey could hardly drag herself out of bed and down to the slope. She felt like a citizen of Troy, throwing back the covers on the morning after the Greeks invaded. Worse, considering the hours she'd spent making about a million flatlanders feel welcome down at the good old hospitable Broken Binding, she felt like she'd helped pull that damned trick horse in through the gates herself.

"You're off today," said Megan when they passed in the kitchen.

"Off to the mountain as usual."

"No. *Off*, I mean. From the Binding." She lifted an empty cup and raised it to Stacey by way of asking if she wanted any. "It's your night off, right?"

Stacey agreed and took the cup and filled it and thanked her. Only when the thin coffee hit her tongue and the faintest suggestion of caffeine nudged her bloodstream did she remember. She slapped herself on the forehead. "What was I thinking? I agreed to sit for the Paxton kids tonight."

"The Paxton kids? How'd that happen?"

Stacey told her.

"Good luck with those two," Megan said.

"Hey—after the crowds at the mountain this week, two lousy kids'll be a walk in the park."

"Lousy," said Megan, "being the operative word."

The day went by in a gaudy blur of fleece and Gore-Tex, a torrent of hip-hop music from the half-pipe, and a cloud of mingled tobacco smoke and mothballs. Plus an occasional hint of marijuana smoke. You never knew what you'd smell on the chairlift.

Stacey skied from the first chair to the last in order to make the most of the day, but her total runs still clocked in well short of the usual. So she wasn't exactly worn out when she got back to the Ramsey place for a leisurely shower and maybe a nap—that last just to be fresh for the late-night run with Chip. There was nobody home—she hollered to make sure—and she was halfway out of her fleece before she even reached her room. Into a stinky pile in the corner it went, and then she fished some clean stuff from the drawer for later on. She put it on the bed, and found on the pillow a note from Megan. Richie Paxton had called, asking her not to bother having supper as long as she didn't mind heating something up for the kids. That'd be fine with her. Any place to eat in town— including Mahoney's, where the sandwiches were better than the surroundings, and that was a good thing—would be shoulder-to-shoulder anyhow. Plus this way she'd save a little money. And Richie'd said he'd pick her up, too, which she guessed was standard practice with sitters who were still in junior high, but it was all right anyhow. It meant a couple dollars' worth of gas money saved.

She napped and showered and charged up her cell phone in case she got a chance to call her mom and dad later. It didn't seem likely, though. With those kids' reputation, she'd probably be hopping every second. And who knew if there was even service at the house? But there was still a chance, and she thought she might as well be prepared.

Richie arrived a little before six, as promised. His big black SKIBUM Mercedes stank of expensive perfume, and Stacey made the mistake of mentioning it.

"Oh, shit," he said, reaching his left hand down to the control pad and opening all of the windows at once.

"I don't really mind that much," she said, zipping up her coat as he finished with the windows and turned his attention to the sun-roof. It must have been fifteen degrees outside. Her hat was in the duffel she'd tossed into the backseat, along with the rest of her ski clothes for later. "Honest."

"It's not you I'm worried about." He gave her a look that would have made her feel conspiratorial if it hadn't creeped her out entirely. It was the kind of look he would never have given a junior high sitter, that was for sure. It confessed what he'd been up to in the car before he'd come here, and it assumed that she'd keep whatever she might figure out about it strictly between the two of them.

Stacey shivered, half from the cold and half from the idea.

The car barreled down the snowy roads and into town, heedless as a locomotive. The lights were on in every window and there were lines of people clear out the doors at Vinnie's and Cinco de Taco and the pizza joint next door to Bud's. That last one went halfway around the block. Everywhere, New Yorkers were stamping their feet and hugging themselves and blowing out thin clouds of steam, waiting for food that they wouldn't have given a nickel for in the city—the worst pizza on earth.

In the window at Bud's, keeping an eye on the crowds and wondering when he'd ever get in to cadge himself a slice or two, stood

Danny Bowman. None of the laundry machines was running and it was cold behind the glass where he stood and his breath bloomed on it. He wore his ratty wool Burton hat pulled down over his ears and he had his hands in his pockets and the look on his face was one of despair and disgust. He looked like a man who'd spent his life convinced that things could never get any worse, only to learn at last that he'd been wrong.

Richie's Mercedes, careening past in a shower of slush, caught his eye and distracted him from his empty stomach. With the windows open and the streets lit up he could see inside a little bit, enough to see Richie and Stacey in the front seat, side by side. He reached a finger up under his gimme hat and scratched at his head, turning as he watched them sail past. He withdrew his finger, examined a whitish crust of something under the nail, and sucked it off with a kind of ugly satisfaction. Then he jammed his hands into his pockets and left the laundromat.

Over the roar of the open windows, Richie turned to Stacey and hollered, "I know I can count on you to keep a guy's secret." Just like that. As if a girl who'd sunk to making a living by serving beer to unfaithful bastards like him couldn't possibly give a damn about the difference between right and wrong.

She didn't deny it. She only kept her mouth shut as they drove along—which to him was probably as good as a promise that she'd keep on doing the same. She was thinking about the alternative, though. And about how maybe his implication was right: Until right now, until she'd confronted the red-haired woman's perfume in the Mercedes and witnessed Richie's panic over it, she hadn't given a whole lot of thought to Jeanette. She certainly hadn't considered telling her what she knew. It was none of her business.

They pulled into the garage and he left the windows down and lowered the door behind them. He opened the door behind the other car—Jeanette's, obviously; a Japanese minivan the color of mud—so that they would take that one instead. Then they went in.

Inside the house, the kids were insane.

Jacked up on sugar cookies and greed, overstimulated by twinkling lights and Christmas music that blared from hidden speakers in every room of the big house, they were practically murderous with anticipation and desire. Christmas morning was still four days away, but either one of them would have strangled his own grandmother to move it twenty-four hours closer.

Jeanette took Stacey's jacket to the mudroom and then introduced the kids, Cameron and Mackenzie. Boy and girl, or girl and boy. Ages eight and nine, or nine and eight. It was impossible to tell. Stacey didn't even catch which one of them belonged to which name, but she figured she'd get the hang of it as the night went along. Fat chance. Right up until their parents left, they ran around calling each other *retard* and *dirtbag* and *moron*. And once Richie and Jeanette were out of earshot, they would effortlessly switch over to *fuckwad* and *asshole* and *shit-for-brains*. She would never hear *Cameron* or *Mackenzie* again. Not tonight, anyway.

Jeanette was nice. She was a good bit shorter than Richie— hardly any bigger than the taller of her kids, really—and although she was immaculately put together for the party there was something about her that suggested it didn't come naturally. Stacey had seen spouses like her at affairs she'd attended with her parents in Boston. The steady one, always slightly in the shadows, more than likely the private heart and soul of the family. Most couples had a component like that, and it wasn't by any means always the woman. In Stacey's parents' case, it had always been her father. She watched Jeanette moving from the refrigerator to the sink to the stove in an exquisitely tailored dress—it must have come from New York or Boston or maybe Hartford, at the closest—and she thought about who would have played that role in the aborted Stacey-and-Brian

Show. Maybe that was the problem. Maybe that was why they'd had to break up the way they did. Neither of them fit the job description.

Jeanette had put together a mac-and-cheese casserole, and all Stacey had to do was put it in the oven and clean up some green beans to go with it. The table was already set, and Stacey figured she had a good idea about who was responsible for that, too. Not the kids. "Please," she said, taking the paring knife from Jeanette and turning on the water to rinse the beans where they already lay in a colander at the bottom of the big double sink. "I think I can handle this. Don't you have something better to do?"

Jeanette allowed that she did, and she vanished back toward where Richie had gone. Above the mechanized drone of Mannheim Steamroller, Stacey called over her shoulder for Mackenzie, asking for a little help in the kitchen please. When there was no answer after a minute or two she called again, this time for Cameron. Whichever one came didn't make any difference to her. But it didn't matter anyhow, because neither of them showed up. She was on her hands and knees, probing in various cabinets for an appropriate pot, when the music died between tracks and she heard Jeanette's voice raised from behind a closed door. Good for her. The kids had it coming. Maybe if she put the fear of the Lord into them a little, they'd be on their best behavior until bedtime—whenever that was.

FORTY

A shooting star dropped from overhead and faded out before it got halfway to the treeline. *That's the way it goes,* Danny thought. *Another planet bites the dust, or something like that.* He remembered reading a story a very long time ago, about a rocket that blew up in space and sent astronauts flying every which way, screaming and burning, until some little kid saw one way high up in the night sky and made a wish on him. So he made a wish himself. He'd forgotten people did that until just now.

He was walking all by himself with his hands in his pockets and his cap yanked down and his chin buried in the collar of his coat, up the mountain access road. There was a certain amount of traffic, which provided more light than was usual up here in the woods. Cars coming and going in the condo lots. People pulling up in front of grand single homes that usually stood empty, lit up this time of year like some kind of landing strips. He took advantage of the light to keep an eye out for that big black Mercedes, wondering where Richie and that girl might have been heading. Thinking that maybe he could catch up with them and figure out what they were up to. Wondering what he would do once he knew.

• • •

The sound of Jeanette's voice rose as a door opened somewhere and then it faded again with the rapid closing of the same door and then it stopped entirely. The nerve of those kids, walking out in the middle of a scolding. And shame on her for letting them. But it turned out that the kids were in the family room, chasing each other around the Christmas tree, and it was Richie who emerged red-faced and boiling into the kitchen.

He looked at Stacey and said, "Maybe now you understand."

"I can be very understanding when I'm tending bar," she said, adjusting the flame underneath the green beans, "but in real life, I'm not so easy."

"Women," said Richie, and he walked away to adjust his necktie.

"Can't live with 'em." She flicked on the oven light, looked inside, and flicked it off again.

Nobody notices a mud-colored Japanese minivan. Especially not somebody trudging up a wet road after dark, with his eyes peeled for a black Mercedes wagon. Danny squinted against the headlights and ducked his head and kept on walking, headed up the hill toward Richie's house while Richie and Jeanette headed down. There was a little dive bar at the next turning, a place called Doc's that catered mainly to skiers who wanted a brew before they hit the road home, and he thought he'd stop in there to warm up. See if maybe they had some free chicken wings or something.

Wow. The macaroni and cheese smelled like paradise. Stacey checked the refrigerator and the trash, too, and she found signs that Jeanette had put it together with no fewer than three different kinds of cheese that you couldn't even get in town. Imported not just from Switzerland and France, but from Rutland. And for what? The way the two kids were carrying on in the other room, Stacey didn't think they deserved anything better than the orange-powdered stuff from Kraft. Not even that, maybe. The generic equivalent, which was probably toxic. All the same, she was glad to be looking forward to something better than that for herself.

The timer showed five minutes, so she went out and told the kids to wash their hands and they ignored her.

Doc's was a squat pile of bricks alongside one of the mountain's second-string parking lots, slumped on a little island of land that had been in the same family since just about forever. The building was already standing when Andy Paxton's grandfather had bought the mountain in the first place, a two-story house occupied in those days by a cantankerous old widow woman who'd resisted Paxton's every overture to buy her out. It had been that way ever since. She'd moved up to the second floor and begun serving whiskey downstairs back around the turn of the twentieth century, and her son had kept it up through her death and straight on through Prohibition. He'd had two sons of his own who'd fought like rabid dogs over the place until one of them either ran the other one off or killed him outright, nobody living could say. The one left standing was Doc. In the 1960s he'd hired a high school kid to paint a twelve-foot likeness of a certain animated dwarf on the side of the building, traces of which were still visible wherever the years hadn't quite finished weathering the paint down to nothing.

As an institution, Doc's was a common enough kind of ski-town parasite, sucking blood from the mountain's customers and sending drunks out onto the local roadways and taking unspoken advantage of somebody else's parking lot. But there was nothing to be done about it. As for Doc himself, he was still around, ninety-some years old and deeply cirrhotic and sucking breath from an oxygen tank on a wheeled cart. His three-hundred-pound son, Doc Junior— who was white-bearded and jolly and resembled the cartoon dwarf more than the twelve-foot painting ever had—ran the place under the old man's watchful and bloodshot eye.

Between the rancid stink of the beer-soaked peanut shells on the floor and the ammoniac stench of the restrooms, between the low funk of sweat-stained fleece and the high reek of mothballs, and the old-man smell of Doc and the fat-man smell of Doc Junior, this was the only place in town where Danny could enter a room without being noticed. He yanked the stubborn door open and stepped in from the cold and sidled up to the bar.

Doc Junior was on duty and Doc himself was nowhere to be seen, which was OK with Danny. The old man's oxygen tank was behind the bar, though, tipped up against a refrigerator full of cold beer and live bait, so he couldn't have gone any great distance. Probably just to the men's room. He'd be back soon, so Danny had to work fast.

"Christ Almighty, it's cold out there," he said to Doc Junior, and Doc Junior nodded. "A feller could catch his death."

Doc Junior smiled from behind his beard. "How about a little coffee, warm you up?"

"I wanted coffee I'd have stayed in town."

The timer buzzed and once more she told Cameron and Mackenzie to wash their hands—using their names this time, although not with any kind of specificity. She spooned portions of the mac and cheese onto each plate and added the green beans and set them out and called to the kids again. When they showed up they were loud and cranky and aghast.

"Mom always puts everything on the table and lets us help ourselves," said either C or M. The girl, Stacey thought, to judge by the high pitch of her whining.

"Clean your plate," Stacey said, "and then you can have some more." By the looks of them, they'd been helping themselves a little too generously for a little too long.

One of the kids dug in and the other one reached for his or her glass and muttered something under his or her breath. Stacey thought it might have been *bitch,* but she wasn't sure. Whatever it was, at least the volume was low. That made it a step in the right direction.

Danny's brand, if he had one, was Genny Cream. There was a green-labeled bottle of it sitting in front of him right now. "The Green Death," people called it, and according to the date on it this one was a few weeks past its prime, but it still suited him. The price was right, and this long after the expiration date what else was Doc Junior going to do with it?

"You know what they say about the expiration date on The Green Death," he'd said when he'd handed it over. "It's whatever day you get low enough to drink it."

"I don't give a shit," said Danny. "You're a generous man."

"Don't tell Doc."

"You can count on me." Danny raised the bottle to his lips. "You can count on me double if you got any more of these old boys back there collecting dust."

"I do," said Doc Junior. "But I don't guess I'll have them for long."

There was nothing left after supper. Not a scrap or a shred. Not a single stiff elbow of macaroni cemented to the bottom of the baking dish. Not even a green bean. Nothing.

Stacey asked the kids to help with the dishes, but the protest that they set up was so appalling that she gave in and did them herself. Not that it was all that much trouble. Jeanette's dishwasher—she couldn't think of it as Richie's, try as she might—was a foreign-made wonder of bright chrome and burnished steel, easily worth twice as much as everything Stacey owned put together (short of the engagement ring). Both fierce and domestic at the same time—imagine a motorized Martha Stewart—it gleamed and sparkled in the low light of the kitchen as if it had somehow managed to wash itself. She latched it shut and let herself admire it and thought about how it was the kind of thing that people with new money, or people who were just new to old money, bought when they couldn't figure out what else to do with their checkbooks. Her parents' place had always been strictly GE, straight from Sears. Then again, her parents usually ate out.

Although Christmas music still blasted everywhere else, the kids had used a hidden switch somewhere to turn it down in the family room. In its place they'd booted up a PlayStation or something like it, and now they were happily ensconced on a pair of matching recliners, wrecking cars and stabbing hookers to the accompaniment of fake rap music that looped back on itself like a boa constrictor. The flat-screen was the biggest Stacey had ever seen. As big as a picture window and twice as lifelike. There was blood on every inch of it.

Joy to the World.

FORTY-ONE

Danny was halfway through his second beer and had started making small talk with the guys next to him—a spent-looking housepainter from New Hampshire with his cousin, a spent-looking lawyer from Connecticut—in hopes of cadging some of the nachos he'd seen them order. "I do love this time of year," he said, a dreamy look in his eye.

"Is that so?" said the housepainter, without looking up.

"Oh, yeah." Danny took a sip of his Genny Cream and savored it like honey. "I do dearly love it."

The housepainter sized him up, sniffing a little, curious. "So. What's Santa going to bring you?"

"I ain't talking about no Santy Claus," said Danny. "That ain't it. What I'm talking about is new faces around this old town. Kind of brightens the place up."

"New faces. I guess that'd be us." Pointing with his thumb toward himself and his cousin.

"You betcha." That was Danny all over. A regular Welcome Wagon.

The lawyer spoke up. "I guess anybody'll get bored of the same old same old. Even in a nice spot like this."

Danny set down his bottle. "Doc's? You're shitting me."

"Oh no," said the lawyer. "I mean the whole town. The mountain and all."

"Oh. Well. Yeah. My point exactly." He finished off his beer and raised a finger and Doc Junior brought him another one because why not. It beat spending some afternoon cracking them open and tipping them out into the utility tub one by one. "I've lived here all my life, when I wasn't in the service."

"Korea?"

"Shit, no. I look that old to you?" He'd have to watch himself. At this rate, he'd be going without nachos.

"Vietnam then." The housepainter said it as if it explained a lot.

"You bet your ass." Tipping up the bottle.

Stacey read magazines and watched the clock. Bedtime was ten o'clock for Cameron and Mackenzie, and she had a pretty good idea that she'd have to get started about an hour in advance if she hoped to make it. Not that she cared whether the little rodents obeyed their parents' rules or got a proper night's sleep. She just wanted a little bit of peace and quiet.

During a lull in the evening's action that could have signified its last gasp, Doc Junior paused in front of Danny. "So how come you're all the way up here this time of night, anyhow?"

"Your warm hospitality."

"Don't give me that."

Danny sniffed. "That the way you treat all your customers? No wonder you don't do a better business."

"Giving away beer's a hard way for a man to make a living."

"I hear you."

Doc Junior laid his forearms, each as big as a monster truck muffler, out flat on the damp bar and leaned his weight on them.

He looked at the empty stools alongside Danny and at the scoured-clean plate on the bar in front of the stools and he shook his head. "You sure as hell didn't come for the nachos."

"Those boys know how to pack it away, don't they? And they're fast on the draw, too."

"They paid for it, they get to eat it."

"Where'd their manners go, anyhow?"

"They left 'em to home, I guess."

Danny sat fuming for a while, and Doc Junior stood taking a load off and listening to the music from the jukebox. The room was paneled with barnboard and decorated with baseball caps that in his younger days Doc Junior used to enjoy nailing to every surface within reach. Once upon a time the place would have been filled with a cloud of cigarette smoke, too, but those days were gone and all that remained of them was a brownish-gray nicotine film on the baseball caps. The sight of it made some of the old-timers, including Doc Junior and particularly Doc himself, nostalgic for the days when a man still had his personal freedoms. Doc Junior stood listening to the jukebox and studying Danny, probably the freest individual he'd ever known. Then he waited until his father's back was turned and brought him another bottle. After a little bit Danny spoke up again.

"You're just a rest stop for me tonight," he said.

"Really."

"Oh, yeah. I got me a ways to go. A long ways."

Doc Junior checked his watch. "Then you better get started."

"I will, I will." He tipped back the green-labeled bottle, then lowered his gaze and his voice too. "I'm on a mission," he said.

"A mission. You and Mother Theresa." Doc Junior laughed, a sound that seemed to come from the bottom of a barrel. "You and Superman."

"Go on, make fun if you want. There's people up there on that mountain doing something they shouldn't, and I'm about to get to the bottom of it."

"Danny. There's a thousand people up there doing things they shouldn't. Two thousand, maybe."

"I don't care about a thousand people."

"You got somebody picked out special?"

"I do. And I got my reasons for it."

"I'll bet." His father sat up straighter behind him and knocked over his oxygen tank and Doc Junior slumped off to give him a hand with it. "I'll bet you do."

Stacey pulled the plug on the PlayStation—literally pulled the plug from the wall; that's what it took—and bulldozed the kids through the living room and into the foyer and up the stairs toward their separate bathrooms. Thinking all the while that yes, it was a good idea to stay as far away from the ski instruction business as possible.

The music was still playing everywhere downstairs and she couldn't figure out how to turn it off. She discovered a complex control panel inside the kitchen door, but every button and knob and slider on it looked to her like it might set off an alarm. That would be the last thing she needed. More noise, to begin with. And maybe even a call direct to the sheriff's office, which would forward somewhere else at this time of night and from there go straight on to Guy at home, relaxing in front of the Franklin stove with the tree up and his feet up, too. She figured she'd wait until the kids were brushed and washed and then ask one of them for help, even though it pained her to give them an excuse to come back downstairs now that she'd gotten them up.

The Rotary Club Christmas party was the usual stone-cold bore. Jeanette couldn't figure out why her husband belonged to the organization in the first place, although it made a little more sense now that they allowed women. He certainly didn't need the business contacts. Spruce was the biggest business in the valley by a factor of what, ten or twenty? More? If you wanted to do business around here, you did it in the shadow of Spruce Peak.

So maybe it was just a goodwill thing on Richie's part, although goodwill had never been his strong suit.

Or maybe he was just trying to walk in his father's footsteps—which was even more important now that his brother David was dead. She sat and listened to the band play "Jingle Bell Rock" and watched Richie dance with somebody from the school board. There were always things about people you couldn't understand. Even people you'd spent fifteen years married to.

Miracle of miracles, the kids were actually ready at a quarter of ten. They trooped down the stairs and showed her their damp hands and faces and their shiny white teeth and insisted that they ought to be able to spend their last fifteen minutes watching something ghastly on MTV—some reality show reflecting a reality that nobody within a thousand miles of planet Earth had ever actually witnessed.

"I don't suppose it could do you any harm," Stacey said, and they gave her looks that suggested they hoped she was wrong.

One of them helped her turn the Christmas music down a little, and then they barreled off to watch television. Stacey took her phone into the living room—there was another tree there, in addition to the oversized one in the family room—turned the lights down, and sat on the couch. She switched her cell on and checked the signal. Not too bad, but when she dialed her parents' house it rang once and then died. Great. Now they'd think she'd had some kind of emergency, and would be dialing her back like crazy people. She went into the kitchen and sat on a stool at the marble peninsula, but the signal wasn't any better there. It might even have been worse. She opened the back door and stood in a corner of unheated porch—man, what a view these people had—where the phone buzzed once and showed her parents' number for about half a heartbeat before the signal died again. Damn. She let herself back in, frankly just as happy not to be out there in the cold anymore, and headed for the garage.

Danny drained his last bottle and put it down. He collected himself and buttoned his coat and looked Doc Junior square in the eye or at least as squarely as he could with three or four hasty beers in his belly. And then, as slowly as a judge passing sentence, he said, "You seen my hat?"

"Check the floor," said Doc Junior.

Danny did and sure enough it was there all right, a dusting of wet peanut shells stuck like cockleburs all over it. He brushed a few of them loose and jammed the hat down over his eyebrows. The Burton logo was somewhere over his left ear, but he didn't give a damn. "I can't be wasting any more of my time here," he said.

"I'm sorry you feel that way."

"Although I do appreciate your kindness." He tilted his head, indicating the bottle.

"I know you do. That's all right."

"It's just I been working on this thing, like I said, and I finally got it figured out."

"That thing you were getting to the bottom of."

"Yessir."

"That mission you were talking about."

"The very same." He fastidiously tucked his ponytail into the collar of his jacket. "I'm on it right now."

The music from the jukebox died out and Doc Junior leaned over the bar and asked, lowering his voice and grinning like a man expecting to receive a present, "How about a hint, before you go?"

Danny twisted up his mouth and gave the whole thing some thought. He waited a minute, contemplating, considering the angles, and then he made his decision. "All right," he said. "Two words: *David Paxton*. I know who killed him."

"Really?"

"It was a two-man job, and I happen to know the two men who done it. I also happen to know that one of them weren't even a man."

Doc Junior marveled. "That's more than two words."

"I weren't counting." And he jammed his hands into his pockets and set out.

FORTY-TWO

The garage light was on a motion sensor and it came on when she pushed open the door. It was cold out there, but not as cold as it had been on the porch, and the cell phone signal was a little stronger. You never could tell around here. A stepladder stood against the wall and she settled her butt against it just as the phone in her hand rang again.

"Hey," she said. "Merry Christmas."

"Honey, pick up." It was her mother's voice, calling to her father. "It's Stacey."

"Hey. Mom."

"Are you on? Jay? Are you on? It's Stacey. I've got Stacey."

"Merry Christmas, Mom."

"Pick up."

"Mom."

"Hang on a minute. I don't know where your father is. I told him I was calling and then—"

"Mom."

"Jay!"

"I can just talk to you for a while."

"Pick up!"

"Mom."

The line clicked a little and the faint buzz of some History Channel voiceover hummed in the background. "Hey, sweetie. Merry Christmas. You coming home for it?"

"No, Dad. I've got to work."

"On Christmas?"

"It's a big day. People still eat. People still go out."

"But Christmas. Jeez."

"Let her go, Jay. She's made up her mind."

"This is a resort town, Dad. Don't forget."

"I know. It's just that we'll miss you."

"I know. I'll miss you, too."

"Turn down the TV."

"I will. Sorry." He laid the phone down with a click. The History Channel got a little louder as he searched for the remote, and then it died entirely once he'd come up with it.

Stacey's mother took advantage of the moment. "I've been worried sick about you," she said. "Don't you ever answer the phone? Don't you ever check your messages?"

"The service here is terrible, Mom."

"You could check your messages."

"You don't leave messages."

"Because you never check them."

"I'm back," said her father.

Stacey stood up from her seat against the stepladder and began pacing the garage. Talking with her mother always went better if she was in motion.

"So did you get the package? I was hoping you'd call to acknowledge it."

"I got it. I think it came yesterday."

"Yesterday? You'd think you lived in Alaska, the mail is so slow."

Stacey paused against the workbench and switched on the overhead light. It was clearly the workplace of a person who didn't need one or at least didn't care to use it. Nothing but broken tools and toys, paperwork bound for nowhere, and odd bits of cast-off clothing—everything covered with a film of dust and grime. "I can't help the mail," she said.

"I know it's not your fault," said her mother. "I'm just glad you got the package."

"I did. Thank you. I'm waiting until Christmas to open it, though."

"Good girl," said her father.

"I couldn't send you guys very much," she said, thinking of the little care package from the sugar house that had taken everything she could spring loose from her pay.

"You don't need to send us *anything,* sweetie."

Stacey thought about the excess that would mark Christmas morning in the Paxton house, and she wondered how much of it would end up out here on the bench—broken or just discarded—in a month's time. How much of it would be piled here with the torn gloves and the broken chain saw and the rusty hatchet and *oh my God.* . . .

"I've got to go," she told her parents. "I'll call you back."

The country club wouldn't have passed muster anywhere but up here in the mountains where time moved slowly and the economy kept pace. It had the look of an old ski lodge, with a sagging barnboard A-frame serving as the foyer and a warren of other rooms added on over the years, one after another after another. None of them were very big and they all smelled moldy, including the ballroom where Jeanette stood looking out the window into the night. The course itself was nice enough, if you didn't mind all the ups and downs. She had to give it that. It was best in the fall, with the leaves changing all around. All those colors.

She stood close enough to the window to feel the cold leaking through from the outside and she watched her husband's reflection as he worked the room. Sometimes at events like this, provided he didn't have too much to drink and let himself turn ornery and petulant, he looked like a man who was running for something. He looked as if he wanted everyone to like him. As if he thought he could make that happen by efforts this limited, when he spent the rest of his life just being himself. The man Jeanette had married.

Still, if only for the moment, it seemed to work. He had a kind of grace—call it the ease that comes with money—that lifted him up as he moved from table to table and couple to couple. People were attracted to him. She watched and understood and didn't mind too much. Not anymore.

The party was about over anyhow.

Stacey slid the phone into her pocket, took a deep breath, and went inside to put the kids to bed. She left the light on over the work-bench the way she used to turn on every single light in the apart-ment if her parents were gone and she'd seen something scary on television. Michael Jackson's *Thriller* video, maybe. The overheads would go off in the garage sooner or later, but she didn't want the stuff on that workbench sitting in darkness. She didn't trust it.

Cameron and Mackenzie had taken advantage of her absence to raid the cookie jar once again, and there were crumbs all over everything. Slow as a pair of cats, they unfolded themselves from the couch and yawned luxuriously and flicked crumbs from their pajamas onto the floor, and although Stacey had half a mind to make them brush their teeth again she decided against it. Their dental hygiene was no concern of hers. Especially not now.

She pushed them toward the stairs. "You guys are getting in bed and you're going to be quiet, because I have some things I need to get done."

"Dad says that sitters have to give us their full attention."

"Is that so? He says that?"

"He says he's not paying them to loaf around and do home-work."

"That's good," Stacey said. "Because I don't have any homework. So you've got nothing to complain about."

"But he says . . ."

She wasn't listening. She was eager to get back out into the ga-rage and she was even more eager to make a phone call. She pushed the kids up the stairs and they staggered and stumbled and made it as difficult as possible, but she was relentless. And once she'd gotten them in their rooms—Cameron was the girl and Mackenzie was the boy, to judge by the color schemes and the trail signs over their beds—CAMERON'S WAY and MACKENZIE'S RUN, painted to look like the real thing—she pulled the doors shut and ran.

Danny was thinking he could have used about one beer less than he'd taken on board at Doc's. He felt plenty warm as he hiked up the hill, warmer than he would have been without a belly full of Genny Cream. He couldn't decide if this was a good thing or a bad one. Didn't those rescue dogs carry little barrels of brandy around their necks? Saint Bernards or whatever? If they didn't know what they were up to, who did? Then again, people said that having a little buzz on when you were out in the cold could screw up your thermostat, make you feel warmer than you really were. That couldn't be good. You could freeze to death. He didn't want to get overconfident and fall down and end up frozen stiff by the side of the road where everything was drifted over and iced up, so he kept moving and stayed right smack on the dotted line as best he could. That was probably dangerous, too, with the cars and the darkness and all, but he didn't exactly have a whole lot of options at this point.

• • •

She pushed the garage door open slowly, and before the automatic lights kicked in she could see the workbench at the other end, standing in the glow of its own little overhead like some kind of shrine.

Ridiculous. She felt ridiculous thinking of it that way, and she acknowledged it to herself. So she swung the door the rest of the way and the lights came on and she went to the bench just as if she were looking for a hammer or a screwdriver and not sizing up the key to a murder. She stopped short of touching anything, of course. She was careful to stand about a foot away and fold her hands behind her back and bend over to check things out, even though she'd been leaning hard against the bench not more than fifteen minutes ago, talking to her parents. That didn't matter. A person had to be careful.

And yes indeed, there it was. Just the way she'd seen it before, down to the last detail. A newish chain saw, hardly a mark or a scratch or a grease stain on it, missing its chain. Alongside it, a hatchet with a blade all dinged up and bashed. On closer inspection of both—which she managed without touching anything, drawing so close to the chain saw's bar and the hatchet's blade that her breath showed on them in the cold garage—she could see the places where they had met. More than that, she was pretty sure she could read their mutual story. There was grease on the hatchet—the same black grease that rimmed the bar where the chain had run, she'd bet anything. And there were dents along the top edge of the bar, where someone who didn't know the first thing about working on a chain saw had hammered at the chain with the hatchet until it had come apart. Someone like Richie Paxton.

She knelt down and looked beneath the bench, and sure enough: There on the floor—lying in the dust but not covered by it, since it couldn't have been there for more than a couple of weeks—was a gleaming and greasy pin, a pin like the one she'd seen Guy knock out of the chain he'd been working on in the basement. Except this one looked like it was maybe bent a little.

She straightened up and went over to lean on the stepladder again, watching the lighted bench as if it harbored a poisonous snake. Then she took out her phone and dialed.

The Paxton place was lit up like a Christmas tree when Danny turned off the road into the great big circular drive. Pretty much *exactly* like a Christmas tree. With a huge illuminated wreath mounted on the oversized masonry chimney, and colored lights picking out the roofline, and candles in every single window, and electric icicles dripping down from where the gutters would have been if houses around here had gutters. Danny shook his head and strained to see in the living room window where the tree gleamed and pulsed and he said under his breath, "Well, deck the fucking halls."

The lights were on in the garage.

He crouched down below the line of sight from the garage door windows and moved toward it, a shadow among shadows. The closer he got, the more invisible he was. In a small windless space where the door met the wall he stopped and gently pushed himself into the corner, not making a sound. He pressed his ear against the door and sat for a while, not hearing anything. Then he reached up and pushed the Burton hat up and pressed the naked ear against the frozen door again. This time he heard a woman's voice, pitched low and secretive, the words coming fast, but try as he might he couldn't make out a single syllable. He adjusted his position against the door and kept his hopes up.

Guy picked up the phone with an airy kind of greeting. "Mmm-yello?" There was Christmas music playing just like at the Paxton place, but it was slower and softer than the stuff that Stacey had finally gotten cranked down to the minimum. It came from a CD, or maybe even from an old cassette or LP, instead of from the god-awful Holiday Music Channel. And it emerged through two lowly speakers instead of a hundred.

No wonder he was in such a good mood.

Stacey hated to spoil it by telling him that she'd found the secret of David Paxton's death, but she didn't hate it enough to hold back.

"That would be interesting," he said after she'd described the chain saw and the hatchet and the bent pin. "That would be interesting, all right."

"I was afraid you'd think I was crazy."

"Nah. On the other hand, everybody within a hundred miles of here's got a chain saw kicking around somewhere. And they're all pretty beat up, for the most part."

"Not this one. The only marks on it are on that arm that holds the chain."

"The bar."

"The bar. Like I said. Other than that, it's brand-new."

She could practically hear Guy thinking on the other end. After a while he blew out air and said, "I'd need a warrant, is the problem."

"I suppose." She hadn't thought of that.

"I can't just come up there and snoop around. And neither can you."

Stacey switched off the lamp over the workbench and walked back to the door that led to the house, thinking. "What if I thought there was a prowler?" she said. "You could come up then. You'd have to."

"You're right," said Guy. "And I'd have to give the place a good looking over, too." He was already pushing forward in the recliner and getting ready to hang up the phone. "You just sit tight," he said.

FORTY-THREE

Richie helped his wife into her coat, which he would never
have done in a less public place. She was accustomed to it,
this double standard, and after fifteen years of marriage she
hardly noticed it anymore. Tonight she made a point of noticing it,
though, watching the other husbands help their own wives into their
own coats and wondering if it was the same everywhere. Maybe,
maybe not.

A husband who helped his wife into her coat for the right
reasons—in the right spirit—would probably open the car door for
her, too. And once they had filtered into the country club lot with
the rest of the Rotary crowd she frankly didn't see a whole lot of
that going on. Then again, it was brutally cold. Which meant every
man for himself.

Danny heard the woman's voice leave off for good and he heard the
door close behind her. After a few tense minutes during which he
sat crouched against the door, burning with curiosity but afraid to
move, the lights in the garage went off and he stood up. He made a
tunnel of his hands and looked in through the window. By the glow

of the Christmas decorations he could make out the shape of the big black Mercedes wagon. So they *were* here, the two of them. Richie and the girl. That must have been the girl, talking in the garage. On the phone, maybe, or maybe to Richie if he'd been out there with her, doing something in the car or having done it. Women. Get them going and you didn't need to say a word.

He stood looking at the house and counting his blessings at last. All he had to do was catch the both of them together, and he'd have something. No wonder neither Richie nor the girl had given him the time of day. They'd been covering up for each other, and covering up this thing they had going on, too. But now he knew. And now he knew that if he caught them at it, he'd have an angle he could work for sure.

He wondered where the bedroom was. Probably on the second floor, which meant he was shit out of luck in that department. He'd never make that climb, not in the dark and not in this cold. And even if he did, he might pick the wrong window—maybe one of the kids' rooms or something—and what then? All that work for nothing.

On the other hand, maybe they were doing it on the couch in the living room. Why not? If they were the only ones home, they could have the run of the place. Get their thrills wherever. Only problem was, they weren't the only ones home. They hadn't counted on their good friend Danny boy.

He righted his hat, which had been sitting cocked up over his ear all this time, and started around to the back of the house. Toward the front the wind had blown the yard nearly clean of snow, but the farther back he went the more deeply it had drifted. Especially a few yards away from the house, where he was angling toward the steps that led up to the deck. The yard sloped downward as it went back, too—it looked as if the basement was exposed on the back side of the house, probably one of those ski-out arrangements—but the snow got deeper at the same rate and soon he was up to his waist. He realized how cold he was and he realized how much beer he'd had earlier and between the beer and the chill on his legs he realized that he had to take a leak, so he backed out and pissed at some personal risk against the cedar siding and then set out again, this time keeping closer to the house and aiming for what looked like an open area below the deck. He ought to check for Richie and the girl down on that level anyhow. There was probably a family room or something down there, with a sliding door. Maybe a wide-screen TV in it, some kind of home-theater deal they'd be relaxing in front of. He was pretty sure he saw light cast on the snow back there, and he headed for it.

Guy turned onto the access road and thought about whether or not he ought to turn his light bar on. It was one hundred percent a matter of discretion as far as he could tell, and it could go either way. Switch it on, and scare the nonexistent prowler into the woods. Switch it off, and maintain peace and quiet in the neighborhood. Which he figured, in the end, was probably his chief obligation right at the moment. So he rolled unobtrusively up the road, taking the long curves one after another, and he went on past the lot at Doc's, and he kept on going uphill without haste and without urgency until he found Paxton's circular drive and pulled slowly into it and killed the lights. He sat there thinking in the soft glow of the Christmas decorations, and then he got out of the car and went to the front door.

The lights on the snowdrifts behind the deck were from a half-dozen more of those goddamned electric Christmas candles. Danny cursed them and cursed his luck and wished he'd waited until he was back here where there wasn't so much snow and the air was dead still to pull himself out and take a leak. He could have frozen his pecker off out there in the open. Then he made for the stairs on the other side of the deck, because those weren't drifted in so much as the ones back the way he'd come.

Stacey was at the door before Guy had a chance to ring the bell, hoping to keep the kids from waking up.

"You reported a prowler, miss?" He lifted his hat and scraped his boots on the mat and she let him in, a finger on her lips to shush him. He got the message.

The garage entrance was only a few steps away from the foyer, down a little hall and through the mudroom, and they both waited until they were there before they spoke.

"Right over there," said Stacey.

"I see it." He walked to the workbench and stood in front of it, half bent, sizing up its contents with slow caution. "Looks to be about the right size," he said. "Of course, we'd have to make sure."

She pointed out the marks on the hatchet and the chain saw and he nodded. She had him kneel on the floor to see the bent pin, and he nodded at that, too. "Somebody took that chain off who didn't know what he was doing," she said, and he didn't disagree.

It was windier up on the deck. The snow there was crusted over with ice, frozen and refrozen into a surface smooth and hard as rock, and Danny had some difficulty navigating. Right away he slid and nearly fell down, but he caught himself at the last second against the sill of the window over the sink. Luckily there was nobody on the other side, getting a drink or rinsing out a glass, or else they'd have both had heart attacks.

He saw footprints in the shallower snow by the glass door. Recent footprints, by the look of them, and he thought he ought to check them out. *This is it,* he told himself. If there was anybody around, he might catch sight of them through the glass. And they might see him, too. So he bent over and made himself as small as he could, and he drew himself nearer to the door.

"How long till they're home, you think?"

They hadn't said, and Stacey didn't know.

"Because I really ought to stick around. I mean I can't exactly seize this stuff and run. Without Richie and Jeanette around and all."

"No?"

"A person might make a case for it, but to my way of thinking it'd be bad form. Plus I wouldn't mind hearing what Richie has to say about it."

A little sadly, Stacey switched off the light over the bench and started toward the door. Guy followed. His feet were dry by now so he didn't pause in the mudroom but went with her straight into the kitchen, where they were surprised by a scrambling and a crashing on the deck that could have been a raccoon but in the end turned out to be Danny Bowman, panicked at the sight of them and fallen with his face pressed up against the glass. He looked bug-eyed and crazy and nearly frozen to death.

"Oh, for Pete's sake," said Guy. "It's The Claw."

They got him inside and sat him at the kitchen table and Guy just stood across from him shaking his head.

"Are you gonna cuff me?"

"You think I need to? You plan on running off?"

"No."

"Good. Don't go getting any ideas."

"I won't." His hat was on his knee and his greasy hair was sticking up like horns in some places and plastered flat in others.

The Christmas music was still playing in the background and Stacey was glad of it for a change, since it was probably keeping the kids upstairs from hearing the interrogation. Or whatever it was.

Danny kept on, defensive. "I didn't come clear up here without a good reason."

Guy just checked his watch and craned his neck to check out the Christmas tree in the next room.

"She's in it with him, you know." Pointing to Stacey where she leaned in the doorway. "That one's in it with Richie. Right up to her neck. I told you about her before, but I didn't know he was in it, too."

"Don't start more trouble than you're already in. Just sit there and warm up and then we'll go."

"I'm used to the cold."

"If I'm taking you into custody, I've got a responsibility to see you don't die from exposure."

"I won't."

"Good."

"You taking me into custody?"

"I'm thinking pretty hard about it."

Danny picked at a peanut shell that was still stuck to his hat. "I'll tell you somebody ought to be in custody." His tone had gone from defensive to petulant.

Stacey stepped out of the doorway, into the light of the lamp that hung over the kitchen table. "Give it up, Danny. I never did you any harm."

"I never said you did."

"Why me? Why all the stuff with my car? The scraping and everything?"

"That weren't me."

"Why can't you just leave me alone?"

"That weren't me on that snowmobile, neither."

Guy just shook his head, and Stacey went off to listen for any sign of the kids at the foot of the stairs. Danny sat up a little straighter and put a look of utter satisfaction on his face. A moment later, all three of them were surprised by the sound of the garage door beginning to groan open.

FORTY-FOUR

Y ou stay put," said Guy.

"I ain't going nowhere."

Stacey went and opened the door to the garage and Guy followed her. On the threshold they both looked back over their shoulders to see Danny beginning to stir, shifting his feet. Guy gave him a hard look and he stopped. If only there'd been a way to get him into the car, this might have been less awkward. "Dang it all," Guy said, then he went back across the kitchen and cuffed Danny to the table. That would have to do.

The garage was ablaze with light. The motion-sensitive overheads and the bulb on the chain opener and the headlights of the van as it eased past Guy's parked car. From the passenger window Jeanette looked out with a combination of surprise and alarm.

Stacey came out into the garage first and stood with her arms folded against the cold. Guy, the old hand at this kind of thing, followed her out and raised his hand in greeting and pasted a big smile on his face. Don't worry, the smile said. The kids are OK. Everything's OK.

Richie pulled the van forward and parked it, and Jeanette was out before he could kill the engine. "What's wrong? Is it one of the kids? What is it?"

The questions came out in a torrent and Stacey stood shaking her head no, no, no—everything's just fine, really.

'No worries," Guy said. "We had a prowler, is all."

Richie was still easing himself out of the van, and anyone could see that if Guy had given him a Breathalyzer he'd have had to take him in.

"A prowler?" said Jeanette. "I didn't think people had prowlers anymore." As if prowlers were like polio or something, a scourge eradicated by modern science.

Richie came around the back of the van, leading with his head tilted to one side. "What on earth?"

"A prowler, honey."

"Huh?"

"A prowler," said Guy. "You know. Outside. Lurking around. Looking in the windows and like that. The usual. A prowler. We got everything cleared up, though."

Richie laughed. "So it was nothing, eh? The city girl gets freaked out in the woods."

"No," said Stacey. "Like Guy said, it was something. Somebody."

"Somebody."

"Danny. It was Danny, the vet."

Richie's mouth dropped open, as if the secrets of the universe had just been explained to him.

"You know Danny."

"I do." He squinted toward Guy's car but couldn't make out much in the dim light of the driveway. "You got him in the car? You taking him in?"

"I'm taking him in. Yes."

That was good enough for Richie, and he thrust out a hand toward the sheriff. "Thanks. Well done. What can I say? Well done. I

appreciate it." Pumping away. Without letting go he turned to Stacey and apologized to her for her trouble, and she said it was nothing.

"You'd be amazed, though," said Guy, extricating his hand, "what
a person finds when he starts poking around a place like this."

"Don't blame the housekeeping on my wife. She's got the best
help in town, and it's not all that great."

"I'm not talking about housekeeping. And no offense to you,
Jeanette."

"None taken." She looked from Guy to the open doorway and
back again, probably wondering how the kids were doing, maybe
thinking about all the heat that was going to waste. Then she
stepped to the wall and pushed the button to lower the door. "How
about we go inside?"

"In a minute," said Guy, moving toward the bench, stepping into
the small space between it and the big Mercedes, not taking his eye
off Richie. "Take a look at this."

"Like I said," said Richie, following, "you can't blame my wife."

Guy ignored him. "I notice things," he said, as if it were a curse.
"I can't help it. And when I came through the garage a little bit
ago? I noticed this." He reached into his pocket and took out a
handkerchief and picked up the chain saw by the handle. "This
missing chain right here? I think it's the by-God double of the one
that choked your brother."

Jeanette put a hand to her mouth.

Richie narrowed his eyes and said that he didn't even know the
chain was missing.

They were all crammed into the narrow space between the car
and the bench now. Stacey backed away to lean against the wall,
disbelief on her face. How could he be that stupid?

"Come on," said Guy.

"Honest," said Richie. "I haven't touched it in forever. Besides—"

Guy advised him not to say a word. He indicated the marks on the bar and put the saw down and using the handkerchief he picked up the hatchet. He pointed out the marks on that, too. "Somebody mangled that chain getting it off," he said. "We knew that already."

Richie shrugged. "If you say so."

"There's a bent pin under the bench, too. The kind that holds the chain together. Unless you take it apart with the right tool or bash it all to hell with a hatchet."

Jeanette ducked down to look under the bench and sure enough, there it was.

"I wouldn't know about that," said Richie.

"Which is why we both need to take a little ride up to Rutland."

"You're kidding me."

"I'm afraid I'm not."

"Honest. I haven't touched that saw since I bought it."

Guy put down the hatchet and shook out the handkerchief and put it in his pocket. "If that's so, you've got nothing to worry about."

Jeanette looked from her husband to the workbench and back again, her eyes wide.

Stacey leaned up against the Mercedes and said to Guy, "It looks like you're going to have a full car."

"It does." He took a half step toward Richie and placed his hand on his arm.

"Don't worry about me," she said. "I'll find my own way home."

"You got somebody you can call? I can give Megan a buzz, if you want. It's no trouble."

"I'll be fine." Thinking she'd have quite the story to tell Chip. It would take the whole way up the mountain, and maybe the whole way back down, too.

Guy took Richie by the elbow and drew him toward the door. There was one step up into the mudroom, and he angled him into going first. Richie had the presence of mind to scuff his feet along the runner in the mudroom, but he stopped short at the doorway the instant he saw Danny at the kitchen table. "You accuse me of killing my own brother," he said over his shoulder, "while this troublemaking sonofabitch is sitting in my kitchen."

"Don't worry about him," said Guy, pushing Richie forward into the room. "And I haven't accused you of anything. So don't go spreading rumors."

"I *knew* he was in on it," said Danny from the table. "Him and the girl."

"Shut up, asshole," said Richie. "What do you know about anything."

Jeanette went slowly and deliberately toward the door, moving like a person walking under water. She let the fingers of one hand trail absently along the workbench.

"I wouldn't touch that stuff if I were you," Stacey told her.

Jeanette jumped, and they went ahead into the house.

It was a strange tableau, that was for sure. The sheriff with his holstered gun, leaning back on the counter. The Christmas decorations and the music. Danny cuffed to the table leg with a mixture of snowmelt and mud and peanut shells pooled around his feet. And Richie slumped against the refrigerator door, stunned and half drunk but recovering by pure will.

Jeanette collected herself before she was through the door, possibly because she could smell Danny from the mudroom. "Get that man out of my house," she said, although she could have been referring to either one of them. She slipped off her heels and turned and stalked off through the family room, taking off her long coat as she went and tossing it on the couch. It slid down, covering a tangle of video game equipment and comic books.

"That's a good woman right there," Danny said. "And I know what she means. I got no place at her table." He moved his feet as if he wanted to rise and go.

"It's my table, too," Richie put in.

"We'll see how long that lasts," Danny said, as if he could see the future. And as if he weren't the one with his arm cuffed to the furniture.

Jeanette came back in a moment, red-faced from running up and down the stairs. She said the kids were still sleeping.

"Good," said Richie. "There's no reason to disturb them. This'll be over in the morning, and it'll be like nothing ever happened."

"I can't say how long it'll take, actually." Guy gave Richie a look that was level and earnest but not the least bit sympathetic. "That's up to the troopers."

"But . . ."

"I'm just saying." Then he pushed off from the counter and went toward the mudroom. "I've got a little bit of evidence to take care of in the garage, if you folks can look after yourselves for a minute."

Stacey said she could stay with the kids for however long it might take, since Jeanette would certainly want to go with Richie.

Danny raised an eyebrow. "Watch out for that one," he said, pointing with his free hand at Stacey. "She ain't no good Samaritan."

Jeanette ignored him completely and told Stacey no, she thought her husband had proven that he could take pretty good care of himself. "He doesn't need *me*," she said.

But the look that he gave her in return said otherwise, and even Stacey and Danny could see it. Maybe this was what it took.

"Then I guess I'm done," Stacey said. "I can get a ride home. Don't worry about me." It wasn't as if anybody had asked or even cared, but there was no use waiting around here. She stepped into the mudroom to get her jacket, was gone for just a moment, and came back shrugging it on. It was loose, one or two sizes too big, and she felt the difference right away.

"Hey. Is this . . . ?" She had her hands in the pockets, but she stuck her elbows out and gave them a quizzical look, as if her arms had shrunk.

Jeanette laughed. "You grabbed mine. Here. Let me—"

"Wait a minute," said Danny. He sat there at the table, massaging his cuffed wrist, looking from Stacey to Jeanette like a man who'd been poleaxed. The skin was rubbed a little bit cleaner where he was working at it. "What're the odds you two'd have the same coat?"

"I only use it for chores," Jeanette said, and Stacey took her meaning. The old yellow Columbia wasn't something she'd be caught dead in otherwise.

"Well, I'll be," said Danny, smacking his lips. "It's a small world, ain't it?"

"Give me a hand," said Stacey, tilting her head toward the mudroom. "And help me find my own."

Stacey kicked a pair of boots out of the way and pushed the mudroom door shut behind them.

"Hey," said Jeanette. "What's with—"

"Hey, yourself," she answered right back. "I thought you might want a little privacy."

Jeanette watched her as she stepped over to the dryer and switched on the light above it. There on the bare white top of the dryer, stark as could be, were the contents of the pockets of Jeanette's own jacket. Some keys on a springy loop. A couple of crumpled paper towels. A pair of perfectly unremarkable work gloves, owned by somebody who didn't do much in the way of work.

"What's this?" said Jeanette.

"The troopers aren't going to find your fingerprints on the chain saw, are they? Or on the hatchet either."

"I don't know why they should. That stuff belongs to Richie."

"No," said Stacey. "That's not the reason." She tapped her finger on the top of the dryer next to the gloves, and it made a low sound that resonated in the little room. "They're not going to find your fingerprints, because you used these when you broke the chain."

She flipped the gloves over. They were fairly new, lightly used for the most part, but their palms were slashed across with a heavy black line of embedded grease. There was grease on the fingers, too, plus something else not quite so dark that might have been dried blood.

"You had them on when you went to David's condo, too. When you . . . you know."

The look that Jeanette gave her had an edge of betrayal to it—the look of a person who has suffered enough and who's thought she's found a sympathetic ear and who's been proven wrong—but the words that she spoke as she leaned back against the door were defiant. "You must be kidding."

"No. I'm not."

"So I touched a chain saw. Big deal. Show me somebody around here who hasn't."

Beyond the garage door Guy's footsteps passed back and forth as he carried things to his car. It wouldn't be long now.

"Besides," Stacey said, "even Danny noticed we've got the same jacket. He's been telling everybody that he saw me leaving the Snowfield around the time David died. But it wasn't me. It was you."

"I don't believe it."

"He told me, and he told Guy, and he told Richie, too. God knows who else. And he was almost right. It all makes sense now."

"David was my brother-in-law. He was *family*. How could I possibly—"

"He was family, all right. Family that owned a third of the mountain."

From outside came the slamming of Guy's trunk.

Stacey went on. "And you, you had a cheating husband who was throwing money away on his new girlfriend. Don't tell me you didn't know."

Jeanette gave her that look of betrayal again, but that was all the answer she made.

"There might not have been much left by the time you got around to divorcing him. So you did what you could."

The garage door opened and Guy stepped in. "Hey," he said, "what's the deal?" And then Stacey showed him the gloves.

Guy didn't turn on his light bar when he left the driveway. Against his instincts, he'd ended up with Danny in the front seat and Jeanette in the back, behind the Plexiglas. It seemed wrong, but there it was. Procedures were procedures.

Still, Danny behind Plexiglas would have been a whole lot more palatable than Danny right in the front seat alongside you. He opened the window a crack to let in some fresh air, but from the backseat Jeanette complained about the cold. Who could blame her? She was wearing the lightweight coat she'd worn to the Christmas party, instead of the warmer Columbia that was now in evidence. Too bad.

Stacey stood on the porch watching their taillights vanish around a long loop in the mountain road, looking up now and then toward the lights in the upstairs windows. She didn't envy Richie the job of telling the kids, but there was no way she'd hang around for it. So she flipped open her cell phone—the service out here was about as good as it had been in the garage, which was OK with her since she didn't want to have to go back inside and make the call—and dialed Chip's number. She told him she'd meet him at Doc's, and then she picked up her duffel and swung it over her shoulder and started down the hill.